Mike cocked his head as, gunning the motor so hard, Claudia swung the Jeep out into the street. She pulled a wide U-turn—missing a parked car by no more that a quarter inch—and started off in hot pursuit of the Santa on snowmobile.

Remembering it was Friday the thirteenth, Mike quickly fastened his seat belt.

Claudia tromped on the gas pedal and the Jeep shot forward. Then, halfway down the block, a dog ran into their path. She slammed on the brakes so hard that Mike would have been a hood ornament if it hadn't been for his seat belt. There was certainly no mystery about why her car was battered.

They sped through town, then along a stretch of dark road that led to a highway. Claudia hit the brakes again. They spun sideways and bounced off the six-foot-high bank of snow lining the side of the road.

Mike glanced right, then left. In the distance he could see a lone set of car taillights. That was all.

"He waved at us," Claudia said. "As if he'd been waiting for us to come out and see him. I think he must have heard you were coming to town and was issuing you a challenge."

"A challenge? You mean he was telling me I won't be able to track him down?"

"That's my guess."

Dear Reader,

This book was inspired by friend and fellow Superromance author Janice Carter, who told me about the Random Acts of Kindness Movement. (I suspect I was one of about three people in North America who hadn't heard of it, but writers spend much of their lives chained to their computers.)

At any rate, Janice started me thinking. What if someone was doing major—although not necessarily random—acts of kindness and nobody could figure out who he was?

I saw a lot of potential humor in the situation, and that's how *Looking for Mr. Claus* came to be. (With special thanks to Senior Editor Paula Eykelhof, who thought up the title.)

As for the frigid setting, I tend to stay away from Northern Ontario in mid-December. But while I was writing this story, Toronto was experiencing one of the coldest winters in history. So it only took sticking my nose outside to get into the right frame of mind for writing a cold scene. (To research the *really* frosty ones, I took the dog to the park.)

Season's greetings and happy reading!

Dawn Stewardson

Dawn Stewardson
LOOKING FOR MR. CLAUS

Harlequin Books

TORONTO • NEW YORK • LONDON
AMSTERDAM • PARIS • SYDNEY • HAMBURG
STOCKHOLM • ATHENS • TOKYO • MILAN
MADRID • WARSAW • BUDAPEST • AUCKLAND

ISBN 0-373-70719-3

LOOKING FOR MR. CLAUS

This one's for Stacy Widdrington, who knows far more than I do about the newspaper business.

And for John, always.

CHAPTER ONE

MIKE O'BRIAN HAD BEEN walking on eggshells for two weeks, and when he came in to file his story he could hear them starting to crack. He read the note beside his computer.

O'Brian,
My office as soon as you're here.

J.E.S.

"Damn," he muttered. He was far from the editor in chief's favorite investigative reporter at the moment, so he'd been doing his best to steer clear.

From the next desk, Howie said, "You'd better grab a flak jacket before you go up. Big Jim didn't look happy."

"And when," Mike asked, shooting his buddy a wry glance, "does he ever look happy?"

"Hmm...good question. I think the last time was January '94. When he heard the quake did major damage to the *Times* offices."

Mike grinned. "Exactly. It's when he's smiling you know you've got trouble." Absently nodding to a few of the other reporters, he made his way across the newsroom.

The offices of the publisher and editor in chief were one floor up, and he climbed the stairs telling himself he had nothing to worry about. Even though rumors of pending layoffs had been running rampant, there wasn't much chance he was in line for the ax.

According to Marketing, his byline drew a lot of readers. And only last year he'd won a Pulitzer for his series on L.A.'s gang warfare. Besides, all he'd done wrong was blow a little of the *Gazette*'s money.

By the time he reached the eighth-floor landing he was silently admitting it had been more than a little. Still, he was hardly the first reporter to pay an informant who didn't deliver. And anyone would have paid those same big bucks to get a story as hot as the one he'd been after.

Of course, it hadn't been hot once his informant took the money and ran. It had gone stone-cold dead. Big Jim, on the other hand, was still as steamed as if that money had come from his own pocket.

Nearing Jim's office, he squared his shoulders. Then he stopped outside the open door.

Jim Souto looked up from his desk. And smiled. It made Mike wish he was off dodging bullets in a Third World revolution.

The chief waved him in, saying, "Shut the door and sit down. I've got something for you."

He was sorely tempted to ask if it was a pink slip but kept his mouth shut.

"Tell me," Jim said, "how much you know about Ferris Wentworth's newspaper empire?"

It took a second for the significance of that question to sink in. When it did, though, Mike began to relax.

Not that being assigned to write a feature about a billionaire newspaper magnate was exactly a plum. And he didn't relish the thought of a trip to New York to interview the guy. Mid-December in the Big Apple could be mighty cold. But he'd known the chief would stick him with the next crummy assignment that came along, and this wasn't anywhere near as bad as what he'd been imagining.

"Well, let's see," he said, turning his thoughts back to Jim's question. "Aside from the *Gazette,* Wentworth owns about twenty more papers in this country—plus a string of others internationally."

"Right. Some big, some small. Some cash cows, some real drains. And he's decided to shut down his losers."

Mike nodded. Luckily for them, the *L.A. Gazette* fell into the cash-cow category.

"Before he does, though," Jim continued, "he's giving them a fighting chance. The ones that can get themselves into the black earn a reprieve. Which is where you come in."

"Uh-huh?"

"Yeah, Wentworth's paired each of his losers with a major paper like the *Gazette.* And I'm supposed to lend our sister paper a name journalist."

"I take it that's me?"

"Right. You'll be doing a local-interest series."

"Local interest? That's not exactly—"

Waving off the objection, Jim said, "Don't worry. The subject will have broad appeal. Wentworth's after the sort of thing a lot of his other papers will run."

At that news, Mike relaxed a little. Local-interest pieces weren't up his alley, but if this one had broad appeal, it might not be *too* bad.

"Wentworth suggested," Jim went on, "an article a day for about a week. He figures that'll give circulation a boost and bring in new advertisers. At any rate, we're paired with a paper called the *Miner's Dispatch,* in Victoria Falls.''

For a moment, Mike was afraid to believe he'd heard right. But there wasn't a thing wrong with his ears, so he grinned and said, "Hey, that's great, Jim. I love Africa.''

"Oh, hell, no, I'm not talking about the Victoria Falls in Africa. This one's in Ontario. You know, up north. In Canada.''

Mike could feel his grin fading. A whole lot of Canada was nothing but ice and snow and polar bears—none of which he was even slightly crazy about. "Exactly *where* in Ontario?" he asked.

"Northern Ontario. Gold-, nickel- and copper-mining country.'' With that, Jim flipped open a book on his desk—which proved to be an atlas—and tapped his finger against a spot that looked to be about a nugget's throw from the North Pole.

"It's a small town,'' he elaborated. "Not more than three or four thousand. But the *Dispatch* is the local paper for all the small towns in the region.''

After staring at the atlas for a few seconds, Mike looked at Big Jim once more. "Come on, I didn't cost us *that* much money. How about some other punishment assignment?"

"Punishment assignment?'' The chief produced a poor imitation of childlike innocence. "O'Brian, that money you wasted has nothing to do with this. I'm giving it to you because you're a single guy. You don't have all the pre-Christmas family stuff that most of my name reporters do.''

"Wait a minute. I have nieces and nephews. And I'm their favorite uncle.''

"Yeah, well, that's not exactly the same thing, is it. I mean, if by any chance you got stuck up there over the holidays, it—"

"What!" Mike's blood pressure leapt ten points.

"Keep your shirt on. It's still a week and a half till Christmas, so you'll probably be back in plenty of time. I'm just saying that if by some fluke you got snowed in or something, it wouldn't be such a big deal for you as it would for a guy with kids."

"Oh, no. No way. I might not have kids, but I've got awfully thin blood. There must be *somebody* else. Maybe even someone who *likes* cold weather."

"Want to suggest anyone? Without forgetting it has to be a *name?*"

He desperately tried to think of somebody, but no one was going to want this assignment any more than he did. Which meant he was toast.

"All right," he said, deciding he might as well give in gracefully. "I guess I can stand playing Nanook of the North for a week."

Hearing that, Jim produced a ticket folder from his pocket. "You're leaving first thing in the morning," he said, tossing the folder across the desk. "Flying American to Toronto, then Air Ontario to a place called Sudbury."

"Tomorrow," Mike pointed out, "is Friday the thirteenth."

"Oh. Well, I didn't know you were superstitious, but I guess you could leave Saturday. 'Course, that would make you a day later getting back."

"I'll take my chances tomorrow. So how do I get from this Sudbury to Victoria Falls?"

The chief shrugged. "You could rent a car and drive. But Iggy—he's the *Dispatch's* editor—said he wouldn't recommend that. Says the roads have been so icy lately you might kill yourself. He suggested finding a bush pilot or something.''

Terrific, Mike muttered under his breath. If he couldn't find a bush pilot, the ''something'' would probably turn out to be a team of huskies.

''And what,'' he asked aloud, ''is the local-interest topic? What's my story?''

A fresh smile appeared on the chief's face. ''Well, O'Brian, you're going to be doing some serious investigative reporting. I wouldn't waste your talents on anything else. But I think I'll let Iggy Brooks fill you in once you get there.

''And O'Brian?'' Jim added as Mike rose to leave. ''Take a mug shot with you. Iggy wants one to run. And he said to bring your warmest clothes and a pair of high boots. They've got a ton of snow up there.''

''Dammit, Jim, the only high boots I own are cowboy boots.''

The chief flashed a final smile. ''Guess they'll be better than nothing.''

WHEN THE CLOCK RADIO came on, Claudia groaned and hit the snooze bar. Then she told herself it was Friday, that she could sleep in tomorrow. But between working all day and lying awake worrying about Santa half the night, she was exhausted. And there was still a week and a half till Christmas.

Before she could bury her face safely against the pillow, Morgan flopped his head onto the side of the bed and pressed his nose to hers. That made her groan again. But if a cold nose really was the sign of a healthy dog, at least he wouldn't be running up any vet bills in the near future.

She opened one eye and looked into his, which was enough to start him happily wiggling his big behind. From the end of the bed, Ghost immediately hissed a warning to keep that tail away from him.

Knowing the cat's next move would be to give Morgan a swipe, Claudia reluctantly got up and let the dog out for his morning prowl. Then she hit the shower and grabbed a quick breakfast. By the time she was dressed and ready to go, Morgan was on the front steps waiting to come back in.

"You," she told him, opening the door, "are a disgrace to malamutes everywhere."

He looked offended, but it was the truth. His ancestors had been sled dogs who'd hauled freight in even the coldest weather. But Morgan much preferred the warmth of the house to ice and snow.

Shrugging into her coat, Claudia grabbed her boots. Or, more precisely, she grabbed the one boot she could find. Its mate was nowhere in sight.

"Morgan," she said, waving the single boot in front of his nose, "you've done it again, haven't you."

The dog curled his upper lip, giving her one of his best smiles.

"Morgan, this is not funny," she told him sternly. "Where is it this time?"

He flopped down onto the floor and lay gazing up at her—the picture of canine innocence.

"Look, I can't stay home with you all day, every day. How many times do I have to explain that if you want to eat I have to work? Now, go get my other boot.

"Rats," she said when he didn't move a muscle. "Morgan, I've got a busy day—two stops before I even check in at the paper."

That made no impression on him, so she started searching the house, carrying the boot along with her. Given the chance, he was liable to hide the first one while she was looking for the second.

He followed her from room to room until she discovered his latest hiding place and dragged the missing boot out from behind the couch.

While she put the pair of them on, she gave Morgan a dire warning about what happened to dogs who persisted in playing this sort of game. Then she hurried out into the frosty day and drove over to the nearby town of Kenabeek to interview Frank Willoughby. He was coordinator for the annual local dogsled races that were always run the week before Christmas.

Once she'd finished talking with Frank, she made her way up to Matachewan and took some pictures of the snow angels the local children had made on the grounds of the church. After that she turned her Cherokee back in the direction of Victoria Falls, stopping only for lunch along the way.

Even so, by the time she parked in front of the *Miner's Dispatch* it was almost two.

When she first walked in she thought the place was empty. All was silent, and Pete Doleman, their other reporter, wasn't at his desk. But the moment she began stomping the snow off her boots, Iggy came zipping out of his office wearing a grin that made her heart sink.

Only one thing would have made her boss as happy as he clearly was. Which meant she wasn't going to get the reprieve she'd been praying for. The *L.A. Gazette* really was shipping them some hotshot investigative reporter.

"Where's Pete?" she asked. Maybe if she didn't give Iggy a chance to tell her the news it would go away.

"I've got him checking on a story. But listen to this. The *Gazette* thing is definitely on. They called me after you left yesterday. And you won't believe who they're sending."

So much for the going-away theory, she silently muttered.

"Well?" Iggy demanded. "Aren't you going to ask who?"

She forced a smile and asked.

"Mike O'Brian!"

Her heart sank even further. She'd read some of O'Brian's stuff. He was among the best in North America.

"I almost phoned you last night to tell you, but I wanted to see your face."

She did her best to smile again, hating to imagine what her face was saying. "Well . . . great," she managed. "When does he arrive?"

"Assuming he doesn't get delayed in Sudbury, he should be here about four. And I want you to come meet him with me."

Nodding, she turned to hang up her coat.

"We can finish putting the weekend edition together before then," Iggy went on. "I've already written our lead—all about the illustrious Mike O'Brian and what he'll be doing here. So as long as he's remembered to bring a photo, the front page is a wrap."

"Good," she said, turning back from the coatrack.

Iggy eyed her for a moment, then said, "Claudia...you realize this changes our approach to the copycat Santa story. I've got to give it to O'Brian and let him run with it."

Even though she'd known he was going to tell her that, hearing the words made her mouth go dry. "I thought you didn't want Santa identified too fast," she said evenly. "I thought we agreed to let him finish delivering all his presents first. You told me not to—"

"I know. I know everything I told you. But that was before Wentworth offered me his deal. And the Santa story's exactly the kind of human interest, investigative-type thing he told me to come up with."

"But what about the people who haven't—"

"Look," Iggy said, running his fingers through his gray hair, "I'd like our Santa—whoever he is—to have all the time in the world, but I've got to think about the paper. And this just might save our bacon."

She simply nodded again. What was there to say when she didn't have a leg to stand on? What else could Iggy assign O'Brian? The district school's Christmas concert? The regional mince pie bake-off?

No, whether she liked it or not, giving O'Brian the Santa story was only logical. But the thought of where that might lead scared her silly.

"You know what?" Iggy said. "I've been thinking we were probably worrying too much. Maybe, when people learn who Santa is, he won't stop making his deliveries at all."

But people simply *couldn't* learn who he was.

"Claudia? It's for the good of the paper, eh?"

"I know. And it's okay. But I almost forgot, I have to make a phone call. A personal one. So in case someone comes in, would you mind if I use your office for a minute?''

CLAUDIA FINISHED delivering the bad news, then sat with the phone to her ear and waited for his reaction—praying he'd say he was going to call it quits.

"Well," he said at last, "I guess I'd better start being a little more careful."

Closing her eyes, she tried to think of words that would convince him the game had gotten far too dangerous.

"Listen to me," she finally said. "It's not a case of simply being more careful. The situation has changed entirely. With Mike O'Brian's byline on the articles, they'll be picked up by a lot of other papers in Ferris Wentworth's chain. Which means that if he identifies you, your picture's going to be splashed across papers all over the United States. And I mean *all* over."

She waited again, hoping the silence at the other end of the line meant he was seriously reconsidering.

She'd been worried about this Santa escapade from the start, worried about the risk of someone finding out who he was. In the beginning, though, even if that had happened, it would only have been local news. The potential danger would have been low. But now, if he was identified, he'd be at *serious* risk.

"I think you're overreacting," he finally said.

"I am *not* overreacting. Don't you see that—"

"Claudia, I appreciate your concern, I really do. But this O'Brian guy isn't going to catch up with me. And even if he did, I'd be out of here so fast that—"

"But what if—"

"Hey, take it easy. Everything's going to be fine. And how can I even think about stopping when I've delivered presents to only half the kids on my list? Just think how the ones who got nothing would feel.''

"Dammit, it's not the kids' feelings I'm worried about at the moment. It's you. If O'Brian catches up with you, if he identifies you . . ." She couldn't bring herself to finish the thought, but they both knew the potential consequences.

"Look," he said. "The minute I finish working my way through the list I'll go completely to ground, okay? So all you have to do is make sure this O'Brian doesn't figure things out in the meantime."

She exhaled slowly, knowing she could argue with him for hours and he wouldn't change his mind. He was just as stubborn as he'd always been.

"*All* I have to do?" she repeated at last. "You make it sound like a picnic in the park."

He laughed, then said, "You can handle it."

"Well, let's hope so. But I'll phone you again later, after O'Brian's arrived and I've had a chance to size him up."

Once they'd said goodbye, she made another quick call. Then she headed out of Iggy's office, telling herself everything really would be fine.

After all, she'd never *expected* Santa would listen to reason. And it wasn't as if there'd been no advance warning, no time to plan.

So she knew exactly what she had to do. Either she got rid of Mike O'Brian—fast—or she led him down enough blind alleys to keep him from the truth.

"Claudia?" Iggy said as she sat down at her desk.

She glanced at him guiltily.

"You're all right with this O'Brian thing?"

"Sure. In a way, I'm even glad. I'll probably learn a lot from working with him."

"Working with him? Oh . . . well, I wasn't actually thinking along those lines. You've got a lot of extra things on your plate right now, what with all the Christmas stuff."

"But I've got enough time to handle everything. And I don't want to give up that story entirely."

"Yeah . . . well . . . I'm afraid we'll have to leave the decision to O'Brian. I can hardly foist you on him if he balks at the idea."

She told herself to remain calm. But she absolutely *had* to work with O'Brian. Otherwise, she couldn't possibly keep the upper hand.

"Iggy?" she pressed. "I don't think you understand how much this means to me. I *really* want to stay with the story."

"Oh." He hesitated, then shrugged. "Okay, then I guess we'd better make sure you do."

"Thanks," she said, trying not to let the full extent of her relief show.

"We'll have to play it by ear," he went on, "but you might want to throw in your line about learning a lot from him. He'd probably like it."

"I'll keep that in mind." The truth, though, was that she didn't really care about learning diddly from Mike O'Brian. The only important thing was keeping *him* from learning too much.

FORTUNATELY, SOMEONE at the Sudbury airport had pointed Mike in the direction of Drew Patterson—a bush pilot who didn't mind taking a short-hop flight.

"I fly anywhere, anytime," he'd said. "Wherever a paying customer wants to go."

Not that Mike actually wanted to go to Victoria Falls, but that was beside the point.

Absently, he glanced around Drew's plane. It was an old single-engine Beaver with a small cabin area behind the pilot. Drew had invited him to ride in the copilot's seat, though, saying the view was better.

The obvious question was, better than what? There wasn't a whole lot to see—just endless gray sky above and an enormous white blanket of snow below. It stretched as far as the eye could see—across open acres of land, forested areas and frozen lakes.

If anyone asked him to guess the biggest winter excitement around Victoria Falls, he'd guess snowmobile races. So that was probably what he'd be stuck covering. That and the church's turkey dinner or something. Maybe the investigative reporting Jim had promised would amount to finding out who got the wishbones.

"That's Victoria Falls up ahead." Drew glanced across the plane, easing the throttle back and increasing their angle of descent. "Landing strip's just north of town."

Mike stared morosely through the windshield, wondering whether just north of town put the landing strip inside the Arctic Circle. If he wasn't lucky, he was going to freeze his butt off up here.

His leather bomber jacket was the warmest thing he owned. But during the walk from the terminal to Drew's plane, both he and the leather had frozen almost solid. Clearly, neither of them were up to tolerating twenty below zero. And his feet felt like two very wet blocks of ice. The Sudbury tarmac had been heavy on snow, and his cowboy boots had been no match for it.

He watched the town as they flew nearer and lower, thinking that if it weren't for the covering of white,

Victoria Falls could be any of the hundred small towns he'd been sent to all over the world.

It was laid out in a standard grid pattern—low commercial buildings lining the main street, and side streets of houses that were mostly small and nondescript. The tallest thing in town was the church steeple.

Once they'd flown over the buildings, he spotted the landing strip. The fact that it looked like a long skating rink was hardly reassuring, but Drew put the Beaver down smoothly, and they only went into a couple of slides as they taxied toward the hangar.

There was a lone car parked beside it, an old blue Chevy, and as the plane taxied nearer, the car's front doors opened. Two people emerged—a short, rotund man who looked sixty and a woman who was about half that age and struck Mike as decidedly interesting.

"That's your welcoming committee," Drew told him. "Iggy Brooks is the editor of the *Dispatch*. Has been forever. And the woman's one of his reporters, Claudia Paquette."

Mike nodded but didn't take his gaze off the woman. "This Claudia," he finally said, glancing at Drew. "Is she attached to anyone?"

He grinned. "Uh-uh."

"Really? A woman who looks like that?"

"Well, she *was* going with someone, but he's been gone for... oh, must be a year or so now. And I don't think there are many men around here who'd interest her. Places like this, most of the young people head south as quick as they can. There's Pete Doleman, of course—Iggy's nephew. I've heard he's got a thing for her, but people say it's pretty one-sided."

While the plane rolled to a stop, Mike looked at his welcoming committee again. More specifically, he looked at Claudia again.

She was mostly hidden under a heavy burgundy coat, but he certainly liked what little he could see. Average height, she had a long brown tangle of what his sister Sarah called wash-and-wear hair, and . . .

His thoughts trailed off as Claudia smiled. She had a smile that lit up her entire face—making her look even prettier than she already was. So good, in fact, that he actually started feeling a little better about this assignment.

"I'm not stopping," Drew said. "Just heading straight back to Sudbury."

"Well, I've got your number, so I'll probably see you next week on my way out of here." Mike grabbed his gear from the floor behind him and opened the door.

The plane wasn't warm, but the air that rushed in at him was absolutely frigid. Victoria Falls was even colder than Sudbury, and climbing down from the plane felt like crawling into a freezer.

He carefully planted his feet on the ground—having already discovered that the smooth soles on his boots weren't much good on ice. Then, giving Drew a farewell wave, he headed over to Claudia and Iggy. The snow beneath his feet was so cold it squeaked with each step.

"Ignatious Brooks—Iggy," the editor said, pulling off his mitt and reaching to shake hands. "And this is my ace reporter, Claudia Paquette."

When Mike turned to Claudia, she smiled—at him, this time. And, close up, her smile was positively devastating. Her mouth was wide, her lips full and lush.

And her eyes, he could see now, were a deep, dark, delicious shade of chocolate brown.

"Let's get into the car where it's warmer," she suggested.

"Good idea," he said, liking her more by the second. He'd always had a soft spot for women who'd rather he didn't freeze to death.

CLAUDIA GOT INTO the back of Iggy's car, using the old "There's more legroom up front" line. Actually, though, she was far less concerned about Mike O'Brian's legroom than she was about having a chance to unobtrusively size him up on the way back to the *Dispatch*.

From reading the lead article Iggy had just written, she already knew that O'Brian was thirty-two, single, and had covered stories in more parts of the world than she'd see in her lifetime. But she wanted to get a more complete fix on him. Fast.

If there was anything that would convince him to ditch this assignment and head back to L.A., she had to figure out what it was.

She watched while he stowed his duffel bag in the trunk and climbed into the front seat with his camera and laptop. He wasn't what she'd been expecting. For some reason, she'd pictured him short and dark. Instead, he was tall, with sun-streaked brown hair and warm blue eyes.

She'd also imagined him on the scrawny side, but from what she could see he had a nicely muscled build. He also had the kind of hard-angled jaw she found extremely appealing.

Reminding herself he was the last man in the world she should be having those sorts of thoughts about, she settled back in the seat.

"Why don't I tell you a little about the *Dispatch,* O'Brian," Iggy said, starting the engine and pointing the Chevy toward town. "There are just Claudia and me full time, plus a second reporter, Pete Doleman. He's my nephew, but there's no nepotism, is there, Claudia."

"None that I notice."

"Then," Iggy continued, "there's old Walter Warnick. He works evenings, putting the next day's issue to bed—handles everything from the layout to the typesetting to the actual printing. Aside from that, we've got free-lancers in some of the other towns. And I pick up the odd thing I like from the wire services.

"All in all, we're a lean operation for a daily. Well, .almost a daily. We publish Tuesdays through Saturdays, so that's when we'll be running your first five articles."

"*First* five? But—"

"I won't need the initial one till Monday," Iggy interrupted. "That'll give you a couple of days to get up to speed on your story."

"And just what *is* my story? Jim Souto didn't give me any details."

"Oh, we've got a real doozy for you. Claudia's been working on it since it broke last week, but she doesn't have anywhere near your savvy."

Even though the remark was undoubtedly true, Claudia took offense. She was glaring at the back of Iggy's head when O'Brian glanced around, caught her at it and grinned. The minute he looked forward again, she refocused her glare and aimed it at the back of *his* head.

If he had so much savvy, why was he wearing that stupid bomber jacket instead of a down-filled parka? And his cowboy boots looked as if they were soaked right through.

She'd bet he didn't have long johns on under those jeans he had tucked into his boots, either. So maybe, if things went well, he'd come down with a fatal dose of pneumonia. That would certainly solve her problem.

"Here's the scoop," Iggy said, intruding on her image of O'Brian gasping his last.

"The economy up here is pretty depressed at the moment," the editor went on. "There's not much work except in the mines. And a few months ago, Hillstead—that's one of the major mining companies—cut back operations and laid off most of its workers. They say the layoffs are only temporary, but everyone who's out of work is worried. So they've really tightened their belts, and Christmas was looking to be pretty bleak until the copycat Santa started making his rounds."

"The copycat Santa," O'Brian repeated.

"That's what we've dubbed him," Iggy explained, "because he's been delivering gifts to the families that have no money coming in. There he is, in the middle of the night—"

"People have actually seen him in the middle of the night?"

Iggy nodded. "And *only* the middle of the night—never any other time."

"The odd insomniac's spotted him," Claudia put in.

"Yup," Iggy agreed. "And his snowmobile's wakened a few light sleepers. They're not exactly quiet machines at the best of times, and his is decked out with sleigh bells, to boot. At any rate, there he's been—flowing white beard, red Santa suit and a sack of presents. The gifts are for the kids, all nicely wrapped with tags saying not to open them until the twenty-fifth. And he's got hampers on his sled, too. Filled with frozen turkeys, canned hams, plum puddings, everything you need for a Christmas dinner."

"So who is he?" O'Brian asked as Iggy pulled up in front of the *Dispatch*. "And why's he doing this?"

Claudia smiled. Unless Iggy was completely in awe of Mike O'Brian, she knew how he'd react. And sure enough, he glanced across the front seat and graced their hotshot with his patented "Are you an idiot?" look.

"Who is he?" he said. "Why's he doing this? Well, I thought I was making myself clear, O'Brian. That's why you're here. That's your story."

CHAPTER TWO

MIKE SET HIS NIKON and laptop down, his gaze lingering on Claudia. She'd just taken off her coat, revealing a trim figure, a dark brown sweater the color of her eyes and tight jeans that emphasized her small hips.

He glanced away before she noticed him watching her, and looked around the newsroom. At the front stood a long wooden counter for serving customers, and off to one side was an office with a tarnished brass plaque on the door that read Editor.

In the center area were two ancient oak desks with computers sitting on them, but if it weren't for that, the place would look like a set from a forties movie.

He could smell printer's ink, and through an open door at the back a printing press was visible—an old lead-castings dinosaur. Clearly Ferris Wentworth hadn't sunk much money into modernizing his losers.

"So," Iggy said, removing one of the two shapeless cardigans he'd had on beneath his parka, "did you remember to bring that photo?"

"Uh-huh. It's out in your car. In my duffel."

"Good, I'll get it before you leave. Need it for tomorrow's edition."

As Iggy pushed up the sleeves of his second cardigan, Mike said, "About your Santa?"

"Uh-huh?"

"You've got me wondering why it's not obvious who he is. I mean, if somebody's buying up gifts and groceries on a grand scale..."

"He's not buying them locally," Claudia explained.

"Then where's he getting them?"

She shrugged. "Maybe in Sudbury. Or there are a couple of other good-sized towns that aren't an impossibly long drive."

"He's putting some cash in the hampers, though," Iggy said. "With notes asking people to spend it in the local stores, so Victoria Falls' merchants don't lose out. Seems to have thought of everything. But let's get back to your series. I want to tell you how I see it unfolding."

Mike nodded, although he'd rather Iggy told him what he'd meant by that remark in the car—the one about the *first* five articles. Surely he wasn't thinking there might be more than that, because even five was at least four too many. Schmaltzy Santa stuff just wasn't Mike O'Brian material.

Iggy passed him a stack of thin tabloids, saying, "These are our last few issues. Have a look at the Santa pieces Claudia's already written, but I want you to take a different approach."

"Different how?"

"Well, I'm envisioning each of your articles like the chapter of a mystery. Each day you write about the clues you've turned up, showing the readers how you're using your finely honed investigative skills to close in on Santa. But each article ends with a cliffhanger, because he's still eluding you."

Mike merely nodded again, resisting the urge to ask how much investigative skill Iggy thought it took to find some guy who was running around in a bright red suit.

"The final chapter, of course, comes when you ID him. Then you tell the readers who he is and what his motivation was."

"All right," Mike said slowly. He'd probably figure out who Santa was tomorrow, but he could somehow milk the story for a week's worth of articles.

"And we want to know where he got all the money for the presents and hampers," Iggy continued. "That really has me stumped. I never thought there was anyone around here with much money."

"Except the Nilssons," Claudia put in.

"Yeah, but we know it's neither of them."

Mike's ears had pricked up. "Who are the Nilssons?"

"Our local millionaires," Iggy said. "Two brothers who made their money back in the early days of computers. Then they retired young, built a place on a lake about fifty kilometers from town and turned into a couple of hermits."

"Oh, Iggy, you know they're not hermits," Claudia told him. "They just don't come into town all that often. But they're actually quite sociable," she said to Mike. "My father's always going out there to play poker with them."

"And how do you know one of them isn't your Santa?"

"Because they're a couple of cheap so-and-sos," Iggy said before Claudia could answer. "I hear that when they have those poker parties they make their guests bring the beer."

"They don't *make* them," Claudia objected. "People just do."

"Well, whatever, the point is that there's not a community-minded bone in either of their bodies."

"But if nobody else has money," Mike said, "then—"

"Trust me," Iggy told him. "It's not the Nilssons. Now, getting back to your articles, I want them warm and humorous. In tune with the Christmas season."

At that, Mike looked away so Iggy wouldn't see him gritting his teeth. His byline promised readers hard-hitting reports on wars, insurrections and serial killers. If Iggy wanted warm and humorous, he should have asked Wentworth to send Dave Barry.

When Mike glanced back, he was just in time to see Claudia poke Iggy in the ribs.

"Oh, yeah," he said, "there's one other thing. Unless you've got any objections, I'd like Claudia to work with you."

That, Mike thought, was the best thing he'd heard since he'd arrived. But he knew better than to let a woman think he was too interested, so he said, "Well, I'm not sure that's a good idea. I always handle assignments on my own."

Claudia nodded. "Yes, we realized you probably do. But I know everyone around here, and the legwork I've already done will get you off to a quick start. Besides, you'll need someone to drive you around."

"Don't feel we're pressuring you, though," Iggy said. "I'd just assumed you might want some help—in case Santa gives you as hard a time as he's been giving Claudia."

"Well, hopefully I'll get lucky fast. In fact, that's something I want to ask you about. Assuming I identify our man right off, you won't care if I just give you the whole series at once and clear out of here, will you?"

"You mean go back to L.A.? Before we run your final article?"

"Well . . . yeah."

"Oh, no," Iggy said, shaking his head. "Oh, no, that wouldn't do. If you left, people would know you'd solved our little mystery in no time, so you can't leave before next Saturday at the earliest."

"But—"

"I don't just mean people here," Iggy interrupted. "The way news travels in this business, if you left any sooner people on every paper in Wentworth's chain would realize your series was a sham—which would make the *Dispatch* a laughingstock."

"But—"

"So you're here for at least a week, O'Brian. Five articles—Tuesday through Saturday. That's the *minimum* Jim Souto and I agreed on."

"The minimum?" Mike repeated, not liking the way Iggy had emphasized the word.

He nodded. "Souto *did* mention you'd be staying until you identified Santa, didn't he? Hell, I don't care if it takes till Easter. The final article's *got* to answer the questions of who he is and what inspired him. Without that, the series would be left dangling."

"True," Mike admitted, thoughts of murdering Big Jim dancing in his head. Of course, there was no way it would take more than a week to find their Santa. But what if, by some remote chance, it did?

Unlikely as that possibility might be, he decided he'd better grab Claudia's offer of help before she withdrew it.

"Okay, Paquette," he said. "I guess it won't hurt me to collaborate this one time. I mean, if you've already been working on the story, it would hardly be fair to steal it away from you entirely, would it."

"Well...O'Brian...if you're sure you don't mind..."

"No, I can live with it. But I'd still better get a car of my own. I generally do a lot of work at night, and I wouldn't expect you to chauffeur me around twenty-four hours a day."

Claudia thought rapidly. A car of his own. So he could get around without her at night—which was when Santa was delivering his goodies.

That was no good. She couldn't have O'Brian skulking off doing heaven knew what. She had to keep an eye on him all the time. But how was she going to manage that?

When she tuned back in, Iggy was saying, "I've booked you a room at the Silver Dollar, O'Brian. I'd have invited you to stay with me, except the wife had surgery last month. She's coming along all right, but she's not up to having a houseguest yet."

"No problem, a hotel's fine."

"Well, *fine* doesn't exactly describe the Silver Dollar, but I'm afraid it's the best we've got."

"Hey, I've slept in the backs of trucks and in mud huts. I'll be okay."

Claudia eyed O'Brian uneasily, able to think of only one way she could keep a close enough eye on him. The last thing she wanted, though, was Mr. Hotshot sleeping under her roof.

No, she silently corrected herself. That was actually one up from the bottom of the list. The *very* last thing she wanted was for him to find Santa.

So even though she was almost certain she'd regret it, she said, "The Silver Dollar really is a pretty poor excuse for a hotel, O'Brian. And I've got a spare bedroom, as well as a printer you can use. The Silver Dollar doesn't have room service, let alone anything remotely high-tech."

Iggy looked surprised. Mike O'Brian looked like the cat who'd just swallowed the canary—which made her wish she could vanish into thin air.

"Well, that's awfully nice of you, Paquette. Awfully nice. And it's what I like best about small towns. The people are so darned friendly."

Oh, Lord, the man was practically leering at her. She hadn't expected she'd be regretting her offer within five seconds of making it, but O'Brian was obviously reading far more into it than she'd meant.

She had to try to wriggle her way out of it. Of course, if she managed that, she'd have to stand guard outside the Silver Dollar or something. Still, it would be the lesser of two evils.

"I guess I should have asked this first," she said, "but you're not allergic to dogs, are you?"

He shook his head.

"Cats?" she tried.

"Uh-uh. The only thing I know I'm allergic to is feathers. Once, in Costa Rica, I got trapped in an aviary and almost sneezed to death."

While Iggy laughed at that, Claudia considered the idea of borrowing Pete's pet budgies. But that wasn't a feasible plan. She'd only have them in the house for two minutes before Ghost would leap on the cage and scare the poor things to death.

"And I can sleep without a pillow," O'Brian was saying, "so if you don't have a foam one it's okay."

"Ahh . . . well, I'm pretty sure I have a foam one," she admitted unhappily.

"Great. Then we're all set. So," he added, turning to Iggy, "unless there's anything more you want to tell me, I guess Paquette can fill me in on the rest of the details."

"Sure, that'll be fine. I always hang around for a while on Fridays, in case there's any late-breaking news before the weekend edition goes to press. So I'll just come out with you and get that photo. Then the two of you can go on ahead and enjoy the evening."

Fat chance of that, Claudia muttered to herself.

IT WAS ONLY A LITTLE after five o'clock, but darkness had already engulfed Victoria Falls. Main Street was bathed in the soft glow of its street lamps—festooned for the season with cedar garlands—and all along the block, store windows twinkled red and green with Christmas lights.

The small-town peacefulness, Mike reflected as they headed for Iggy's car, was so far removed from the frenetic activity of L.A. that he might as well have been sent to a different planet. An incredibly *cold* different planet.

He pulled his scarf more tightly around his neck, thinking that, given the three-hour time difference, it was still sunny and warm back home.

"Here, I'll carry your laptop," Claudia said, taking it as Iggy hauled the duffel bag from the Chevy's trunk.

After Mike dug out his photo, Iggy said, "If anything comes up, feel free to call me. I'll just give you my card and . . ." Iggy froze, his hand halfway to his pocket. "What was that?" he asked quietly.

"What was what?" Claudia said.

"I thought I heard . . . sleigh bells."

The three of them stood like statues while a lone car drove by. Then Claudia said, "Iggy, I didn't hear a—"

"Shh!" he whispered furiously, pointing down the street.

Mike stared, then blinked, then stared again. Half a block along, someone on a snowmobile had appeared from an alley between two buildings. A man with a full white beard and dressed in a Santa suit. He pulled out onto the snow-packed surface of Main Street, then stopped beneath a streetlight and looked straight at them.

"It's him," Iggy whispered. "It's our Santa. O'Brian! Can you get a shot?"

He fumbled with the snap on his camera case, his fingers so cold he could hardly make them move. He'd need a hell of a long exposure time, but if Santa stayed still long enough . . .

He didn't. The jingle of sleigh bells drifted through the air. Then, giving them a leisurely wave, Santa roared off into the darkness.

"Well, aren't we going after him?" Mike demanded.

"Damn right!" Iggy said. "But we'll take Claudia's car. She's got four-wheel drive. Follow me," he added, darting away with surprising speed.

Mike started after him, completely forgetting about the smooth soles on his boots until his feet flew out from under him. A second later his butt unceremoniously crashed onto the icy sidewalk.

"You okay?" Claudia asked, skidding to a stop beside him.

"Yeah, except for the excruciating pain, I'm—"

"Hurry!" Iggy urged them.

Shoving himself to his feet, Mike gingerly limped the final few yards to where the editor was climbing into the back seat of a battered old Jeep Cherokee.

"You get in front, O'Brian," he ordered. "Toss your bag in here with me."

Mike threw it onto the back seat, then climbed into the front, pain shooting through him as he sat down.

Gunning the motor to life, Claudia swung the Jeep out into the street. She pulled a wide U-turn—missing a parked car by no more than a quarter inch—and started off in hot pursuit of the snowmobile.

Remembering it was Friday the thirteenth, Mike quickly fastened his seat belt.

"Faster!" Iggy shouted from the back. "He's got a big lead."

Claudia tromped on the gas pedal and the Jeep shot forward. Then, halfway down the block, a dog ran into their path. She slammed on the brakes so hard that Mike would have been a hood ornament if it weren't for his seat belt.

He grabbed the armrest and hung on for dear life, thinking there was no mystery about why her car was battered. Or about why Iggy had ordered him into the front. Iggy'd ridden with Claudia before, so he knew better than to risk the suicide seat.

They sped through town, then along a stretch of dark road that led to a highway. As they neared it, Claudia hit the brakes hard again. They spun sideways and bounced off the six-foot-high bank of snow lining the side of the road.

When his already throbbing hip smacked against the door he muttered, "Dammit, Paquette, has anybody ever mentioned you drive like a maniac?"

She flashed an icy glare in his direction, then looked back at Iggy. "Which way?" she demanded. "Did you see which way he turned?"

Mike glanced right, then left along the highway. In the distance he could see a lone set of car taillights. That was all.

"We've lost him," Iggy said. "He must have taken off cross-country."

"But what the hell was he up to?" Mike asked. "There was no sled full of presents. And I thought you told me nobody's ever seen him except in the middle of the night."

"Nobody has," Iggy said. "Until now."

"He waved at us," Claudia reminded them. "As if he'd been waiting for us to come out and see him."

"Exactly," Iggy agreed.

"Exactly *what?*" Mike demanded, his frustration level rising rapidly. He hated it when people talked in a shorthand he didn't understand.

"I think he must have heard you were coming to town," Iggy explained. "And he was issuing you a challenge."

"A challenge? You mean he was telling me I won't be able to track him down?"

"That's my guess," Iggy said.

MIKE O'BRIAN DIDN'T utter a word on the way back to town. He was so obviously annoyed, though, that Claudia could barely keep from smiling.

He wasn't a *blatantly* arrogant man, but she knew he figured he'd be able to solve their little puzzle with one hand tied behind his back. Of course, if she had her way, he'd be in for a big surprise.

In the meantime, she liked the way that challenge had taken him down a peg or two. But she didn't like not having a clue about what was going on.

Despite Iggy's assumption, the man on the snowmobile hadn't been their Santa. So did that mean they now had a second Santa running around? She mentally shook her head. She already had enough to worry about without any added complications.

When she pulled up in front of the *Dispatch*, Iggy quickly climbed out, saying he had to go in and rework the morning's lead article.

"Thank heavens this happened before I put my piece on the wire," he added. "Because it's what's going to let all our sister papers know your series is starting on Tuesday, O'Brian. They'll have my article to run in their Sunday or Monday editions—as a teaser. So it's really great we've got this challenge angle to add excitement."

O'Brian muttered something under his breath.

"See you two Monday," Iggy said. "And here's my card, O'Brian, in case you need to reach me." With that, Iggy slammed the car door and hurried off toward the building.

"You figure we'll make it to your place without any *more* excitement?" O'Brian asked, sticking the card into his wallet.

Her place. Remembering they had a little something to straighten out about that, she flicked on the interior light and glanced over at him.

He gave her a wolfish smile that made her blood run cold. She knew exactly what he was thinking, and she didn't like it one bit.

"Look," she said. "Before we get going, I want to be sure you're clear about why I offered to let you stay with me. It was because the Silver Dollar's a dump. Period."

The astonished expression that appeared on his face was worthy of an Academy Award. "Paquette, you don't think I figured ... Hell, I can tell the difference between a come-on and a gesture of kindness. And you don't have a thing to worry about from me."

"Good. As long as there's no confusion." She could feel her face growing hot, so she quickly switched off the light and pulled out into the street.

Then, to change the subject, she said, "I'm having dinner at my father's tonight—with him and my stepmother. So unless you want to risk the restaurant in the Silver Dollar, which I wouldn't advise, you'd better come with me."

"A stepmother, huh? Good or bad?"

"Oh, Lucille's a really nice lady."

"You're lucky. My parents are divorced, and I've got one of those stepmothers from hell. My two sisters have been known to start plotting murder after an evening with her."

"But she doesn't bother you?"

"Oh, yeah, she bothers me. Sometimes, though, I end up on an assignment when she's arranged a get-together. Which means I don't get as much exposure to her as they do."

"Well, Lucille's terrific. And she's always been like an aunt to me. Before my mother died, they were close friends."

"Your mother died a long time back?" O'Brian asked quietly.

"Ten years ago." She turned off Main and onto her own street. "My father married Lucille about five years ago and . . . They're good together. You'll see."

"You don't think they'll mind your bringing an extra dinner guest?"

"No. I'll call and explain that you're staying with me. But even if you weren't, I'm sure they'd want to meet you."

Pulling into her driveway, she wondered what O'Brian would think if he knew Lucille and her father were already half expecting him for dinner or that she'd told them he was on his way to town as soon as Iggy had informed her. Or if he knew that, barring the unexpected, her father had already put part of their plan into motion.

Claudia parked behind a tarpaulin-covered shape that Mike assumed was a snowmobile, and when she cut the ignition he simply sat looking through the windshield. The cloud cover had cleared since he'd arrived, and her place made him think of a moonlit scene from a Christmas card.

The house, a cozy-looking frame bungalow, was as white as the snowdrifts surrounding it. A huge wreath hung on the front door, and in the yard a fir tree sparkled from top to bottom with tiny white lights.

"That looks really nice," he offered.

She smiled. "I like Christmas."

Glancing at the house again, he began thinking about the prospect of sharing it with her. Merely the thought was enough to start a stirring in his groin. Maybe she *had* only offered him a room because the hotel was a dump. But even if that was true, a week alone together in the same small house . . .

Just as his imagination began running wild, a dog started howling inside—reminding him they wouldn't be entirely alone.

"That's Morgan," Claudia said, opening her door and reaching for the laptop again. "He's a bit protective, but don't let him scare you. Just be careful of your camera."

Mike eased his aching body out of the car, tucked his camera bag safely under one arm and slid his duffel bag from the back seat. As he stiffly climbed the two front steps, Claudia opened the door.

When she ushered him inside, he took a couple of steps into the shadowy entrance area, then stopped dead—his heart hammering.

"Ahh...Morgan's actually a wolf?" he said as calmly as he could. It was hard to remain even marginally calm, though, when he was looking a wild animal in the teeth and it was growling deep in its throat.

"No, don't be silly," Claudia told him, switching on the light. "He's an Alaskan malamute. They only look like wolves.

"It's okay, Morgan," she added to the dog. "This is company."

Morgan began edging forward, still growling.

Mike casually put his duffel bag down between them.

The beast scuttled past it, reached Claudia and instantly turned into an immense gray bundle of affection.

"See?" she said, bending down to give him a hug. "The vicious routine is only an act."

"Right." It was one hell of a good act, though. If the dog lived in Hollywood, he could make a fortune in the movies.

Claudia put Morgan outside, a move Mike heartily approved of, then pulled off her boots and set them on the mat.

He tried to bend over to remove his, but the motion made his backside hurt like hell.

"They're so wet you're going to have trouble getting them off," Claudia pointed out, hanging her coat on the coat tree. "So maybe you'd better sit down."

Sit down. On his bruised butt. Now, there was an appealing idea. Since he didn't have much choice, though, he lowered himself cautiously to the floor— then groaned. He hadn't been nearly cautious enough.

"That fall hurt some, did it?"

"Some," he agreed, trying to pull the legs of his jeans out of his boots. When they wouldn't budge, he had a shot at just yanking off one of the boots. It might as well have been cemented to his foot.

"Need help?" she finally asked.

"Apparently, yes."

She knelt down in front of him and began tugging away. "These are absolutely sopping," she said. "Do you have something else to wear when we go out again?"

"A pair of hiking boots, but they're not very high."

"Well, anything will be better than these. Lord, your jeans are soaked right up to your knees," she told him, managing to work the boots off. "And your socks are half ice. Can you even feel your feet?"

He wasn't sure, and before he could decide, she had his socks off and was poking at his toes.

"Well?" she demanded.

"Yes, I can feel them. And they feel as if they've got a zillion pins sticking in them."

"That's because you have frostbite."

"It's not fatal, is it?" he joked.

She didn't smile—simply shook her head and said, "No, it's not fatal. But I'll have to get you to the doctor. She'll probably want to amputate before gangrene can set in."

His heart was suddenly in his throat.

"Just kidding, O'Brian," Claudia said.

"Very funny," he muttered, thinking he'd like to take her swimming off Santa Monica, get her out a few hundred yards, then tell her the water was infested with sharks.

"They don't really look *too* bad," she told him, "but come on. You'd better hit the bathtub and soak for a while." She rose and started down the hall.

He carefully pushed himself up, grabbed his duffel bag and limped after her, the pinprick sensations getting sharper with each step.

Trying to ignore them, he glanced into the living room on the way by. From what he could see, with only the hall light, the room looked comfortable— furnished with overstuffed pieces and decorated with brightly colored wall hangings.

"Sorry there's no Christmas tree in there yet," Claudia said, glancing back. "I've been too busy to get one, but I will."

He nodded. There was something about her that said she'd never dream of not having one.

At the back of the house, the hall ended in a T-shape. The bathroom was straight ahead, with one bedroom on either side of it, their open doorways facing each other.

Claudia started water running in the tub, then came back out into the hall. "That's my room," she said, pointing to the right.

"There are messages on your machine," he told her, in case she hadn't noticed the red light flashing in the darkness.

"Mmm. There are always messages on my machine. If somebody's kid builds a snow fort, I get a message telling me the paper should run a picture of it. At any rate," she added, turning left, "this is the guest room."

She switched on its light, revealing a white cat lying on the bed. It looked at them, blinked a couple of times, then jumped down and scurried off.

"That was Ghost," she said. "He's not very sociable, so he'll probably stay out of sight while you're here."

"It's okay if he doesn't. Cats don't bother me."

"Well, get undressed and into the tub. Soak for at least half an hour. My father and Lucille eat late, so we're not in any hurry. In fact, I'm going to make coffee. Would you like some when you're done?"

"Sure. Sounds great."

She started to turn away, then said, "Oh, don't run the water any hotter than I've got it or you're liable to cause tissue damage."

"You practice medicine in your spare time?"

"Just do as I say. Frostbite isn't exactly an exotic disease up here. Everybody over the age of two knows how to treat it."

As she headed for the front of the house, he limped into the bathroom, closed the door and stripped off his clothes—then realized he hadn't brought any clean stuff in with him. Which meant that either he went and got some dry clothes now or he'd have to drip his way into the bedroom later.

Since that decision was a no-brainer, he turned off the water and checked the towels on the shelf. They were all pink, which wasn't his color, and none of them were terribly large. He only had to go a few steps, though. And with any luck, Claudia was still busy making the coffee.

Wrapping one of the towels around his waist, he hobbled to the door, cracked it open a couple of inches and peered out. The light in her bedroom wasn't on. The coast was clear.

Opening the door the rest of the way, he stepped into the hall. And that was when he heard her in the dark bedroom. The hall light reached far enough into her room that he could see her standing with her back to him, talking quietly on the phone.

He was about to skulk along to his own room when she said, "I realized that. So I invited him to stay with me. He's here now."

There was such an anxious tone in her voice that he didn't move. She sounded as if she wished he were staying anywhere in the world except with her. But if that was true, why had she invited him?

"Yes," she murmured, "I *do* think it's a good idea. Otherwise I wouldn't have asked him."

That made him wonder who she was talking to—who *didn't* think it was a good idea for him to be staying with her?

It had to be her father, he decided. She'd called to explain the situation and let him know there'd be extra company for dinner. And, like any normal father, hers didn't like the prospect of a strange man staying with his daughter.

Mike found that fact a little unsettling, considering he'd soon be eating dinner at the man's house. Just as he was wondering if Mr. Paquette and Lucille kept a handy supply of rat poison in their kitchen cupboard, Claudia glanced around and caught him listening.

And at that exact second he felt his towel beginning to slip.

CHAPTER THREE

STARTLED, CLAUDIA STOOD staring at a near-naked Mike O'Brian—six-plus feet of lean muscles, golden brown chest hair and California tan.

He was wearing nothing except a horrified expression and a hot pink towel. And he was just about to lose the latter.

Then he grabbed at it with both hands, mumbled, "Sorry," and rapidly limped to his bedroom.

Forcing her gaze from his retreating form, she turned her attention back to the phone. "I've got to go," she whispered. "I'll call again later. And whatever you do, don't leave any messages on my machine while he's here."

Hanging up, she frantically replayed the conversation in her head, then told herself to calm down. Even if O'Brian had heard every word she'd said, her side of things hadn't been enough to clue him in.

She'd assumed, though, that he'd gotten safely into the bathtub. Now it was clear she couldn't count on him to do what she expected. Which meant she'd have to be far more careful.

Just as she was telling herself it was a good thing she only had the one phone, that he was probably into picking up extensions, he reappeared—wearing a jade monogrammed bathrobe.

"I...ahh, forgot to take my robe in there with me," he explained. "But I won't make a habit of wandering around in a towel."

She nodded, hoping he meant that. Since she obviously had to be on her guard, she could do without distractions. And O'Brian wearing only a towel definitely qualified as a distraction.

Not that she had the slightest interest in him. Not in *that* department. But she'd admit he was an attractive man even with his clothes on. Without them, he was the stuff sexual fantasies were made of.

"And I'll try not to eavesdrop again, either," he promised. "It's just become kind of a habit over the years."

"I know." She managed a smile. "You can never tell when you might overhear a great lead."

That made him laugh. "I like the way you think, Paquette. You're a woman after my own heart."

She smiled again, but Mike O'Brian's heart was the last thing on earth she was after.

"So," O'BRIAN SAID as Claudia backed out of her driveway, "does Morgan always go visiting with you?"

She glanced into the rear seat and told Morgan to stop drooling on their guest's shoulder. Then, to O'Brian, she said, "No, he only goes places he's welcome. And feel free to tell him when he's bothering you."

"I'd feel a bit freer if his teeth weren't so big. But how about filling me in on some of the Santa details? Your father might want to talk about what's been happening."

She nodded. O'Brian could safely bet his bottom dollar her father would want to talk about it. And Lucille, too. "Well, you had a look at my articles," she said, shifting into drive and starting down the street. "Santa's been delivering gifts every night for more than a week now. And at the rate he's going, it looks as if he intends to visit every family that was hit by the layoffs."

"Uh-huh, but..."

She glanced across at him and waited—unable to get a good read on his expression with only the dim light from the dash. "But what?" she finally pressed.

"Well, don't take this wrong. I thought your stuff read just fine. And you had some nice quotes from people he's already visited. But none of the articles were exactly heavy on hard facts."

"That's because I haven't turned up many hard facts."

"But you've been on this from the beginning, haven't you?"

"It isn't the *only* story I've been working on," she said defensively. He obviously figured she'd had three times as long as she should have needed to crack the story.

"No, no, of course. You've had other things to cover. But you must have come up with *some* sort of plan by now. Some idea of how to identify him."

She swung out onto Main Street before answering. "Actually," she admitted at last, "I wasn't intending to identify him."

"Oh, sure you weren't. And if I buy that, you've got a hundred acres of frozen tundra to sell me, right?"

Their conversation, she decided, was well on its way to being ironic. As far as the subject of Santa went, saying she hadn't been intending to identify him was probably one of the few truthful things she'd be telling O'Brian. And he hadn't believed her for a second.

"Look," she said, "can you keep a secret?"

He nodded. "I once spent two days in jail for refusing to reveal a source."

"All right, then. Don't say a word about this to anyone. Not even Iggy, because he wouldn't like me telling you. But when Santa first began making his rounds, Iggy and I decided we wouldn't really work at identifying him."

"You're serious?"

"Yes. I know my articles sound as if I've been hot on his trail, but I haven't."

"Why not?"

"Because we were afraid that if I actually did catch up with him, he'd quit distributing goodies. And we didn't want to risk that. I mean, when somebody's playing Good Samaritan, why take a chance on stopping him? So even if I'd gotten iron-clad proof of who he was, we wouldn't have told people. Not until he was finished, at least."

"But Iggy said I'm *supposed* to ID him."

"That's because Iggy rethought things. You see, it wasn't until late yesterday that your editor confirmed he was definitely sending someone. And after he did, after Iggy really started thinking about how your articles would get picked up by major papers and everything..."

"Yes?"

"Well, it was one thing for me to pretend Santa was outsmarting *me*. But Iggy could hardly tell you he wanted *you* to look incompetent. Aside from anything else, it would have taken the edge off your series, and he couldn't have that—not when he's hoping it's going to save the *Dispatch*."

O'Brian shook his head. "Hoping one short series will save a paper is hoping for a hell of a lot."

"I know. But the *Dispatch* is Iggy's whole life, so if there's even a chance... Well, as I said, he's re-thought things."

"And you're okay with that?"

"Iggy's the boss," she said, not liking the way O'Brian was eyeing her. If he was *already* suspicious, it didn't augur well.

"Paquette, I didn't ask who the boss was. I asked if you're worried about how Santa will react when we unmask him."

"I think the term would be unbeard him." She'd hoped the remark would make O'Brian forget his question, but it didn't.

He gave her a quick grin, then said, "Okay, un-beard him. Either way, you're still worried he might stop making his deliveries, aren't you."

"Well...yes. But Iggy's decided that might not happen."

"Then Iggy's into wishful thinking. Santa's got to be getting a big kick out of his anonymity. Otherwise he wouldn't be skulking around in the dead of night. So the thrill will be gone once somebody figures out who he is."

O'Brian was silent for a few seconds, then added, "And if I'm the *somebody*, that would kind of make me the Grinch who stole Christmas, wouldn't it?"

Claudia held her breath, hoping their hotshot had a softer heart than she'd expected.

Then he dashed her hopes by saying, "Well, I guess nobody can really predict what he'll do. And hell, I've got no choice about tracking him down. You heard what Iggy said. I'm stuck here until I write that final chapter—even if it takes till Easter. So let's figure out how we're going to nail the guy. Why don't you give me a quick summary of everything you know."

She exhaled slowly, warning herself to be careful what she said. She was far from a first-class liar, and mixing lies with the truth was going to put her at high risk of tripping herself up.

"Well," she began, "as I explained in my articles, even when he's delivered gifts to houses outside town, where people have been able to follow his tracks, they've always led onto a snow-packed road."

"And tracks from snowmobile skis don't show up on packed snow, right? No more than tire tracks do."

"Exactly. That's obviously why he's using roads, even though it isn't legal to drive a snowmobile on them."

"No?"

"No. But of course it wasn't legal for him to be driving one around town, either. And even though people don't worry much about the side streets, most of them wouldn't go driving down Main."

"Okay, then we've got a starting place. We can rule out all the strictly law-abiding citizens, as well as everyone who can't drive a snowmobile."

"Around here?" She couldn't keep from giving O'Brian a superior glance. "That would let you rule out most children still in diapers and a few ninety-year-olds."

"Oh. Then we'll have to try another angle. Have you got a list of everyone who was laid off? Everyone he'll have slated for a visit?"

She nodded, turning onto her father's street. "I made a point of getting all the names. As I said, we wanted to make people think we were seriously trying to track him down. But he hasn't been making his visits in any obvious order, so it won't be as easy as just figuring out where he'll show up next and waiting there for him.

"At any rate, we're here," she said, pulling into the driveway and stopping behind her father's truck.

When O'Brian opened his door and slowly maneuvered himself out of the Cherokee, it reminded her that the fall he'd taken had been pretty bad. From the looks of him, he wouldn't be moving very quickly for a while.

That made her feel a tiny bit better about things, because Santa had always been a very fast runner.

TEN MINUTES AFTER they arrived at Raymond and Lucille Paquette's, Mike decided he didn't have to worry about them putting rat poison in his food.

They were clearly kindly people. They even kept a supply of rawhide bones on hand for Morgan. And the way Raymond had sat Mike down on the couch next to Claudia, then offered him a drink, had made him feel right at home.

While Claudia was filling the couple in about Santa's unexpected appearance on Main Street, he glanced around the living room.

Most of the decorations on the Christmas tree were homemade, which seemed right for the Paquettes. But he was surprised to see there were no photographs on display. They'd struck him as the sort of people who'd have pictures all over the place.

He looked back across the coffee table at them, wondering if any of his other first impressions had been off base. But he was pretty sure he had a good read on them.

They were both in their early fifties—Lucille with short dark hair, an easy smile and a few extra pounds; Raymond, Victoria Falls' jack-of-all-trades, a large, solid man who might well have been a hippie in his youth.

He wore his long brown hair pulled back in a ponytail and had a graying beard. He also had a generous pouring hand and excellent Scotch whiskey.

Mike took another sip of it, savoring its smoky smoothness. Then something funny in Claudia's voice drew his attention back to what she was saying.

"No, I have *no idea* who he was," she told the others.

It took a second for him to realize she was still talking about Santa, and another second to begin wondering what had caused the funny tone. Then he grew even more curious as Lucille and Raymond exchanged puzzled glances.

When Santa had pulled out onto Main Street, he'd been about a hundred yards away and all dressed up in his suit and beard. So surely it should be no big surprise that Claudia hadn't known who he was.

"Well, Mike," Raymond said, looking over at him. "You got quite the introduction to our Santa, eh? Is that what you'll write your first article about?"

"No, Iggy told us he'd cover it in tomorrow's edition."

"Santa's going to have quite the scrapbook by the time he's done," Lucille said. "There've been stories about him in every issue since he began his deliveries.

Claudia's written all of them so far, and they've been wonderful."

Mike nodded. "I read them. I only hope mine turn out half as good."

"Oh, puh-leez," Claudia whispered beside him. "Keep that up and we'll need a shovel."

"What did you say, dear?" Lucille asked.

"I said I'm sure his series will be great."

"But do you think," Raymond asked, waving his glass in Mike's direction, "you'll have any trouble proving who Santa is?"

"Well, we can't go getting ahead of ourselves. First we've got to *figure out* who he is. Then we'll worry about *proving* it."

"Figure out who he is?" Raymond glanced at his daughter. "You haven't told him?"

Mike looked curiously at Claudia. Until this moment, he'd been under the impression that nobody had the slightest clue about Santa's identity.

She neatly avoided eye contact with him and said, "Dad, not everyone is as certain they have the answer as you are. And O'Brian and I simply haven't gotten around to discussing suspects yet."

"Why don't we do it right now," Mike suggested, seizing the opportunity. "Who do you think Santa is, Raymond?"

"Well, hell, there are only two people it could be. A couple of poker buddies of mine—two brothers named Gord and Norm Nilsson."

"Those are the fellows you and Iggy were talking about," Mike said to Claudia.

"Uh-huh."

"They're millionaires," Raymond offered.

"Don't you think it's multimillionaires, dear?" Lucille asked.

"Whatever. They're loaded—made a bundle in computers."

"Iggy mentioned that," Mike said. "But he also told me it couldn't possibly be them," he added, trying to remember *exactly* what Iggy had said.

"Iggy," Raymond muttered. "Sometimes Iggy Brooks sounds so dumb I wonder if he's brain-dead."

"It couldn't be anyone *but* one of the Nilssons," Lucille put in firmly. "Or both of them. That's what I figure. They're in it together."

"I think she's right," Raymond agreed. "I'll bet they hatched the scheme between the two of them. They're quite the couple of characters."

"And you're *sure* it's them?"

"Has to be. Nobody else around here's got nearly enough money."

Mike looked at Claudia again, managing to catch her eye this time.

She shrugged. "I've talked to them. They denied it."

"And you let it go at that?"

"You know what I told you," she murmured, clearly intending the words for his ears only. "Identifying Santa wasn't on the original agenda."

"Claudia, do you have a sore throat?" Lucille asked. "You keep speaking so quietly I can't hear a word you're saying."

"Sorry. I was just telling O'Brian that you and Dad are making a valid point. The Nilssons are the most obvious suspects."

"Then why," Mike asked, "did Iggy dismiss them with such certainty?"

"Bad blood," Lucille said.

"Between Iggy and the Nilssons," Claudia elaborated. "When O'Brian first got here," she explained to the others, "Iggy was telling him that Gord and Norm are cheap. And not community-minded."

"Is he ever going to stop riding that horse?" Raymond muttered.

"It isn't true, then?" Mike asked.

"Well, I've never seen them throwing money around on Main Street, but that hardly means they're cheap. When Iggy gets an idea in his head, though, he never lets it go."

Glancing at Claudia once more, Mike began wondering if anyone was ever going to tell him the full story.

"Here's what happened," she said—much to his relief. "The *Dispatch* has been losing money for years. And Iggy's been worried all along that Ferris Wentworth would eventually pull the plug. So, a couple of years ago, he tried to convince the Nilssons they should ask Wentworth to sell it to them. But they didn't go for the idea."

"Of course they didn't," Raymond said. "They're intelligent men, so why would they want a money-losing paper? Telling Iggy they weren't interested was the only sensible thing to do."

"That's not how Iggy saw it, though," Claudia explained. "He thought that if they were the least bit civic-minded they'd have jumped at the chance to take over ownership and ensure the *Dispatch* would survive."

Mike nodded, but the cause of the falling out between Iggy and the Nilssons wasn't the important thing here. What he should have sunk his teeth into earlier, rather than letting Iggy mislead him, was the fact that there were only two people around with enough money to be playing Santa. So regardless of what Iggy chose to think . . .

He looked at Claudia again, annoyed that she hadn't set him straight about the Nilssons. How could she be earning her living as a reporter when she didn't bother distinguishing important facts from filler?

When he'd asked her for details about the story, the very first thing she should have told him was who the prime suspects were. Hell, the only *possible* suspects, from the sound of it. Instead, she'd launched into that big explanation about how nobody could follow Santa's tracks. Which didn't matter in the least. Not if the whole town knew where he lived—or *they* lived, as the case seemed to be.

"I guess you figure I should have explained right away that Iggy has a biased opinion of the Nilssons," she said.

He was about to tell her that was exactly what he figured, but the anxious look in her big brown eyes stopped him cold. There was nothing to be gained from making her feel like a fool.

"Well," he offered, "I probably should have asked more questions than I did. At any rate, we've got things sorted out now."

The smile she gave him made him glad he hadn't taken her to task. Besides, maybe he was expecting more of her than he should. After all, being a reporter on the *Miner's Dispatch* was a far cry from covering stories for the *L.A. Gazette*.

"Does *anybody* think," he finally asked, "that it might not be the Nilssons? Anybody aside from Iggy, I mean?"

"Sure," Claudia said. "A few people don't think it can be them because that would be just *too* obvious. Right, Lucille?"

"Ahh...yes. Yes, of course." Lucille looked at Raymond. "I guess we were being a little too emphatic, weren't we, dear. I mean, what Claudia's saying is true. Not everyone's certain it has to be Gord and Norm."

"Then who else do people think it might be?" Mike asked.

"Oh, there are a variety of theories floating around," Claudia told him.

"Such as?"

"Well, one thought is that maybe somebody's secretly gotten rich—has been stashing money in his mattress for years, and now...

"All right, I know that doesn't sound likely," she hurried on at Mike's skeptical glance. "But it's not *definitely* the Nilssons. I mean, they haven't come right out and admitted it or anything. And it would be worth trying a few other angles first, wouldn't it? Especially since you have to write a whole series of articles."

He merely sat gazing at her, deciding she really *wasn't* reporter stuff. It was perfectly obvious that the Nilssons were playing Santa. So if she figured it would be a good idea to go running around town looking for a nonexistent mattress stuffed with money, she was completely out to lunch.

Then he thought back to their conversation in the car and realized she might not actually figure it was a good idea at all. Maybe she was simply trying to buy time for the Nilssons. Time for them to deliver more of their presents before they got unbearded, as she'd called it.

If that was what she was up to, he could hardly blame her. And, actually, he didn't mind the idea of stringing things out a little—would have to, in fact, to get a week's worth of articles. But there was no way he'd make a fool of himself by pretending not to have a clue who Santa was. No, it would be clear from the start that the Nilssons were his prime suspects.

After all, he was an investigative reporter with a reputation for ferreting out facts no one else could get at.

He took another sip of Scotch, unhappily thinking that, in this situation, there were no facts to be ferreted. Which meant his stupid articles would be a farce from square one.

MORGAN YAWNED AND LOOKED at the door, obviously eager to get going, but Lucille didn't seem ready to let them escape yet.

"Now," she said, "is there anything else you're going to need to survive up here?"

"I don't think there *could* be," Mike told her, enunciating his words carefully. Something had caused his tongue to get a little fuzzy, although he wasn't sure whether he should be blaming that fine Scotch, the wine he'd drunk with dinner or the . . . *stuff* Raymond had pressed on him afterward. *Moose milk,* he finally remembered. It was a mixture of home brew and milk—heavy on the brew and light on the milk, from the taste of it.

He sneaked another look at Claudia, who'd passed on both the Scotch and the moose milk. She seemed perfectly sober. Which was just as well, given the erratic way she drove.

Thinking about that reminded him he wanted his own wheels, so he turned to Raymond. "You won't forget the car?"

Victoria Falls, he'd learned, didn't boast an auto rental place. Raymond, though, had offered to line something up.

"I'll ask around in the morning," he said. "Get you one as soon as I can."

"Great. Really appreciate that." Lucille and Raymond, he mused, were two of the finest people on earth. As for Claudia...

He risked glancing at her once more, even though he knew he'd been doing it far too often. But she was so darned good to look at, he couldn't seem to stop himself. And she was awfully nice.

Those sterling qualities had almost made him forget she wasn't much of a reporter. Or maybe he'd decided that didn't matter.

He liked her sense of humor, too. And she had a very kind heart. She'd saved him from a stay at the Silver Dollar, treated his frostbite, and tonight she'd rummaged through her father's closet with Lucille to find warm clothes he could borrow.

She caught him eyeing her again, so he quickly looked away. Which left him staring at himself in the hall mirror.

The image staring back looked as if it weighed three hundred pounds. The knee-length parka of Raymond's was very bulky and very hot. Just as hot as those... *things* they'd lent him to wear instead of his hiking boots.

"What are they called again?" he asked, pointing down at them.

"Mukluks," Claudia said.

"Muuuk...luuuks," he repeated. Made of seal-skin. Worn by the Inuit as far back as the beginning of time, or some such story. And under them were the three pairs of heavy socks they'd found for him.

"Oh, we *did* forget something," Lucille said, turning and hurrying off down the hall.

He glanced longingly at the front door. He'd never have believed the thought of getting back out into that cold would be appealing. But the parka and wool scarf and those things on his feet were becoming warmer by the minute.

"Here," Lucille said, reappearing with a box in her hand. "These were going to be one of Raymond's Christmas presents, but I can get him another set."

Mike fumbled the lid off the box and peered at the bright red fabric inside.

"Hmm," Raymond muttered. "When you get another set, could you get a different color?"

"But red is such a Christmasy color, dear."

"It's...a long-sleeved T-shirt?" Mike guessed.

"Thermal underwear," Claudia told him.

"A top and bottom," Lucille added.

When he prodded at the material, sure enough, there were two pieces. "Ahh...thermal underwear. Great."

He produced a smile for Lucille, but since his body temperature had already climbed to about a hundred and forty degrees, it was a darned good thing she hadn't thought about the underwear earlier. If she'd made him put it on along with everything else, he'd be melting into a puddle.

"Well, we'd better get going, O'Brian," Claudia said. "You said you want to head out and interview the Nilssons first thing in the morning."

"Right." He watched her take his bomber jacket and hiking boots from the hall closet, thinking that first thing wasn't sounding as terrific as it had earlier. But once he got out into the cold he'd probably stop feeling as if he wanted to sleep for a week.

"Don't forget the mitts," Lucille told him. "And the toque."

Collecting the rest of the things the Paquettes were loaning him, he profusely thanked them for their hospitality, then followed Claudia and Morgan out into the frigid night—realizing his body didn't feel nearly as sore and stiff as it had earlier. Raymond must have been right. That moose milk really did cure whatever ailed a man.

By the time he made it down the steps, Claudia was already over at the Jeep, unplugging its block heater. In Northern Ontario, she'd told him, engine heaters were critical if you were leaving your car sitting for more than a couple of hours.

He watched her drag the extension cord past the truck and snowmobile that were parked in the drive, his gaze lingering on the moonlit snowmobile. "Raymond," he said.

"Pardon?" Claudia glanced at him as she looped the cord over a hook on the garage.

"Raymond," he repeated, pointing to where the name was scrolled along the side of the chassis.

"Oh. Right. It's kind of corny, isn't it," she said, starting back toward him. "He wanted to have Lucille's name put on hers, too, but she said no way."

"Hers? Where is it?"

"Oh . . . Gee, I don't know. They must have taken it in for some work or something."

"Ahh. I can drive those things, you know."

"You can, can you?"

"Uh-huh. Learned years ago. When I was doing a piece on skiing, at Lake Placid." He'd been going to tell her more, but a sneeze seized him.

"Gesundheit," she said, letting Morgan into the Jeep.

"Thanks."

They'd barely climbed in themselves before he sneezed again.

"Oh, dear," she murmured, backing out to the street. "I was afraid you'd end up paying for walking around in those wet cowboy boots. You're coming down with something."

He sniffed. He *was* beginning to feel congested.

"We'll have to keep a close eye on you. I'll bet leaving the warmth of L.A. and landing here in the cold is enough to cause pneumonia."

"I'll be fine." As they started off, he settled back in the seat, feeling warm and cozy in all his northern clothes. And he was also feeling . . . cared about.

Glancing across the dark car, he decided it was kind of nice to have someone worry about his welfare. Then he gave the thought a little more consideration and decided the moose milk had muddled his brain.

He was perfectly capable of taking care of himself. And given the life he led, flying all over the world on a moment's notice, the last thing he normally wanted was anyone worrying about him.

No strings, no commitments. That was the only philosophy for a man like him. He'd seen too many of his colleagues' marriages go down the tubes to have any doubts about that, he mused, trying to ignore the tickle in his nose and the scratchiness in his throat.

When O'Brian sneezed a third time, Claudia flashed him the best look of concern she could muster. Then she focused on her driving again and went back to worrying about that little goof she'd made by mentioning Lucille's snowmobile. Finally telling herself O'Brian wasn't going to remember much in the morning, she turned her worries to the way her father and Lucille had sounded so positive about Santa's identity.

She was afraid that, instead of merely ensuring O'Brian would suspect the Nilssons, they'd convinced him Santa couldn't be anyone else.

Glancing across the Jeep once more, she wondered just how awful O'Brian was going to be feeling tomorrow. Anyone drinking moose milk for the first time usually woke up with a head the size of Toronto. And the down filling in that parka had his allergy kicking in nicely.

Of course, he'd probably realize what the problem was sooner or later. But in the meantime, if there was just some way of convincing him he should sleep in the parka tonight...

The only idea that came to her was turning off the heat in the house and pretending the furnace was broken. But she could hardly do that. If she did, her pipes would freeze.

Maybe, though, if he was *highly* allergic, he'd still be stuffed up come morning. And if the moose milk left his head feeling as if trains had been running through it...

Well, with a little effort, she might manage to convince him he should be flown home to a hospital in warm, sunny L.A.

CHAPTER FOUR

O'BRIAN PROVED TO BE more resilient than Claudia had anticipated. She hadn't expected him to crawl out of bed before noon, but by the time she'd showered and thrown on jeans and a sweater, he was sitting at the kitchen table in his bathrobe.

He'd already made a pot of coffee, had the radio turned up higher than she normally played it and was in the midst of a game of tug-of-war with Morgan.

"Your dog's decided he likes me," he announced cheerfully.

"Good. That only leaves the cat to win over." She eyed him for a moment, thinking that at least he looked a little green around the gills.

"How about bacon and eggs?" she suggested, hoping the mere thought of fried food would do him in.

It didn't. In fact, he offered to help cook.

She let him take care of the toast, watching him surreptitiously while she handled the rest.

"You're not stiff from your fall?" she asked when he didn't seem to be having any trouble moving around.

"Hardly a bit. Surprising, isn't it?"

"Yes. Amazing." It wasn't good, though. He was obviously a hard man to slow down. A fall like that would have left her limping for days. And the moose milk, which had a devastating effect on most people, clearly hadn't taken much of a toll on him. If it had, he wouldn't have that radio blaring away.

He wasn't sneezing, either. A night's sleep, with the down parka hanging out in the front hall, had apparently cleared up his allergy problems.

So much for convincing him a trip to some far-off hospital was in order. It looked as if she might as well forget about trying to get rid of him and simply concentrate on buying time. She only hoped she could buy enough. The danger to Santa was becoming far too real for comfort.

After O'Brian had gone to bed last night, she'd phoned Santa again—and made him promise to finish his deliveries as quickly as he could. But he still needed a few days, which meant it was just as well she had more tricks up her sleeve.

"Santa was busy again during the night," she offered, glancing at O'Brian.

He stopped buttering midslice. "Yeah? How do you know?"

"A couple of people called, first thing, to tell me he left them gifts."

"Really? I didn't realize you had a Santa hot line."

There's a lot you don't realize, she said silently. Aloud, she said, "Well, everyone knows I've been covering the story, and they've been keeping me up to date. So I thought we could drop by their places later. That would give you a chance to see the hampers and—"

"Oh, no, there's no point in bothering anyone. Your articles have covered the gifts and hampers just fine."

Rats, she muttered under her breath. They could have wasted hours with Santa's most recent beneficiaries.

"Besides," O'Brian went on, "we're going to visit the Nilsson brothers this morning, remember?"

With another silent "rats," she put his plate in front of him.

"Hey, this is great," he said, taking a couple of bites.

"You're sure you still want to head for the Nilssons'?" she tried, sitting down across from him. "Their place is a fair drive, and it looks as if we're in for snow."

"So? Doesn't it snow up here most days?"

"A lot of them," she admitted. "But don't you at least want to wait around for a while? See if my father turns up a car for you?"

"No, let's just go dig up some proof that it's the Nilssons. Then I'll only have to figure out how to fabricate a week's worth of articles."

Wonderful. Just as she'd feared, her father and Lucille had done *too* good a selling job last night. So how was she going to convince O'Brian not to start with them? She could hardly come right out and say that she wanted to save them for the main event.

"More coffee?" O'Brian asked, pushing himself up to get the pot as he spoke.

Uneasily, she watched him stride across the kitchen. He obviously felt right at home in her house, while she was feeling more than a little uncomfortable with him here. Especially when he was wearing that darn bathrobe.

Not that it was anywhere near as revealing as yesterday's towel, but she'd feel better if he were fully dressed. There was something decidedly disturbing about his bare legs. Not to mention how sexy he looked with a day's growth of beard. She hated to admit it, but O'Brian's presence had been doing funny things to her insides since the moment she'd walked into the kitchen.

Forcing her eyes from him, she told herself the problem was simply that her hormones were trying to make up for lost time. She hadn't made love in almost a year. Not since the provincial police had transferred Chet Summerly to Red Lake, a good sixteen hundred kilometers away. Which made it hardly surprising that when there was an attractive man staying right in her house...

An attractive man, she firmly reminded herself, who represented a serious threat to Santa. Which made O'Brian the enemy. And that meant sitting here thinking she found him attractive was very foolish. She had to stay focused on outwitting him.

"So," he said, sitting down again and pouring the fresh coffee. "You think we can just show up at the Nilssons'? I like having the element of surprise."

"Oh, no, that's not a good idea with Norm and Gord. For some reason, they don't like people just dropping in, so we'd really better phone first."

And that, of course, would give them a chance to put her off. Then she could try to convince O'Brian there really were a few other viable Santa suspects they should be talking to.

"Are you going to call them now?"

"Sure." But before she actually had to make good on that, someone rang the doorbell. Morgan went flying from the kitchen in fierce watchdog mode, but by the time she followed him to the entrance hall he'd stopped barking and gone into a demented dance routine.

When she opened the door, her best friend was standing on the steps—a copy of the Saturday paper in her hand.

Morgan pushed forward for a pat. Annie gave him a quick rub behind the ear, then scooted him outside and closed the door against the cold.

"What are you doing out so early?" Claudia asked. "Is my calendar wrong, or wasn't yesterday the last day of school?"

"No, your calendar's not wrong. The blessed dog-sled races start on Monday."

Claudia smiled. Schools in their region closed a few days earlier than most did for Christmas vacation— because of the races. And Annie always said it gave the teachers a chance to regain their sanity before Christmas Day.

"And I know," she was going on, "that I traditionally celebrate a break from the little monsters with a leisurely breakfast in bed. But word has it . . ."

Pausing to wave the *Dispatch*'s front-page picture of O'Brian under Claudia's nose, she dropped her voice to a whisper. "Word has it this hunk is staying with you. And word is right, isn't it."

She glanced pointedly at the coat tree, where both O'Brian's bomber jacket and his borrowed parka were hanging.

"Lord, are there *no* secrets in this town?"

"You know there aren't. Well, except for who Santa is. That's not exactly a secret, though, is it."

"No, and you don't have to whisper. In case you haven't noticed, the hunk has the radio turned up pretty loud."

Annie nodded, unfolding the paper. "Since everyone knows who Santa is, why's Iggy saying that your roomer's going to have a hard time identifying him?"

With the paper fully open, Claudia could see that Iggy had changed his headline before it went to press. The final version read, Santa Thumbs Nose at L.A. Reporter.

Frowning, she skimmed the lead article's first few sentences. Just as Iggy had promised, he'd rewritten it to let the readers know how Santa had welcomed their guest reporter. But his description of the encounter was highly exaggerated. It was also the last thing she needed.

O'Brian already wanted to track Santa down just as fast as he could, and a story that played up the challenge angle was only going to make him more determined.

She silently uttered a few unkind comments about her boss, then told herself she shouldn't be blaming Iggy. He wouldn't be intentionally making things more difficult for Santa—not to mention her—if he knew who Santa was and why his identity had to remain a secret.

"What's the matter?" Annie asked.

"Nothing," Claudia said quickly. Best friend or not, she couldn't share the Santa secret with Annie any more than she could with Iggy. Not after she'd sworn she wouldn't.

"Well, then? Aren't you going to tell me what the deal is? How Iggy's L.A. reporter ended up under your roof?"

"I...he was booked in at the Silver Dollar and I just took pity on him."

Annie shot her a "Sure you did" look.

"Really. You'll see. There's something about him that says he'd have been absolutely miserable at the Silver Dollar. But why are we standing here in the hall when I know you're just dying to meet him?"

"Me? Dying to meet a Pulitzer-winning journalist whose picture looks like Alec Baldwin? Whatever gave you that idea?"

Claudia grinned. "The drool stains on your *Dispatch,* for one thing. But look, there's something you've got to do for me."

"What?"

"Well, it's really two things. First, I don't want him to see the paper yet, so can I have it?"

"Sure. It's got drool stains on it, anyway."

Claudia rolled it up and glanced around for a hiding place. Her snowmobile boots were tucked behind the coat tree, so she stashed it in one of them.

"Boy," Annie said. "You really don't want him to see it, do you."

"No. And the other thing is that I'm...well, I'm trying to convince him Santa might not be one of the Nilssons, so—"

"Why?"

"I'll explain later, okay? There isn't time now. But here's what I need you to do."

ANNIE ROBIDOUX, Mike quickly learned, had been Claudia's best friend forever, was the French teacher at the district school and was single. That last detail really made him think there must be something wrong with the men in Northern Ontario. Otherwise, how could both Claudia and Annie be unmarried?

With her green eyes and shoulder-length blond hair, Annie was a very good-looking woman. Maybe not in

Claudia's league, but he hadn't met many who were. Every time he looked at those full, lush lips of hers...

He forced his thoughts from that track when Annie said, "Claudia mentioned you two are off to visit the Nilssons this morning."

"Uh-huh. As soon as I get showered and shaved."

"I guess she told you she's already talked to them? And that they claimed they didn't know anything?"

"Yeah, she did. But I still figure it's worth asking them a few questions."

Annie shrugged. "I can see why you would. But they aren't Santa."

"They're not? Then who is?" He leaned forward, his interest piqued.

"Didn't you tell him about Wayne Greenaway?" Annie asked Claudia.

She shook her head.

"Who's Wayne Greenaway?" Mike demanded.

"He's the manager of Hillstead Mines," Claudia said. "The company that cut back operations and laid people off."

"And I think *he's* our Santa," Annie added.

Mike glanced at her again, certain she must be having him on. She looked perfectly serious, though.

"You're telling me that you figure the guy who put people out of work is now running around playing Santa to them? Doesn't that seem just a little farfetched?"

"Not necessarily," Claudia said, "because it wasn't him who laid them off. I mean, he had to do the dirty work, but the decision wasn't his."

"Then whose was it?"

"It came from head office. Wayne's top dog as far as the site work's concerned, but he reports to the company's CEO in Toronto. And that's who decided on the layoffs."

"How do you know?"

"Wayne told me," Annie put in.

"He has three kids in school," she added when Mike looked at her again. "And they're all in my classes. So I was talking to him and his wife at the last parent-teacher night—which was only a week ago. And he...no, I think it was actually Maureen. At any rate, one of them was saying how awful he felt because everyone blames him for the layoffs."

"Awful enough to be out running around in the dead of night?"

"Well, my money's on him."

Mike leaned back in his chair, considering this latest wrinkle—and wondering whether he'd ever have heard about Wayne Greenaway if it weren't for Annie. The number of things Claudia hadn't bothered to tell him were certainly adding up. And rapidly enough to make him figure she was deliberately holding out on him.

"Have you talked to this Greenaway?" he finally asked her.

"No, I hadn't quite gotten around to it. I explained," she added with a meaningful look, "that Iggy and I weren't...you know."

"Yeah, but you said that was before Iggy rethought things," he reminded her, trying not to sound half as irritated as he felt. "At this point, you and I should be checking out all the possibilities. So why didn't you mention Greenaway last night instead of telling me about that crazy idea of somebody having a mattress stuffed with money?"

"That isn't the *only* thing I told you about. I said there were several theories floating around."

"But why didn't you elaborate on them?"

"Because Lucille and my father are convinced it's the Nilssons. So I thought I'd leave telling you about Wayne until later."

"And then you just *forgot* to even mention he existed?"

"No, I didn't just *forget*. But in case *you're* forgetting, you weren't exactly in the best of shape by the time we headed home. My father," she explained to Annie, "introduced O'Brian to moose milk."

"Ahh."

"But what about the money?" Mike demanded before either of them could say anything more. He didn't like the way Claudia had delivered her "best of shape" line with a distinctly holier-than-thou tone. And he could certainly live without a rehash of his introduction to moose milk. Both his tongue and his brain were still feeling fuzzy.

"Does this Greenaway guy have enough money to be buying all those presents and hampers?" he pressed.

"Well," Annie said, "mine managers are very highly paid."

Mike glanced at Claudia to see what she'd say.

"Wayne's certainly far from poor," she offered slowly. "And he does run the show up here. Which means he likely has access to . . . discretionary funds."

"You're suggesting he's spending company money to buy things for their laid-off workers?"

"I'm saying he *might* be able to manage something like that. I don't know for sure."

Mike sat rubbing his jaw and telling himself the idea sounded utterly crazy. He knew better than to ignore a lead, though, no matter how bizarre it seemed.

And if Santa *was* the fellow who'd laid people off in the first place, it would be one hell of a neat twist to the story. The more he thought about that, the more he hoped it *would* turn out to be Greenaway.

"Do either of you," he said at last, "know what this Greenaway does on Saturday mornings?"

"I think he usually sticks around the house on weekends," Annie offered. "He spends a lot of time with his kids."

"And where does he live?"

"Just outside Elk Lake," Claudia said. "That's a little town about thirty kilometers from here."

"Which in real distance is . . . ?"

"Nineteen or twenty miles. Why?"

"Well, I was just thinking that maybe we should go talk to Greenaway first. Hit the Nilssons second."

"Oh. I guess we could. If you want."

"Yeah. Let's do it that way."

Claudia nodded. Then she gave him such a funny little smile that, for a split second, he wondered if he'd somehow just been bamboozled. But that couldn't be. Not when *he'd* suggested the change of plans.

CLAUDIA LET MORGAN IN while O'Brian was lacing up his mukluks, then she glanced at him expectantly.

He hadn't put his parka on yet, though. Instead, he was standing with it over his arm, watching her— wearing the same suspicious expression she'd been aware of since well before Annie had left.

"Something wrong?" she asked.

"Yeah. I didn't notice last night, but there's a label on this parka that reads Natural Down."

"Uh-huh?"

"Down? You know? As in feathers?"

"Feathers," she repeated, doing her best to look innocent. "Oh! Feathers! Lord, and you said something about being allergic to feathers, didn't you? I'd forgotten that, but no wonder you sneezed all the way home."

"Right. No wonder." He hung the parka back on the coat tree and reached for his bomber jacket.

She hesitated, then decided she'd better speak up. Leading him down the garden path was one thing; letting him freeze to death was something else again. "Are you wearing that thermal underwear Lucille gave you?" she asked as he slung his Nikon over his shoulder.

"No, I didn't bother with it."

"Well, maybe you'd better go put it on. At thirty below, jeans and that jacket just aren't warm enough."

"I'll be fine."

"No, you won't, you'll be cold."

When he ignored that, she told herself to let it go. She could hardly drag him into his bedroom and re-dress him. "Well, okay, but don't forget your toque. You lose a lot of heat through the top of your head."

"We're only going to be in the Jeep, aren't we?"

"Probably, but—"

"Then I won't need the toque."

Resisting the urge to suggest he at least get the heavy mitts from the parka's pockets, she grabbed her own camera and wool hat, then opened the front door.

O'Brian was obviously too stubborn for his own good, but if he wanted to go out dressed for a spring day she didn't intend to argue about it. On the other hand, she wasn't above tormenting him a little to make him smarten up.

"Mind unplugging the block heater?" she asked as they reached the Cherokee.

When he dropped the plug and had to dig into the snow for it with only his thin leather gloves for protection, she could barely keep from smiling.

She started the Jeep while he was getting in, then switched the heater onto high. "Takes a few minutes to warm up," she explained as icy air rushed out of the vents at them.

By the time she could feel the first hint of heat, O'Brian was rubbing his hands up and down his thighs for warmth. Seeing that did her heart good. Maybe next time, he'd listen to her.

Only a few minutes after they'd left Victoria Falls behind, the threatening snow started to fall—in big, fluffy flakes that swirled around the Jeep and skimmed across the highway in front of them.

"You know," O'Brian said, finally breaking the silence, "both my sisters have two kids, but not one of them has ever seen real snow. They'd absolutely love this."

Claudia glanced over at him. He was smiling a little, and the suspicious look was gone. She was surprised at how much better that made her feel—even though there was no doubt she'd be seeing the look again. Probably very soon.

"Well, it works both ways," she said. "I'll bet a lot of the kids up here would absolutely love to be in southern California at this time of year."

When Claudia looked back at the road and said nothing more, Mike decided he hadn't simply been imagining things. She was definitely ticked off at him. And he figured he knew why.

That snarky remark he'd made earlier, about her *forgetting* to tell him Wayne Greenaway even existed had hurt her feelings.

Staring out at the falling snow, he wished he'd kept his sarcasm to himself. After all, even if she *had* been holding out on him, it was no big deal. And he could understand what had prompted the behavior.

She was afraid Santa would stop delivering his goodies if they identified him. So the longer that took, the better she'd like it.

And on top of that, the Santa story had originally been hers. Even if she was trying to make the best of someone else walking in and taking it over, it would only be natural if she felt some resentment.

He glanced at her again, thinking that he didn't want her resenting him. Or even annoyed at him. He'd far rather they were back on friendlier terms.

Actually, more than friendly would be even nicer, but he doubted she'd be having any ideas along those lines. Not the way things stood right now, at least.

"So, what about you?" he finally asked. "In the nieces and nephews department, I mean. Do you have any?"

"No, not a one."

"Does that mean you're an only child?"

When she didn't reply for a second, he almost asked her if that was a difficult question. He caught himself, though. She might not realize he was teasing— might think he was being sarcastic again.

"'Only child' is one of those emotionally loaded terms, isn't it," she said at last. "Everybody always thinks only children get spoiled rotten."

"And did you?" he asked, smiling so she'd be sure he was kidding.

She smiled back—warmly enough to make his pulse skip a beat.

"I don't think I was *very* spoiled as a child," she said. "But look, that's the town of Elk Lake up ahead. We're almost there."

BY THE TIME CLAUDIA had driven though town and they were on the side road that ran past Wayne Greenaway's, the gray sky had deepened in color and the snowfall was growing more serious.

Very promising, she told herself. If there was enough accumulation by the time they'd finished talking to Wayne, she'd be able to convince O'Brian they should go straight home, that it would be best to forget about the Nilssons until tomorrow.

"This is it," she announced, turning into Wayne's drive. There were no cars parked out front, but that likely only meant they were in the garage. She'd tried to call ahead and had gotten a busy signal, so the Greenaways were undoubtedly home.

"Nice house," O'Brian said as she pulled to a stop.

She nodded. A big old stone place, owned by Hillstead, it came with the job of mine manager.

When they headed up the front steps and rang the bell, Maureen Greenaway answered the door. Claudia introduced O'Brian, then explained that they'd come by to talk to Wayne.

Maureen shook her head. "I'm afraid you've made a trip for nothing. He's taken the boys ice fishing."

"Did he say which lake?" Claudia asked.

"Uh-huh. Kenogami."

"Well, great, we can catch up with him there. I know which parts are the best for ice fishing, so he'll be easy to find. Is he driving the Blazer?"

"Yes, but do you really think you should go looking for him? This snow's already coming down pretty heavily."

Claudia glanced at O'Brian. He didn't look very worried about it. Certainly not worried enough to make it easy to convince him to go home, so she said, "Oh, we'll be fine. Come on, O'Brian."

With a quick goodbye to Maureen, Claudia turned and started back down the steps, feeling as if a gift from the gods had just landed in her lap. O'Brian had seemed to accept her evasive answers about her family, and with any luck, she could drive around until dark without finding Wayne Greenaway.

And even if she spotted him, how would O'Brian know? All kinds of people who went ice fishing drove Blazers.

CHAPTER FIVE

WHILE CLAUDIA GUNNED the motor and wheeled down the drive, Mike gazed unhappily out at the falling snow. Whoever had coined the phrase "winter wonderland" must have done it on the basis of seeing a picture.

If they'd been exposed to the real thing, they'd have called it "winter freezerland" or something. He'd almost turned blue just standing on Maureen Greenaway's steps. And the last place he wanted to head for next was some frozen lake.

"You're sure it's a good idea to try finding Wayne Greenaway?" he ventured, glancing across the Jeep. "Maybe we should revert to our original plan. Visit the Nilssons this morning, then catch up with Greenaway later." Preferably, in his nice warm house, where they could talk in front of a roaring fire.

"Kenogami Lake isn't very far," Claudia said, rubbing the windshield with her mitt. The engine couldn't have been shut off for more than five minutes, but the air inside the Jeep was cold enough that their breath had fogged up the glass.

"Far or not," Mike tried, "if he's got his boys with him . . ."

"Oh, they'll get a kick out of it—an L.A. reporter making a big effort to track down their dad."

L.A., he thought longingly. Where the temperature was probably in the eighties. He casually stuck his hands in front of a vent that was feebly pumping out heat.

"And you know," Claudia went on, "interviewing someone while he's fishing will add local flavor to your article. We can take a picture to run with it. You and Wayne crouched over a hole in the ice."

"Well, I don't know. I—"

"O'Brian, Iggy says having Santa out delivering presents is the steak, but the sizzle is that he's running around way up north here. That's what'll make a lot of southern papers jump on your series. Their readers will figure Santa's workshop is just around the corner from Victoria Falls."

"You mean it's not? It sure *feels* as if we're at the North Pole."

Claudia shot him a sidelong glance. "The pole's still a *few* miles farther north. But the point is that readers will love all the arctic-type stuff. So we want to play it up, don't we?"

"Yeah, I guess you're right. A picture in the great white wilderness would be a nice touch."

He looked out at the snow again, trying to convince himself it wouldn't be *too* cold on that lake. But he knew it would be nothing short of numbing.

"And if we're really lucky," Claudia added, "Wayne will get a big bite while we're there. Then I could shoot you reaching down through the hole and dragging a fish out headfirst."

"Hey, we can only hope. Sticking body parts into freezing water is one of my favorite pastimes."

When she laughed, he stopped while he was ahead. Sometimes he wasn't quite sure whether she was joking or not, but if that was actually how you had to get fish out through the ice . . .

A mental picture began forming—of his editor in chief's reaction to a shot of Mike O'Brian up to his elbows in Kenogami Lake.

It would definitely make Big Jim smile. Hell, it would probably have him chortling with glee. After all, how many of his previous punishment assignments could have turned a reporter into a human Popsicle?

"Those are the Hillstead Mine offices," Claudia said after they'd driven a few miles from Greenaway's house.

Mike glanced in the direction she was pointing and saw a long building that looked as if it dated back to the 1920s or 1930s. "Why's it out in the middle of nowhere?"

"It wasn't when it was built. The original Hillstead mine is on that property, so it made sense to put the offices there, too. But that mine ran dry years ago. The ones they're working these days are spread all over the place."

"Which now makes the office conveniently central?" Mike said dryly.

Claudia smiled. "Something like that."

She lapsed into silence again until they reached the lake and stopped on its frozen shoreline. Parked about fifty yards out on the ice were close to a dozen 4×4s, snowmobiles and pickups. Beyond those stood a few tents that looked like canvas telephone booths, and still farther out were the fishermen.

"Is Wayne Greenaway's Blazer there?" Mike asked.

"No, but I'll ask if anyone's seen him." With that, Claudia hit the gas once more and headed onto the lake, driving far too fast for Mike's liking.

Just as he'd started imagining the brakes failing and the Jeep skidding out onto thin ice, she pulled up behind a truck.

"You can stay in here where it's warm," she told him. "I'll only be a minute."

He climbed out and started after her. He knew if he waited in the Jeep, these locals would figure he was a total wimp, but by the time he'd walked thirty feet, he was wondering why he cared. The wind was whipping his face so wickedly he felt as if his corneas were about to freeze. Only his feet—encased in Raymond's mukluks and heavy socks—weren't bitterly cold.

"Hey, Fred," Claudia greeted the first man they reached. "Have you seen Wayne Greenaway?"

Mike glanced down at the hole in the ice Fred was standing beside.

It was a lot smaller than he'd expected, not more than about eight inches in diameter, which meant Claudia hadn't been teasing him, after all. Someone really would have to reach down into the water to maneuver a big fish out—a decidedly chilling prospect.

"You're the guy whose picture's in the paper this mornin', ain't you?" Fred said, eyeing him. "The guy who's come to catch Santa. Iggy wrote a big article 'bout you."

Claudia quickly introduced Mike to Fred, then turned the subject back to Greenaway.

"Why'd you wanna bother lookin' for him?" Fred muttered. "Nobody wants to read 'bout anythin' he's gotta say, I can tell you. But I guess you could try Polar Bear Cove. Hear he's been goin' up there on his own. Guess he don't feel too welcome round some of us."

"Ahh. Well, we'll try there, then. Thanks." With a wave in the general direction of the other fisher-men—several of whom were looking over at them—Claudia started back toward the Jeep.

"Sounds like Annie was right," Mike said, falling into step. "Greenaway isn't exactly Mr. Popularity."

"No, and he won't be until Hillstead starts bring-ing its operations back up to speed. People are really afraid the temporary layoffs might turn out to be per-manent."

They walked the rest of the way in silence, Mike concentrating on not shivering so hard that Claudia would notice. He could live without her saying she'd told him he'd need that thermal underwear.

"Polar Bear Cove," he said as they drove off the lake. "That's just a name, right? I mean, polar bears don't actually hang out there . . . do they?"

"O'Brian, remind me to show you an atlas when we get home. Victoria Falls isn't *that* far north. You have to go practically to Hudson Bay to see polar bears. For the most part, we only have black bears around here."

"Ahh. A lot of them?"

"A fair number. They hibernate all winter, though—unless they get really, really hungry."

Glancing at her, he tried to decide whether she was joking this time around. As far as he knew, black bears hibernated all winter no matter how hungry they got. But maybe she knew something he didn't.

Now that they were back on the road again, she was zipping along so fast the landscape was a blur of white. He gazed out at it for a minute, telling himself that, if she was serious about those bears, at least they'd likely spot a black one coming at them through the snow.

Then another mental picture began forming and he shook his head to banish it. Local flavor or not, he'd draw the line at letting her take a picture of him being charged by a starving bear.

WHEN THEY REACHED Polar Bear Cove, Claudia swore under her breath. That was definitely Wayne Greenaway's red Blazer parked on the ice. Nobody else drove one with a Toronto Blue Jays sticker plastered across the back window.

Neither Wayne nor his boys were in sight, though, so she might be able to breeze a lie by O'Brian. "Looks as if we're out of luck," she said. "Wayne must have gone to another spot. But I know a few more places we can try, and—"

"What are you talking about?" O'Brian interrupted. "That's his Blazer right there."

"No, it's not. His is—"

"Paquette? I'm not blind. I can see the license."

She glanced at it and silently swore again. Why hadn't she remembered that Wayne had one of those stupid personalized plates? But maybe she could still manage to brazen things through.

"Oh," she said. "Yes, of course you'd assume WAYNE G was Greenaway's plate. But it's not."

"No?"

"No, it's Wayne *Gretzky's*. He's Canadian, you know, just like most pro hockey players. And he grew up around here, in a little town called Matachewan. He comes back to fish whenever he can."

O'Brian simply stared at her for a minute. Then he said, "Very funny, Paquette, but if you want to pull my leg you'll have to try a little harder."

"But I'm not—"

"Look, the Kings might have traded the Great One, but nobody in L.A.'s forgotten him. And I'll bet even people who don't follow hockey know he grew up in a town called Brantford."

"Which is in Ontario," she tried, even though it was clear she wasn't going to get away with this.

"Right. It's in Ontario. But hardly *Northern* Ontario. In fact, the last time I saw a map, it was close enough to the American border that it was practically in New York State. So let's go find Greenaway. You think he's in that tent?"

"Probably." Claudia unhappily got out of the Cherokee and started for the shelter. It was another of the modern ones that looked like a canvas coffin standing on end. There wasn't much room inside them, but apparently they were easier to put up and take down than a standard tent.

"It's okay to just leave a rod sitting there?" O'Brian asked, gesturing toward the deserted hole.

"Uh-huh. That ice pick the rod's attached to is dug in pretty deeply, so it's just a matter of keeping an eye on it. But what about Wayne? How do you want to handle him?"

"Let's try focusing on the big picture first—how the mine layoffs have got everybody worried. We can work our way around to talking about Santa from there."

She nodded, but O'Brian could forget the *we*, because she intended to keep her mouth shut. He'd rule out Wayne as a suspect fast enough on his own.

"Wayne?" she called as they neared the shelter.

A second later, the flap opened and he stepped outside—his two boys, who were about eleven and twelve, on his heels. When she introduced O'Brian to them, it was obvious they hadn't looked at the morning paper.

She started to explain who he was, then paused uncertainly. Wayne's face was red from the cold, but she'd swear it had lost a shade of color while she was saying "investigative reporter with the *L.A. Gazette.*"

Then he grinned at O'Brian and she told herself she was imagining things.

"You're up from L.A.?" he said. "Hell, you must be freezing out here, then. Boys, you go pack our gear, eh? While I talk to Claudia and Mike?

"Good thing you arrived when you did," he added, pulling back the tent's flap and ushering them inside. "We've got all the fish we wanted, so we were just about to leave."

There was room for three adults in the tent, but barely. O'Brian ended up standing so close behind Claudia that his body was pressed against hers. Even through her coat, she could feel the solid hardness of his chest. And that, combined with the faintly woodsy scent of his after-shave, made her very aware of his maleness—which, in turn, made her extremely uneasy.

The more time she spent with the man, the more attracted she was becoming to him. Not that she had the slightest intention of acting on that. Aside from anything else, O'Brian would be flying out of her life next week. But not doing anything about an attraction and trying to deny it existed were two different things. And she couldn't see any point to pretending there weren't hormones and pheromones and Lord only knew what other "mones" hard at work.

She had to keep a step ahead of O'Brian, though. And that would be a lot more difficult if her knees started going weak every time he got close.

"So," Wayne was saying. "What can I do for you two?"

"We wanted to ask a few questions about the lay-offs at Hillstead," O'Brian said.

He was speaking over Claudia's shoulder, and the warmth of his breath fanned her cheek, making it difficult to concentrate on watching Wayne. She did her best, though, and this time she was almost certain she wasn't imagining things. The mine manager looked decidedly nervous.

But why on earth would that be? He'd been running Hillstead's operations for years, had probably answered a million questions about them.

"Oh?" he said slowly. "Surely layoffs in a mine way up here wouldn't interest anyone down in L.A."

"You'd be surprised," O'Brian told him. "At any rate, what prompted them?"

"Well, as I explained a few months back, to the *Miner's Dispatch* reporters among others, our operating profits weren't what they should have been, so—"

"Why was that?" O'Brian interrupted.

Wayne shrugged. "Fluctuations in the market prices of metals. Some shafts that weren't producing as expected, others drying up. Higher costs from a few suppliers. A variety of things. A temporary shutdown was in the company's best interest."

"But I gather the miners don't see it as being in *their* best interests. There seem to be some pretty unhappy campers around here."

"Tell me about it. And I really feel for them. But I've done everything I can to assure them the layoffs are only temporary."

"That's definite?"

"Of course. Once a few strategic decisions have been made, we'll be operating at full tilt again."

"And in the meantime, there's Santa."

Wayne stared blankly past Claudia's left ear.

"I mean," O'Brian elaborated over her shoulder, "at least someone's doing what he can to make people feel better."

"Oh. Right."

"You have any ideas about who he is?"

"Santa?" Wayne said. His expression had gone from blank to puzzled.

"Yeah."

"Well...I gather people figure he's one of the Nilssons."

"That's not what everyone figures," O'Brian told him. "In fact, some people think he might be you."

For another moment, Wayne still seemed confused. Then something Claudia read as a flicker of relief crossed his face. She had no time to wonder about it, though, before he smiled and said, "Wait a minute. Is *that* what you came to ask me about?"

"Mostly," O'Brian admitted. "I got sent to Victoria Falls to write a series of articles about this copycat Santa. And I might as well tell you that you're going to be in at least one of them."

"You're here all the way from California to write about our Santa?"

"Yeah, I know. Nuts, isn't it. But let's not waste time with the whys and wherefores, because I gather Iggy has an article in today's paper that explains them. The bottom line is that I'm here to ID Santa and you're on my list of suspects."

"I'd never in a million years have figured anyone would think it was me," Wayne said with a quiet laugh. "Not when the prevailing sentiment around here is that I'm giving Scrooge a run for his money."

"But you *are* Santa."

Claudia admired O'Brian's style. He'd uttered the statement with such certainty that if Wayne actually was Santa, he'd have figured they had him dead to rights.

He wasn't Santa, though, so she was surprised when he didn't immediately deny it.

"Whoever Santa is," he said instead, "he doesn't want to be identified."

"You're sure about that?"

"It's pretty obvious, isn't it?"

"Yeah, it seems to be. Unfortunately, my assignment's to name him."

"Then I guess you and Santa are at cross-purposes. But I'm afraid there's really nothing I can tell you, except that I'm not your man."

There was the denial she'd been expecting. But if she hadn't known better, that strange smile of Wayne's would make her think he was lying. What the heck was he playing at?

"If you *were* Santa," O'Brian said, "I imagine you'd still be telling us you weren't."

The strange smile grew. "Of course I would. If I was him and didn't want anyone to know."

MIKE HAD NEVER BEEN so cold in his life, and if a big fish didn't bite soon his blood was going to freeze in his veins.

Even though Wayne Greenaway's boys had loaded up all their equipment, their father had obligingly dug a rod back out so that Claudia could get the picture she wanted. But since they'd been standing around the hole, they'd hooked nothing except a couple of little sunfish, which they'd tossed right back.

"O'Brian?" Claudia said.

He glanced across the hole at her.

"I *really* think we'd better get going," she told him for the third time. "You've got be dying out here."

"I'm fine," he lied, glad to discover he could still move his lips. Since he couldn't conceivably get any colder, he was damned if he was quitting now. After all, Greenaway had said the fish were really biting today, so how much longer could it take?

"Look," Claudia pressed, "maybe you're not cold, but I think my camera's about ready to freeze up. So let's just forget the picture."

He was on the verge of giving in when Greenaway's line went taut.

"That's a big one, Dad," one of the boys hollered.

"It sure is." Greenaway played the fish a little, gradually reeling the already short line even shorter. "Okay," he said at last. "This should be exactly what we wanted, so you just reach down through the hole, O'Brian, and grab him."

He yanked off his leather jacket and tossed it onto the ice. Then, telling himself nobody'd ever died from putting their arms in cold water for a couple of seconds, he shoved up the sleeves of his sweatshirt and knelt beside the hole. When he asked Claudia if her camera was ready, his teeth chattered.

"Ready," she assured him. "Wayne, you kneel down beside O'Brian. And boys? Huddle in right behind them. This is going to be a great shot. Just let me get focused."

"Will it be on the front page?" one of the boys asked.

"It'll be on the obituary page if she doesn't hurry up," Mike muttered.

"All set," she said. "Go for it."

Against every ounce of his instinct for self-preservation, Mike plunged his hands into the water—barely managing to keep from yelling out as they hit it. He felt as if someone had stabbed right through his arms with jagged icicles. And the idea that he couldn't conceivably get any colder had been dead wrong.

"Make sure you've got a good grip on it," Greenaway instructed. "Fish are real slippery."

By this point, his hands were so numb he could hardly wrap his fingers around the damn thing, never mind get a good grip on it. But, telling himself that if he didn't do it right the first time he'd only prolong the agony, he managed to tighten his hold and yank the fish up through the ice. It was big, greenish brown and dripping water.

"Hold it!" Claudia cried.

If she told him to say cheese, he knew he'd feel like throttling her. She didn't, though. She simply clicked off a few shots.

"Wow, beauty!" one of the boys exclaimed as soon as she lowered her camera. "Must be eight or nine pounds, eh, Dad?'' he added while the fish tried to flop out of Mike's hands.

"That's a northern pike you've got there," Greenaway said. "They're good eating, so if you'd like it for dinner, I'll give you something to wrap it in."

"Put it back," Claudia said quietly. "We only wanted the picture."

When Mike looked over at her again, an unfamiliar feeling of tenderness seized him. Most reporters he knew were tough as nails. But Claudia looked as if she'd cry if he didn't let the fish live.

He removed the hook—as carefully as he could with his stiff fingers—then lowered the pike into the water and glanced at her once more.

"Let's get going," she murmured, giving him such a warm smile that he almost forgot he was freezing to death.

CLAUDIA STARTED the engine, wishing the heater didn't take forever to begin throwing out warmth. Then she dug her emergency blanket from the cargo area, climbed back into the driver's seat and tucked the blanket around O'Brian. He was shivering all over, which made her feel incredibly guilty.

She should never have let him stand out there on the ice for so long. Not that he was exactly the type of man you could order around, but there must have been some way she could have made him leave sooner.

"Give me your hands," she said, taking them in hers.

"Frostbite again?"

"No, just awfully cold." She rubbed them for a minute, torn between wanting to warm him up before they started off and thinking they should just be on their way.

"At least we got my first article," he said. "And I can probably even manage the humorous slant Iggy wants. How does Santa-Seeking Sleuth Practically Perishes Catching Pike sound for a headline?"

She smiled. "Kind of wordy, but you've got to start somewhere." Giving his hands a quick squeeze, she let go of them and shifted the Jeep into drive.

"I'm going to head straight home, okay?" she asked as they started off. "Since you've got your first article, we don't really have to hit the Nilssons' today, do we?"

"No, I guess not."

"Good. Then I'll just stop by Iggy's for a second and give him my film. He does most of our developing himself. After that, we can go home and get warm."

"I don't think I remember what warm feels like. But maybe if I put on every stitch of clothing I've got and you turn the thermostat up to about a hundred and twenty..."

"And if we have something toasted for lunch? Or maybe grilled cheese sandwiches. And hot chocolate?"

"With marshmallows?"

"Of course," she said, glancing at him. "What's hot chocolate without marshmallows?"

When he grinned at her, she felt a fluttering sensation around her heart. Forcing her gaze from his, she looked ahead at the road again, aware that she was finding it more and more difficult to keep thinking of him as the enemy.

But he's not exactly the enemy, an imaginary voice whispered. *He's only dangerous until Santa finishes his deliveries and goes completely to ground.*

By then, though, she reminded herself, O'Brian would be packing for his trip home. And L.A. was a world away from Victoria Falls.

"You figure it's Greenaway?" he asked.

It took her a second to put the question into context. Then she almost blurted out a "no," without thinking.

She just *had* to be more careful. The longer O'Brian spent on the wrong track, the better. "I don't think we should rule him out, do you?" she finally said.

"Not for a minute. I assume he's got a snowmobile?"

"Of course. Almost everybody up here has."

"Then I wish we'd thought to poke around the garage while we were at his place—see if he had sleigh bells. And you know, that was a triple garage, wasn't it. There'd be plenty of room in it to store hampers and presents. Although he might not be keeping them there. If he did, his kids would have figured things out. And if he doesn't want anyone to know who he is . . ."

O'Brian paused for a moment, then shook his head. "That part puzzles me. If everybody's got a big hate on for him, why didn't he admit he was Santa? Wouldn't you think he'd *want* his identity revealed? Want people to know what a good guy he is?"

"Well...maybe he's just trying to prolong things."

"Why?"

"I don't know. Maybe he figures that if he took credit the minute you confronted him, people might figure he'd started the Santa thing purely to get a big pat on the back."

"Mmm. You really think there's any logic in that?"

"I guess it doesn't sound *perfectly* logical. But he might have figured it would be better in the long run if it looked as if you just couldn't make him admit what a good guy he is."

"Yeah...I guess that could be it."

"You're certain it *is* him, though?"

"No, not *certain*. I learned, years ago, never to be certain until I had proof. But he's definitely a man with a secret. I could see that the moment you said I was an investigative reporter."

"I know. I saw it, too." Wayne Greenaway was hiding something. But she knew it wasn't that he was Santa, so what was it? And why did she have the sense that he wanted them to believe he *was* Santa?

"You think that your father will have turned up a car for me by now?" O'Brian asked.

"I'm not sure. Why?"

"Well, I'll have to do some surveillance at Greenaway's tonight, and there's no point in both of us losing sleep."

"Surveillance?" She glanced at him. "You mean you're going to sit in a cold car all night?"

He shrugged. "If I want proof, how else am I going to get it?"

"Good point."

"Then, if your dad hasn't found a car, you wouldn't mind my borrowing the Jeep, would you?"

"No. Of course not."

It had started snowing again, so she turned on the wipers, absently wondering how upset O'Brian would be if he learned her father had no intention of getting him a car.

Not when the current situation was ideal. As long as she was playing chauffeur, their guest reporter couldn't go anywhere without her knowing about it.

, "Or," she said, glancing over at him, "I might go along with you. To Greenaway's tonight," she added at his puzzled expression. "I don't have any plans, and Saturday night television leaves a lot to be desired."

When he merely nodded, she went back to watching the road, thinking there was absolutely no *might* about it. There was no way she could let him out on his own. What if he saw something he shouldn't? Like the real Santa making his rounds?

"You know," O'Brian said, "before I do any surveillance I should go shopping. Pick up a parka that isn't filled with down."

"Actually, it would be a good idea for you to have a snowmobile suit, too."

"Oh?"

"Sure, they're really warm, so it would be terrific for surveillance. And if we end up wanting to use my snowmobile sometime, you'll need one. But there's no point in buying a lot of clothes you'd probably never use again. You should just borrow some more things from my dad."

"No, I don't think I'd better. I've already got half his wardrobe. I don't want him thinking I'm the biggest mooch going."

"Oh, he won't think that. I'll tell you what. Iggy's place is practically around the corner from Dad's, so after we drop off the film, we can stop in. I'm positive he's got a spare snowmobile suit kicking around. And I'll bet he has a different parka he could lend you, too."

"You think so?"

She simply nodded. It wouldn't be wise to admit she *knew* so. Or that, last night, she and Lucille had intentionally chosen the down one instead.

CHAPTER SIX

MIKE FLIPPED THE GRILLED cheese sandwiches, then went back to watching Claudia stir the hot chocolate—thinking she had the cutest little behind he'd ever seen.

"You know," he said at last, "I haven't had hot chocolate in years. I'd forgotten how good it smells."

When she glanced over, her delicious smile started an itch of arousal. He tried to ignore it, reminding himself about that little lecture she'd given him. She'd offered to let him stay with her because the Silver Dollar was a dump. Period. As in "Don't get any funny ideas, mister."

But that had been yesterday, and since then they'd been through a lot together. He figured they'd bonded, to use one of his sister Rachel's phrases. He just wasn't sure whether or not that meant Claudia—

"Would you mind getting the marshmallows?" she said. "They're in the cupboard above the fridge."

And the fridge was next to the stove, which put him right beside her. He dug the marshmallows out from the back of the shelf, deciding she smelled better than the hot chocolate. Even though he hadn't forgotten how cold it was outside, the scent of her perfume put him in mind of a sultry summer evening—and made him desperately want to kiss her.

He was just trying to decide how she'd react to that when something solid thwacked his calf. Morgan, he discovered, had a snowmobile boot in his mouth and was trying to shake it to death.

"Bad dog, Morgan!" Claudia said as he hit Mike's leg again. "Sorry, O'Brian. He has a thing about carrying boots around the house."

"And he hides newspapers in them, too?" Once she'd rescued the boot, Mike pulled out the paper, unrolled it and stood staring at his own picture. And at the headline.

"Santa Thumbs Nose at L.A. Reporter?" he muttered. "Nice. Makes me sound like an idiot."

"I didn't think you'd like it," Claudia said.

"So it wasn't the dog who hid it."

She shook her head, then glanced over at the sandwiches. "Those look ready."

"Oh. Right." He tossed the newspaper onto the counter, thinking he could live without reading Iggy's article, then frowned at Morgan. Thanks to the dog, he'd missed his chance to kiss Claudia.

Of course, they had the entire afternoon ahead of them. And possibly the entire night. After all, she'd said she might decide to come along to Greenaway's, and if she did...

Normally, he hated surveillance. It was mind-numbingly boring. But the idea of spending hours in a dark car with Claudia was decidedly appealing. Snuggling up to keep warm would only be sensible, and who knew where that might lead?

He slid the sandwiches onto plates while she poured the hot chocolate. Then, just as they were sitting down, the doorbell rang—sending Morgan into his vicious guard dog routine.

"I'll only be a second," Claudia said, heading from the kitchen and ordering Morgan to stop barking. Mike could hear the door opening and her saying, "Oh…Pete…hi. Morgan, you go on out for a while, okay?"

The name Pete, Mike recalled, had been mentioned yesterday. The *Dispatch*'s other reporter was called Pete. Iggy's nephew, who, according to Drew, the bush pilot, had a thing for Claudia.

When Claudia reappeared with the guy on her heels, sure enough, she introduced him as Pete Doleman from the paper. He didn't look like serious competition. He was thirty-something, on the short side, and his dark hair was thinning.

"Sorry I missed you yesterday," he told Mike by way of greeting. "You get settled in okay?"

"Fine, thanks."

"Good, I…" He glanced at the sandwiches, then at Claudia. "Hey, I didn't mean to interrupt your lunch. I just wanted to meet Mike."

"Well, why don't you have some hot chocolate with us while we eat."

Doleman jumped at the offer and grabbed a chair. "So," he said to Mike. "What did you think of Iggy's article? You figure he's right? That it's gonna take you a while to catch up with Santa?"

"I sure hope not. Claudia had me out interviewing one of the suspects this morning and I almost froze to death."

"Oh? Who'd you talk to?"

"Wayne Greenaway."

"Greenaway?" Doleman repeated, shooting Claudia a curious look.

"You don't think it's him?" Mike asked.

"Could be, I guess."

"But who do *you* figure it is?"

"Oh, I've been keeping my ideas to myself. After all, it was *Claudia's* story."

The disgruntled look that flickered across Doleman's face said he'd resented Iggy's giving the Santa story to Claudia. And that now he resented an outsider taking it over.

The irony of that almost made Mike laugh. If he could, he'd happily hand it to Doleman. Then he'd head home to the warmth of L.A. and never give Victoria Falls another thought. Claudia, on the other hand, wouldn't be so easy to forget.

He glanced at her, the thought taking him by surprise. Apparently they'd bonded more than he'd realized. At least, he had.

"Pete," she was saying, "just because it wasn't your story doesn't mean you can't have an opinion."

Doleman gave her a knowing smile.

"Go ahead," she told him. "Who do you think Santa is?"

"You don't really want me to say... do you?"

"Of course I do. You're being ridiculous. Both O'Brian and I would like to know."

"Well... okay, then." He glanced at Mike. "I figure it's Claudia."

"What?" she demanded, looking flabbergasted.

It only took a second for Mike to realize that wasn't possible. "Can't be," he pointed out. "Claudia was with Iggy and me when we saw Santa yesterday."

"Oh, but that wasn't Santa. It was me. Iggy and I set up that little welcome to start your visit off with a bang."

CLAUDIA SAT SEETHING while Pete dawdled over his hot chocolate and shot the breeze with O'Brian.

If everything went incredibly well, she just might manage to continue stringing their guest reporter along for the entire time he was here. But that would never happen if he started thinking he shouldn't trust her. So the last thing she needed was Pete spouting insane accusations.

"That's great hot chocolate," he hinted, putting down his empty mug and glancing over at the saucepan.

"Thanks," she said. Instead of offering him seconds, she made it clear the time had come to leave. Then she walked him to the front door, threw on her coat and stepped outside with him. There was no radio blaring at the moment, and only last night O'Brian had admitted that his eavesdropping was habitual.

"What on earth were you trying to do?" she demanded, closing the door and following Pete down the steps to the driveway.

"Eh? What's wrong?"

"Don't try to play innocent, because you can't pull it off. What the hell was that bit about suspecting *me* of being Santa?"

Pete shrugged. "I just figure the way everyone assumes our Santa's a man is kind of sexist. Don't you?"

"Since when have you worried about what's sexist?"

"Hey, lighten up. I know you don't want O'Brian proving who Santa is too fast. It would make you seem pretty inept, wouldn't it. So I just thought I'd help you, give him something else to think about."

"Well, if you come up with any more helpful ideas, keep them to yourself."

"Claudia, what's the big deal? It's no mystery who Santa is. Everybody knows. Hell, even Iggy's gotta know. He's just too stubborn to admit it. So I'm surprised O'Brian wasn't off talking to the Nilssons first thing this morning."

"Will you *think*, Pete? Iggy wants a whole *series* of articles from O'Brian. And the Santa story's going to be picked up by papers all over North America. There's no reason *their* readers won't believe we've got a real mystery on our hands, but they'd never buy that if O'Brian only writes about Gord and Norm."

"Well . . . yeah, I guess. But you figure he can make *Greenaway* sound like a real suspect? How'd you even get O'Brian to go talk to the guy?"

"Would you do me a favor? Just let *me* worry about what's happening with O'Brian?"

Pete jammed his hands into his pockets and glanced back at the house. "Maybe somebody should worry about what's happening with you," he muttered.

"And what's that supposed to mean?"

"It means when Iggy told me you'd asked O'Brian to stay here, I couldn't believe it. And now that I've met the guy, I'm even more amazed. Hell, it's like Little Red Riding Hood inviting in the Big Bad Wolf."

"Oh, puh-leez! I'm not a character from a fairy tale, and O'Brian isn't a wolf. In fact, he's been a perfect gentleman."

"Yeah? Well, don't count on that lasting. Maybe he's the kind of guy who can suck women in, but he doesn't fool me for a second. I'll bet he's got more notches on his bedpost than Morgan has fleas."

"My dog does *not* have fleas."

"All dogs have fleas. Lots of them. And guys like O'Brian have lots of notches. Trust me on this, Claudia. If he's been a gentleman till now, it's only part of his act.''

BY STANDING AT THE CORNER of the living room window, Mike could watch Claudia and Pete Doleman out on the driveway without being seen. Or maybe they were just too busy arguing to notice him.

Either way, watching them wasn't doing him a darned bit of good. He couldn't make out what they were saying through the Thermopane window. And since he was a washout at reading lips, he gave up trying and let his thoughts drift back to Doleman's suggestion that Claudia was Santa.

She wasn't, of course. So what was Doleman's game?

''I guess,'' he finally said to Ghost, ''old Pete was trying to make me think she's yanking my chain.''

The cat, half-asleep on the couch, ignored him—but he elaborated, anyway. ''If Doleman's got a thing for her, he's jealous that I'm staying here. And he probably figures that if I get suspicious she's up to something, it'll make me keep my distance.''

But surely Doleman could have thought of a better red herring than he had, because the idea of Claudia being Santa was ridiculous.

Whoever was playing old Saint Nick had deep pockets. Not that he had to be *immensely* wealthy. Even though a lot of people were convinced only the Nilssons had enough money, Santa didn't really have to be a millionaire. Nevertheless, this caper *was* costing tens of thousands, so unless Claudia had an inheritance tucked away...

Of course, it was possible her mother had left her money. But even if Claudia was as rich as Rockefeller, she wasn't Santa. Last night, she'd been right here in this house while Santa was out making his rounds. Hadn't she?

Mike eyed her for a minute, thinking that, thanks to Raymond's moose milk, he'd been dead to the world the minute his head hit the pillow. Which meant Claudia could have been gone for hours without him knowing. Or maybe...

Now that his suspicious nature was rearing its head, he realized there might not actually have been any deliveries at all last night.

He looked over at the cordless phone Claudia had left lying on the coffee table, wondering why he hadn't heard it ring this morning. Possibly because nobody had really called her Santa hot line? Because she'd simply *said* Santa had been busy during the night?

Glancing at her snowmobile, sitting in the driveway under its tarp, he realized there could be a sled stored nearby. And the only other thing she'd need was sleigh bells, which she'd be smart enough to hide from him.

"You're thinking crazy, O'Brian," he said to himself. If Claudia was Santa, she'd never have invited him to stay with her. Unless, of course, she was really, really devious. Or had a helper making some of the deliveries.

Slowly, he surveyed the living room, but nothing struck him as a likely hiding place for bells. And she was too smart to stash them in the kitchen or bathroom. The spare bedroom he was using was out, as well, which only left her room, the linen cupboard or the basement.

That, he decided, was the most likely place. She'd figure he wouldn't have any reason to go down there.

With a final glance outside to make sure she and Doleman were still arguing, he headed for the basement stairs. As he passed the side door on his way down, he invented an excuse to use if Claudia caught him poking around where he didn't belong. He'd say he wanted to wash a few things and had wondered whether she had a washer and dryer.

Outside, snow was piled up over the entire height of the basement windows, so he could barely see when he reached the bottom of the stairs. He waited a few seconds for his eyes to adjust to the darkness before starting slowly forward, groping for a light switch.

He'd taken half a dozen steps when he was seized by the eerie feeling that he wasn't alone. He froze, listening intently.

For a moment there was only silence. Then he could hear the faint sound of someone slowly exhaling—so close behind him that he could almost feel warm breath on his neck.

He wheeled around. And even in the dim light, there was no mistaking who he was looking at. Red suit, black boots, flowing white beard, arm raised.

Arm raised? Just as Mike was registering that fact, the arm came crashing down, his head exploded with pain and darkness enveloped him.

WHEN CLAUDIA MARCHED back up the steps and into the house, Santa was standing in the hall.

She stopped in her tracks, flooded with panic. He'd promised not to come into town unless he was making a delivery. And even then, it was only supposed to be in the dead of night.

"Are you out of your mind?" she whispered the instant her brain began functioning again. There were so many more other questions racing around inside her head that she didn't know which one to ask next. What was he doing here? Why was he decked out in his Santa suit? Why did he have that long black cloak slung over his arm and why was he clutching a brass candlestick?

"What on earth do you think you're up to?" she finally said. "O'Brian's right in the kitchen!"

"No, O'Brian's...busy. And I just came looking for something."

"In broad daylight?"

"I left the truck down the block and nobody noticed me."

"Walking around in that getup?"

"I had my beard pulled down and the cloak on over my suit—with the hood up."

"Oh, great, then you only looked like Dracula. And nobody'd ever bother taking a second glance at him."

"Dammit, Claudia, I still had the Santa suit on from my deliveries, okay? It was practically dawn when I made the last one because you told me to get the rest finished as fast as I can, remember?"

"And how much longer's that going to be? If it's more than another day or two, you'll turn me into a complete nervous wreck."

He shrugged. "It won't be much longer. With any luck, I'll be able to finish up on Monday or Tuesday."

"Then you'll lie low? You promise?"

"I've *been* lying low."

"You call coming here like this lying low?"

"How did I know you two would get back so soon?"

"What? Now you're blaming me for showing up at my own house?"

"No, but when you called last night it sounded as if you'd be at the Nilssons' half the day. You surprised the hell out of me."

"Well I'm *terribly* sorry. But you still haven't told me what you were looking for. That candlestick? You have a formal dinner party in the works?"

"No, it was nothing important. Just something I thought you'd have."

"What?"

"Claudia, it's *not* important. But while I was trying to find it, you and O'Brian pulled up, so I hid in the basement. Then he went down there and . . . Well, I'd been looking through a few cartons, and the candlestick was in one of them, so when I heard him coming... I'm afraid I had to knock him out with it."

"What?" She pushed past Santa and headed for the stairs, her heart racing.

"He'll be okay," he said, following right behind her. "I didn't hit him hard."

"Oh, sure. Just a light tap's enough to knock somebody unconscious. You'd better not have seriously hurt him or I'll kill you, I swear I will." Flicking on the basement lights, she started down the stairs.

"Claudia, he'll be okay. And what else could I have done? What the hell was he doing in the basement, anyway?"

She reached the bottom of the stairs and her heart began racing even faster. O'Brian was slumped on the cement floor, making moaning noises. At least he was alive, she thought with relief. But he must also be coming to.

"Get out of here!" she ordered, whirling around and poking Santa in the chest. "I'll call you later. And make darn sure you answer the phone, because I've got a whole lot of questions. But think about this one in the meantime. If you aren't going to stick to your side of the deal, why should I keep helping you?"

He smiled at her. "Because you love me?"

"Get going" was all she said. But, of course, he was right.

MIKE LAY ON THE COUCH while Claudia tried to take his pulse and talk to the doctor at the same time.

"No," she said into the phone, "there's no bleeding, just a bump. And yes, his pulse seems regular."

He started to tell her he was really all right, aside from the pounding sledgehammer inside his skull, but she ordered him to hush once more.

She'd barely let him say a word since he'd come to, telling him to keep quiet until she was sure talking wouldn't make things worse. And since she so obviously enjoyed playing Florence Nightingale, he'd gone along with it. Which actually wasn't any hardship.

He liked having her perched on the couch beside him, holding his hand, the sultry scent of her perfume making him think erotic thoughts. They were doing a lot to take his mind off the pain in his head— as was the warmth of her hip pressed against his.

"I don't know *exactly* what happened," she was telling the doctor, "but somebody obviously came into the house—I never lock my side door. And when O'Brian went down to the basement the guy hit him.

"With what?" she asked after a moment. "I don't know that, either. O'Brian, what did he hit you with?"

"Something damn hard."

"We're not sure," she said into the phone. "No," she added, "I didn't see anything at all. By the time I found O'Brian, the man was gone."

Mike closed his eyes, thinking what a big surprise she was in for. Maybe *she* hadn't seen his assailant, but he certainly had.

"Did you feel dizzy?" she asked. "When we were walking up the stairs?"

"Just a little," he said, opening his eyes again.

"Just a little," she repeated into the phone.

"Does the doctor say I'm allowed to talk?" he demanded.

Claudia relayed the question, then nodded. "Okay," she went on after a few seconds. "We'll be here. Thanks so much and...the police? Oh. Well, yes, I guess we *should* report it."

Report it to the police? That suggestion went a long way to driving those erotic thoughts from Mike's head. Then Claudia put down the cordless and gave him an anxious smile.

"The doctor says she'll stop by as soon as she's finished her office appointments but that you're probably okay."

"Exactly what I've been trying to tell you."

"Unless," she added as if he hadn't spoken, "you begin throwing up or get double vision or start exhibiting any other symptoms of concussion."

"And if I do, your doctor will want to amputate my head before gangrene can set in, right?"

"Very funny," she said.

He could see, though, that she was hard pressed to keep from smiling.

"Don't move," she ordered when he tried to sit up. "You're supposed to stay quiet until she's had a look at you."

"Fine." He shoved himself the rest of the way up and planted his feet on the floor. "I'll stay quiet sitting up. Now, do you want to hear who hit me?"

"You know?"

He started to nod, but it made the hammering worse, so he simply said, "It was Santa."

"Oh, Lord," she whispered. "He hurt you worse than we realized. You're hallucinating."

"I'm *not* hallucinating. I may not have seen what he hit me with, but I had a good look at him. And he was Santa."

"But... What would Santa be doing in my basement? And why would he hit you?"

"How the hell should I know? Could be he came here trying to find out where I was going with my articles—hoping I'd left some notes lying around or something."

"He figured he'd find your notes in the basement? And he came looking for them dressed in his Santa suit? Doesn't that seem a little illogical? I mean, wouldn't he want to be a *tad* less conspicuous?"

"Any *sane* person would. So, hell, maybe your Santa's a few reindeer short of a team. At any rate, I know who I saw. And by the way, no police."

"Excuse me?"

"Your doctor's idea that we report this. Forget it."

Claudia felt a distinct surge of relief. The absolute last thing she wanted to do was call the police. Not that they'd likely put out an A.P.B. on Santa because of a minor assault, but she'd feel better if they didn't hear anything about what had happened.

"Don't argue with me on this, Paquette."

O'Brian, she realized, looked extremely worried that she might. But why would he care when he was the victim? Curious enough to want an answer, she said, "Well, we really *should* call them."

"And make the incident public knowledge? Oh, that would be just terrific. Iggy'd love it."

"What does Iggy have to do with it?"

"Iggy? Of the stupid Santa Thumbs Nose at L.A. Reporter headline? Just think where he'd go with a follow-up. Something like Santa Fells Survivor of South L.A. Snipers. I'd be a damn laughingstock."

"Ahh," she said, suppressing a smile. "I see your point. But has anyone ever told you your headlines need work? They're too long and alliterative to be punchy."

He glared at her. "Yes. In fact someone mentioned it recently. But I believe your phrasing last time around was 'kind of wordy.'"

Mike O'Brian, Claudia thought fleetingly, was even more gorgeous when he was angry. It made his blue eyes positively spark fire. And the way his jaw tightened only accentuated its strong angle.

"Well, getting back to what happened," she said, forcing her gaze from his jaw, "if we're not going to call the police, we should at least try to make sense of things. Because I just can't believe that was Santa in the basement.

"I don't mean I doubt you saw a man in a Santa suit," she hurried on when O'Brian opened his mouth to object. "I just can't believe it was the *real* Santa. Because, if he doesn't want you to identify him, why on earth would he risk a face-to-face confrontation?

If you'd yanked down his beard, it would have been game over."

"Too bad I missed my chance," O'Brian muttered. "But what are you saying? That there's a whole herd of Santa clones running around town? I mean, yesterday it was Pete and today it's somebody else?"

"Well, we know it wasn't Pete today. He was standing out on the driveway with me."

"I *realize* that, Paquette. Getting knocked out didn't give me amnesia. But what I meant was, what's with this town? Does every guy around have a Santa suit stashed in his closet? So he can play dress-up whenever the whim seizes him? I mean, is this a weird Canadian custom or something?"

"Of course not."

"Then maybe it *was* the real Santa who conked me. Maybe he was trying to make me realize that he *seriously* doesn't want his identity revealed."

"I guess that could be it," she agreed slowly. "And if he's prepared to go to extremes... You know, maybe we'd better talk to Iggy. Convince him you should change the slant of the series."

"Change it how?"

"So that you're just covering Santa's escapades, not really trying to ID him at all."

"What? And let some local yokel in a red suit best me? Paquette, are you out of your mind? Iggy's story, playing up that stupid challenge, has already gone over the wire. It'll be appearing in major papers as a lead-in to my series. Do you want him sending off a second one that says I wasn't up to the challenge?"

"But that challenge was just a setup, remember? To add excitement to your arrival."

"To let your editor write a more colorful story, you mean. And at this point, nobody'd believe for a second that it was only a setup. If I backed off on identifying Santa, everyone would figure I was conceding."

"Well surely that wouldn't be the end of the world. And if you don't, you might get hit over the head again. Or worse."

O'Brian glared at her once more. "Do you have any idea what backing off on something like this would do to my reputation? Hell, I'd never be able to show my face around the *Gazette* again."

"But—"

"Oh, no, Paquette. We're not calling the police and we're not talking to Iggy. We're going to identify Santa."

CHAPTER SEVEN

"I'M SURPRISED HOW COZY this is," Mike said, glancing across the Jeep at Claudia.

She had her fuzzy pink hat pulled down over her ears, but the moonlight was highlighting the rest of her hair with silver. He couldn't help thinking it made her look positively ethereal. At least, the part of her that wasn't cocooned beneath her sleeping bag.

"Two hours out here," he went on, "and I'm really not that cold. In California we'd never think to go on a surveillance wearing snowmobile suits, blankets *and* sleeping bags."

"In California the temperature doesn't dip below minus thirty overnight."

When he smiled at that, she smiled back, but she seemed very anxious. And the only thing that could be making her nervous was him—which certainly gave him pause.

For more than an hour he'd been considering the old stretch-your-arms-and-end-up-with-one-of-them-around-the-woman ploy, but her nervous smile was enough to make him rethink it one more time. And besides her smile, there was the fact he was so bundled up that stretching his arms would be very tricky.

Looking down the road at Greenaway's house, he tried to figure out what the hell was going on in Claudia's head. There was so much electricity between them that the Jeep was humming with it. But she seemed to be doing her damnedest to ignore it, while he couldn't have ignored it if he'd tried.

Every time he looked at her his pulse began to race and his heart started hammering so hard that cardiac arrest was a distinct possibility. Finally deciding he'd rather risk rejection than a heart attack, he worked his arms free from beneath the sleeping bag. The icy air immediately began nipping at his bare hands.

"Oh, more coffee?" Claudia said. "Good idea."

Muttering under his breath, he unscrewed the thermos, poured a little coffee and passed it to her.

"You don't want any?" she asked.

"We'll share." He reached for the cup after she'd had a sip, letting his fingers linger on hers.

"I'd better warm up the engine again," she said, sliding her hand free. "We don't want to find it doesn't start when we need it."

"No. We don't." He drank a little of the coffee, beginning to wonder if she could possibly be sending off negative vibes that he was missing. Then she smiled at him again, and the rush of arousal he felt made him certain there wasn't a negative vibe for miles.

After Claudia started the car, she didn't let herself look at O'Brian again. Instead, she gazed out into the moonlit night, thinking that sitting here with him was one of the most difficult things she'd ever done. Because despite the biting cold, each time her eyes strayed to him she felt warm tingles inside.

That, of course, merely proved what she'd known all along. She should never have come with him tonight. She should have simply called Santa and warned him not to go anywhere near Greenaway's place. Then she could have safely stayed home and let O'Brian do the surveillance on his own—which was exactly what she'd have done if it hadn't been for that conk on the head.

Her gaze flickered to him again. Doc Bennet had declared him fine after she'd checked him over. And he *seemed* fine. He'd even written his article about Greenaway and their ice-fishing adventure, then insisted on taking it over to the *Dispatch* so it would be waiting for Iggy on Monday morning.

But still, she hadn't thought it would be wise to let him drive up here on his own. And since he'd been bound and determined to come, there'd been little choice about coming with him.

There *was* a choice, though, about whether anything was going to happen between them. And nothing was. Nothing at all. *The last thing you need, Claudia,* she reminded herself, *is yet another complication.*

Her resolve firmly in place, and the Cherokee a couple of degrees warmer, she cut the ignition.

"It doesn't look as if Greenaway's going anywhere tonight," O'Brian said.

She started to agree, then her gaze met his and the words caught in her throat. Even in the darkness of the Jeep, she could see that those blue eyes of his were warm enough to heat Alaska. Then he reached out and brushed his fingers gently down her cheek, starting an aching sensation deep within her.

"O'Brian, I don't think this is a good idea," she said shakily, her resolve draining away faster than water from a sink.

"No?" he whispered. "Why not?"

"Wayne Greenaway. What if we miss seeing him leave?"

"We couldn't miss hearing his snowmobile."

O'Brian's lips were mere millimeters away from hers; the warmth of his breath was seductively hot in the cold air.

"So why don't we try just one little kiss?" he suggested. "If we don't like it, we'll stop."

That sounded like an eminently logical proposal—although she did suspect his nearness was playing havoc with her thought processes. But since it was nothing more than a suspicion, and with every nerve ending in her body urging her to kiss him, she did precisely that.

As soon as she did, she wondered what insanity had made her want to resist, because kissing Mike O'Brian was unlike anything she'd ever experienced—and like everything she'd thank her lucky stars for if she could experience it throughout eternity.

His mouth was soft and warm against hers. His jaw was rock hard beneath her fingers, his skin enticingly rough with its day's growth of beard. And when his tongue began to tease hers, she almost melted. He tasted faintly of coffee. He smelled subtly of a woodsy cologne. And being in his arms felt absolutely perfect.

She leaned into the kiss, sliding her hands to the back of his neck and slipping her fingers beneath his scarf. His skin felt hot, and its heat flowed through her entire body, making her oblivious to the cold.

"So?" he finally murmured against her lips.

"So what?" she whispered.

"Do you like it or should we stop?"

"Very funny, O'Brian."

He grinned at her. And then he proceeded to kiss her senseless—until they heard a car door slam and the distant sound of an engine starting.

"That's Wayne!" she said, scrambling out of O'Brian's embrace and into a sitting position behind the wheel.

"But in his Blazer, not on a snowmobile," O'Brian added as the 4×4 wheeled out of the driveway and onto the road.

Claudia started the Jeep, saying, "Thank heavens he turned the other way or he'd have spotted us for sure." She shoved the Jeep into drive and headed after the Blazer. "Maybe he's got his Santa snowmobile hidden somewhere. And the presents, too." But she knew that wasn't true, of course, so what *was* he up to?

"Claudia?"

When she glanced over at O'Brian he seemed decidedly nervous. "What?"

"Don't you think you should turn on the headlights?"

"No, then he'd know someone was following him. But don't worry. Between the moonlight and the snowbanks, I can see the road perfectly well."

O'Brian looked far from convinced and proceeded to do up his seat belt.

They followed Greenaway through the night until he reached his destination—which proved to be the Hillstead Mine offices.

"Maybe this is where he's got everything hidden," O'Brian said as she pulled to a stop just before they reached the driveway.

"Maybe. Should we just sit here and see what happens next?"

"I guess."

Greenaway parked his Blazer, then headed over to the front door of the building. He stood there for a moment, obviously unlocking the door, then went inside. A minute later, a light went on.

"I think that's his office," Claudia said. "I've been in it, and that's about the right location."

They waited, but no other lights came on.

"We'd better take a closer look," O'Brian finally suggested.

They climbed out of the Jeep, quietly closed the doors, then trudged down the driveway.

"Don't let him see you," Claudia whispered as they neared the office window.

"What kind of investigative reporter do you think I am?"

They crept over to the edge of the window and O'Brian peered in, then glanced back at Claudia. "He's sitting at his desk, working."

"At this time of night?"

"That's what I call a workaholic. But we'll go back to the Jeep and hang around for a while. Just in case he's going to play Santa later."

"IT'S MORNING," O'Brian said softly.

"Mmm?" Claudia murmured. Her face was buried against his shoulder. His arm was comfortably around her. And she knew that if she moved even a fraction of an inch the cold would attack her. Which added up to a very strong argument for staying right where she was.

"I said it's morning," he repeated. "And if Greenaway's Santa, he decided to take last night off."

Braving the icy air, she opened her eyes and looked outside. O'Brian was right. A pink streak, so pale it was barely visible, had appeared on the horizon, and they certainly hadn't heard Greenaway going anywhere on a snowmobile. His Blazer was still parked where it had been earlier.

"You know," she said, "his coming in to work like that is very strange. I mean, the offices are officially closed for the Christmas holidays. And with the mines virtually shut down, how much work can he have?"

When O'Brian merely shrugged, she stretched, then asked, "Did I actually fall asleep or was I just dozing?"

"You fell asleep. An hour or two ago."

He punctuated his words by giving her a quick kiss. It made her realize her lips were swollen from all their previous kissing.

"You snored, too," he added.

"I did not." She sat up straighter and glared indignantly at him. "I never snore."

He grinned. "Well, maybe it was a little more like moaning."

"I don't moan, either."

"Next time we spend the night together, I'll bring my tape recorder."

Looking away, she ran her fingers through her tousled hair. She hadn't intended on a first time, never mind a next time. And if they ever did spend another night together, it probably wouldn't be in a cold car with umpteen layers of clothes and sleeping bags between them. Being too near O'Brian practically made her forget her name, never mind her good intentions.

"Should we get going?" he suggested, starting to shove the sleeping bags and blankets into the back seat. "I'm starving."

The engine complained about the cold but eventually turned over, letting them head for home. And fortunately O'Brian wasn't in a talkative mood, so Claudia had a chance to think.

Today was Sunday, and she'd neatly managed to keep him off Santa's trail since Friday. She really wasn't doing badly at all. And hopefully she'd only have to keep playing this game for another couple of days.

She began considering where she should try leading O'Brian next, then made the mistake of glancing across the Cherokee. Merely looking at his rugged profile was enough to make her forget about her planning. Suddenly, all she could think about was how very soon he'd be leaving and that, after he had, she'd never see him again.

The prospect made her throat tight, and telling herself that was an overreaction didn't help a bit.

You barely know the man, she tried—which didn't work, either. There was absolutely no doubt she'd miss Mike O'Brian once he'd flown out of her life. Miss him a lot. And since she'd reached that stage already, how was she going to feel by next weekend?

That, she decided, wasn't a question she wanted to think about. She was too afraid of what the answer would be, especially if she allowed things to go any further between them. Clearly, she'd be very foolish to let that happen.

They got to Victoria Falls a few minutes later, and when they reached her house Morgan spent a good three minutes bouncing ecstatically around the hall.

"That's his dance of the deserted dog," she explained to O'Brian. "He likes to make me feel guilty if he figures I've been gone too long.

"You could have come with us, you know," she added to Morgan, "but you wouldn't have enjoyed it a bit. We almost froze."

"Oh, I don't know," O'Brian said. "I was pretty hot some of the time."

She let Morgan out before replying, trying to find the precise words she wanted. When she turned back from the door, O'Brian was eyeing her expectantly.

"Look," she said softly, "I'm not saying I didn't enjoy what happened last night, but I'm not sure it should have happened. Well, no, actually I'm sure it *shouldn't* have. The circumstances we're in aren't exactly..."

"Aren't exactly what?"

She shrugged. "I'm going to be blunt, O'Brian. Obviously I find you attractive. But I'm not into one-night stands. Or one-week stands, as the case might be. And I don't want to discover myself doing something I'll regret."

For a long minute he didn't say a word. Then he nodded and said, "Okay. That's not hard to understand."

"Then ... you're all right with it?"

"I didn't say I was all right with it. I said it wasn't hard to understand. And I'll do my best to keep it in mind. I'd hate to find myself banished to the Silver Dollar."

For some reason she didn't quite fathom, the smooth way he'd handled her rebuff made her feel like crying. Or maybe the problem was that she'd gotten what she wanted and it wasn't what part of her really wanted at all.

"Hey," he said quietly. "Maybe I've mentioned having a couple of sisters? Rachel and Sarah?"

She nodded.

"Well, when we were all teenagers, they stapled a picture of a guy they knew to a board and threw darts at it. I decided then I didn't want to be that kind of guy."

"Okay," she said, forcing a smile. "So you'll remember Iggy's got a photo of you. And that I can borrow it any time I like."

MIKE GAVE HIS JAW a final stroke with the razor, still wishing he'd said more to Claudia. But what else could he say?

He wiped his face clean, then stood staring at his reflection in the mirror, wondering if he should at least have told her he really liked her and hadn't been thinking of her in terms of a one-week stand.

Yes, he decided, pulling his sweatshirt over his head, he probably should have. But when they both knew they couldn't have any longer than one week, where would talking about things have gotten them?

Nowhere, he answered himself. Given the situation, there was little point to getting into a big discussion. But dammit, keeping his distance from her was going to kill him.

He rinsed off his razor, then headed for the kitchen, where Claudia was just starting to get things organized for breakfast. Although she'd showered before he had, her hair was still damp. And the way it was drying into a wild tangle of curls made him want to bury his fingers in it.

Trying to ignore the urge, he wandered over to the counter and asked if she wanted him to make the toast again. When she smiled at the offer, he began to reconsider the idea of discussing things, but before he could say another word, the phone started ringing. At the moment, it was sitting on the counter right next to him, so he glanced questioningly at her.

"I'd better answer it," she said. Then she practically flew across the kitchen and grabbed it.

Turning away, he walked over to get the bread, feigning disinterest. But he was curious about why the thought of his answering the phone had spooked her. It was no secret he was staying here. He could easily name half a dozen people who knew. And in a small town like this, that meant a lot more did, too. So who had she figured might be phoning that she didn't want him talking to?

He opened the fridge freezer and took out a half-used loaf of bread, listening intently. Claudia wasn't saying much, though. Her caller was doing almost all the talking.

"That's great, isn't it," she finally said.

"Oh, did you really?" she added a moment later. "I don't think he's going to forget a single person."

There was another little silence, then she said, "Well, thanks, and I'll mention it to him. But he figures my articles covered that angle, so we probably won't. I'll call back if he'd like to, though."

She hung up, looking glum. "So much for Wayne Greenaway merely taking last night off," she said, starting back across the kitchen.

Mike noted that she was carrying the phone away with her. For whatever reason, she really didn't want to risk his answering it.

"While we were watching Greenaway," she went on, "Santa was busy again."

"Oh? That was one of your Santa hot line calls?"

"Uh-huh." She began arranging slices of bacon on a dish for the microwave. "It was May Nowiki, whose husband's one of the laid-off miners. When they woke up this morning, there was a hamper on their porch, along with gifts for their four kids."

"So Greenaway can't be Santa," Mike said thoughtfully. "Not unless he sent an imposter out to make the deliveries last night."

"What?"

He shrugged, trying not to let Claudia see that he was teasing. "You never know. Maybe he figured we might decide to keep an eye on him and he wanted to throw us off. Hell, with all the spare Santa suits that are floating around town, he'd have had his pick of people to send out."

"Yes. Yes, you're right!" she said excitedly. "That's probably what he did. Which would mean he's our Santa after all."

Mike hesitated. He certainly hadn't been serious about the idea of an imposter. It was a highly unlikely possibility, and Claudia had to know that. So what was with her act? She seemed to *want* him to believe Greenaway was Santa.

His reporter's instincts on full alert, he said, "I don't really think we should get carried away with the imposter hypothesis. In fact, I think Greenaway should go to the bottom of our suspects list. Which means I'd better pay the Nilssons a visit today, huh?"

Glancing at his watch, he decided it was too early to call her father about that car. But he *did* intend to try to keep his distance from Claudia, and it would be a whole lot easier if he wasn't depending on her for transportation.

"But we're barely home from our surveillance," she said, sticking the bacon into the microwave.

"Aren't you too tired to head off into the country again?"

"No, I can hang in for a while yet. But if *you're* too tired, just give me the directions and I'll go on my own. You wouldn't mind lending me the Jeep, would you?"

"No, but I'd rather go with you."

He watched her set the timer, wondering if she had any idea that being with her for more hours on end would seriously test his resolve. Then, when she turned away from the microwave, he said, "What did the woman who just called want?"

"May Nowiki? I told you, she wanted to let me know about Santa."

"No, I mean what else? You said something about your articles and that you'd mention whatever she was talking about to *him*—which I assume has to be either me or Iggy. Then you told her you'd call back if he wanted to."

"Oh...*that*. She asked if you'd like to come over and see what Santa left. But I knew you wouldn't because you didn't want to go look at those other hampers yesterday. Besides, she's only hoping to get her picture in the paper and she'd be disappointed."

"Why? I don't mind taking a few shots of her."

"Maybe not, but Iggy wouldn't run one because he doesn't like her. So we'd be wasting our time going there."

Mike was half listening, half still trying to figure out what Claudia was up to. A minute ago she'd been pretending she thought Greenaway still could be Santa. Now she was not very subtly trying to persuade him he didn't want to go see this Nowiki woman.

He didn't know why she'd do either. But whatever her act was in aid of, it was getting curiouser and curiouser.

Visiting the Nilssons could wait a little longer, he decided. First, he intended to find out why Claudia didn't want him talking to May Nowiki.

"You know," he said, "I might have been a bit hasty yesterday. Maybe it wouldn't hurt to go have a look at what Santa brought these people. Even if Iggy *won't* run a picture."

"I *really* think we'd be wasting our time."

He shrugged. "Even so..."

"All right," Claudia said, reaching for the carton of eggs. "But you'll regret it."

BY THE TIME CLAUDIA pulled into the Nowikis' drive, she was congratulating herself for at least the tenth time on how well she'd manipulated O'Brian into wasting the morning.

The man was a born sucker for reverse psychology. As soon as she said they shouldn't do something, he became determined to do it. And with May Nowiki being such a talker, they'd be lucky to get out of here before noon.

Surely by then O'Brian's lack of sleep would be catching up with him. In which case, she should be able to persuade him to leave the Nilssons for yet another day.

No, persuading him wasn't the approach, she corrected herself. She'd *insist* they should drive out to see

Gord and Norm after lunch. Then O'Brian would decide he was too tired.

They'd barely climbed out of the Cherokee before May opened the door—freshly made up and dressed in a long white scoop-necked sweater pulled down over green leggings that looked as if they were stretched to their limit.

A couple of years older than Claudia, May had been very popular back in school. One of those perky, blond cheerleader and prom queen types, she'd dated half the football team each fall and half the hockey team during the winter.

Now, after a dozen years of marriage and four kids, she was a more frazzled and heavier version of her former self.

"Oh, but come in out of the cold!" she exclaimed after Claudia introduced her to O'Brian. "And you brought a camera," she added, looking at the Nikon slung over his shoulder. You aren't going to take pictures of me, are you?"

O'Brian gave her a killer smile. "I sure am if you'll let me."

Claudia mentally rolled her eyes.

"Well," May was saying, "I made a fresh pot of coffee as soon as you called back, Claudia. And the kids have gone off with Tom, so they won't be interrupting us. They were as excited as Mexican jumping beans about Santa's presents and they were driving me crazy. So when Tom was leaving to drive Tom Junior up to Kirkland Lake for his hockey game, I said, 'You just take all four and get them out of my hair for a few hours.'"

"I guess four can be quite a handful," O'Brian said.

"You'd better believe it. And with my Tom off work, it's like having *five* kids underfoot. I don't know how I'll survive now that school's closed for Christmas vacation. But you two just make yourselves at home and I'll get the coffee."

"Nice tree," O'Brian said as May disappeared into the kitchen.

Claudia nodded. It *was* nice—and so big it took up half the living room. "Those are the parcels Santa brought," she offered. "The ones wrapped in that red foil and topped off with green bows. I've seen a lot of them in the past week or so.

"And that's the hamper, of course, sitting in the corner. There'd have been a turkey in with the rest of the things, but I guess May's already put it in the freezer."

O'Brian wandered over to have a closer look at the hamper. "There aren't any markings on it," he said, glancing back across the room. "I figured there might be a store's name or something."

"No, I already checked a few of them for that."

"But all the presents have been done up like these ones?"

She nodded. "Why?"

"They look store-wrapped, don't you think? Professional?"

"Ahh . . . I guess they might be."

O'Brian picked up one of the gifts, inspected it, then looked over at her again. "You told me Santa hasn't been buying locally."

"Right," she said uneasily. She was beginning to wonder whether maneuvering him into coming here had actually been a good idea.

If he put forth a little effort, he'd learn which store was wrapping its gifts like that this year. And she'd rather he didn't have any leads to follow. Other than the ones she fed him, that was.

"Okay, here's what I think," he said, putting the box back under the tree. "These presents are *definitely* professionally wrapped. And not on the cheap, either, which means Santa's buying at an upscale store. So what's the nearest big—"

"Here we are," their hostess sang out, reappearing with the coffee.

Claudia smiled. She'd never been so glad to see May Nowiki in her life.

Her relief was short-lived though. By the time May had finished telling her story about how Tom Junior had been first to discover the gifts, O'Brian was taking her picture and practically charming the leggings off her.

Clearly he was leading up to something. And Claudia couldn't imagine it was anything she'd be happy about.

He clicked off a few more shots, then said, "May, I wonder if you'd mind helping me out a little more."

"Oh, of course not," she simpered.

"Great." He gave her a warm smile that Claudia found absolutely infuriating. It made her feel . . .

The word *jealous* popped into her head, but she quickly forced it back out. Being jealous over a man she was definitely *not* going to get involved with would be both stupid and petty.

"I'd really like to see what some of those presents are," O'Brian told May. "Do you think we could open a few and have a look? Then rewrap them so your children won't know they've been touched?"

"You might tear some of the paper," Claudia quickly objected, her uneasiness growing by leaps and bounds. She didn't know what theory O'Brian was formulating, but the less information he had the better.

"Oh, I think if we're careful it would be all right," May said.

O'Brian graced her with another killer smile, then followed her over to the tree.

"Where do you want to start?" she asked.

"Well, let's see. It looks as if there are three Santa gifts for each of them, right?"

May nodded.

"Then how about opening one per kid—so I can get an idea of the sort of thing he's giving different age groups."

Claudia sat on the couch and fumed while May tentatively unwrapped the first present.

"Oh," she said, taking the top off the box. "I don't believe it! A Maple Leaf hockey jersey. And it's number sixteen, exactly the one Tommy wanted."

"Really." O'Brian looked at the jersey with interest. "I wonder how Santa knew?"

"Why... I can't imagine. We don't see a lot of the Nilssons in town, so I doubt they'd be able to pick Tom Junior out from half a dozen other boys, let alone know what he wants for Christmas."

"The Nilssons," O'Brian repeated. "You think they're Santa?"

May shrugged. "Most everybody does. But I'm sure you've heard that before. Heck, I'll bet you've even talked to them by now."

"Well, I haven't quite gotten around to it yet. Let's look at another present.

"Paquette?" he added, glancing over at her. "How about giving us a hand here? Maybe you could do the rewrapping."

"If you need tape and scissors," May said, gesturing toward an end table, "try that drawer."

Unhappily, Claudia dug out the tape and scissors, then began putting the paper back on the box that held the hockey jersey.

"Oh, my!" May exclaimed. "And look at this for Becky."

"A doll," O'Brian said.

"Not just a doll," May told him. "It's a Baby-Walks-and-Talks! Becky's going to be positively thrilled. She wanted one for her birthday last month, but we couldn't afford it. When she didn't get it she was so disappointed she almost cried."

From the corner of her eye, Claudia could see the meaningful look O'Brian was giving her. She pretended not to notice and went on with her wrapping.

"Oh, this is absolutely amazing," May murmured, opening a third gift.

"Beginner's in-line skates. Just what little Vance has been asking for. And I know that huge package is the toboggan he wants. And that other big carton's got to be his carpenter's bench. Tom will probably have to spend half of Christmas morning assembling it. But you know, Mike, I think I'll open everything I'm not entirely certain of, because now I'm dying to know if Santa got *all* the gifts right."

Sure enough, each present May opened proved to be something one of her children was just dying for. And each time she announced the fact, Claudia found O'Brian's glances more difficult to ignore.

"Well," he said when May was done unwrapping the final gift, "I can't tell you how much I appreciate this. But assuming it *is* the Nilssons playing Santa, who could have told them what your children wanted? Was it you? Or your husband?"

"Oh, no." She shook her head firmly. "We haven't so much as caught sight of either of them in weeks. And even if we had, we'd never have dreamed of being so... What's the word?"

"Presumptuous?" Claudia supplied.

May nodded. "I guess someone could have heard the kids talking about what they wanted and passed it on. But for anyone to bat a thousand like this...

"You know," she went on after a moment, "like most people, I've been assuming the Nilssons were behind this Santa thing. But now I'm starting to wonder. I mean, I don't know who else it would be, but could they *possibly* have known exactly what to buy?"

"I guess that's something Paquette and I had better find out," O'Brian said, shooting her a smile.

She made herself smile back, but she couldn't help thinking his expression was chock-full of suspicion.

CHAPTER EIGHT

CLAUDIA SAT ON THE COUCH stroking Ghost—who was in one of his rare affection-seeking moods—and watching O'Brian.

He'd called her father the minute they'd arrived home from May Nowiki's, and now he was pacing back and forth across the living room, the cordless pressed to his ear.

"Well, sure, Raymond," he said. "If you still haven't been able to find anything, I guess there just isn't anything to find."

Ghost had begun to knead her sweater, so she captured his front paws with her hand as O'Brian went on.

"Yeah, okay, that sounds good. Just give me a call if something *does* turn up. And thanks for all your effort. I really appreciate it."

When he put down the phone and sank onto the far end of the couch, Claudia assumed her best innocent expression. "Dad still hasn't turned up anything?"

"No. He said with the weather being this cold, a lot of people are having battery trouble, which means nobody's got an extra car just sitting in their driveway. But maybe I should try asking around myself. At least drop into that garage on Main Street. They've got to have a loaner or two."

"Whatever they have must already be out, because that's the first place Dad would have tried. The owner, Earl, is another of Dad's poker buddies."

"Well, what other possibilities are there? How about Iggy? Do you think he might—"

"O'Brian? Dad would be awfully insulted if he heard you were trying to line up something on your own. He'd think you figured he hasn't been trying his hardest."

"Oh. Yeah, I guess you're right."

"Besides, I really don't mind driving you around. It's interesting to see how someone with all your experience works."

"Well, so far," he muttered, "I haven't worked very impressively, have I. Chasing Greenaway to his fishing hole might have gotten me a story, but since he's not Santa, that surveillance last night was nothing but a waste of time."

Claudia's face began to grow uncomfortably warm. Then O'Brian quietly said, "Oh. Sorry. I wasn't referring to *that* part of it."

She nodded, feeling as awkward as he sounded. "I realized what you meant. But you've ruled Wayne Greenaway out completely?" she asked, shifting the conversation back to safer ground. "I thought you were only dropping him to the bottom of the suspects list."

"No, the idea he'd send someone out in his place is just too farfetched. He can't possibly be Santa. But, as I said yesterday, I'm sure he's a man with a secret. And I can't help wondering what it is."

"Me, too. He was really pretty shifty-eyed, wasn't he."

"Yeah. The minute I started asking him about the mine layoffs he got awfully nervous."

"And it was almost as if he was relieved when you accused him of being Santa."

O'Brian gazed at her for a moment, then said, "That's it exactly. He was glad to get off the subject of Hillstead, which makes me wonder if these temporary layoffs are really so temporary. What was the rationale behind them?"

"Nobody's really sure. What Greenaway said at the time was what he told us yesterday—that there were a variety of reasons. But the miners didn't buy it when he said there was a problem with ore quality. As far as they could tell, all the working shafts have been holding up fine."

O'Brian rubbed his jaw thoughtfully. "And the guys in the trenches usually know what's what, don't they?"

Claudia could feel her excitement mounting. Victoria Falls was hardly a hotbed of crime and corruption, so she'd never had a chance to do any serious investigative reporting. But if O'Brian's instincts told him there was something up at Hillstead, she wanted to check it out. And doing it with him would be on-the-job training from an expert. Not only that, but if they could shift their focus from Santa...

"Why don't we try to convince Iggy he should let you investigate Hillstead?" she suggested. "Instead of worrying about Santa, I mean."

O'Brian shook his head. "He'd never go for it. But if we got the Santa mystery wrapped up fast, I'd still have lots of time before I leave. We could do some poking around about Hillstead then. Good idea?"

"Great idea," she agreed. But his words had thrown cold water on her excitement. Since she didn't intend to let him wrap up the Santa mystery at all, never mind fast, she wouldn't be able to check into Hillstead until after O'Brian was gone.

FOR A MAN WHO HAD TO BE running on empty, Claudia thought, O'Brian was still annoyingly alert. Instead of falling asleep in his soup at lunch, he'd been bouncing ideas off her.

"And what about those presents?" he asked, slipping Morgan a piece of sandwich when he thought she wasn't looking. "You figure Santa's been delivering exactly what *all* the kids want? That he's got a master list? And if he has, where did it come from?"

"O'Brian, you just asked ten questions in a row and—"

"Four. I only asked four."

"Well, I don't know the answer to any of them, so I guess we'd better go visit a few more people who've had deliveries. Check out what Santa left some of the other kids." *And kill the rest of the day for a bonus,* she silently added.

"No, that would waste too much time," O'Brian objected. "Let's just go talk to those Nilsson brothers."

She mentally kicked herself for forgetting to use reverse psychology. She should have suggested they *not* go visiting other people who'd had deliveries.

"I've been thinking about something else that points to them," he added.

"Oh?"

"Uh-huh. Santa can't have wall-to-wall neighbors, because either he's been getting some darned big deliveries or he's been going shopping and arriving home with tons of goodies. And if he had close neighbors, the grapevine would be *certain* who he is."

"Well . . . yes, you'd think so."

"Which means he must live in the country, and the Nilssons live in the country."

"Ahh, that *is* something else that points to them." She forced a smiled, telling herself to think before she said anything more. She didn't intend to blow the reverse psychology approach twice in a row, because she was running low on tricks. Which meant that the longer she could keep him away from the Nilssons, the better.

"Okay," she said, "let's not even bother doing the dishes. Let's start for their place right now."

"Hey, you're not getting any argument from me. I'm ready to leave whenever you are."

"Well...super. I'll just give them a call to say we're coming." Unhappily, she checked the number and punched it in.

"Claudia," Gord's voice greeted her a minute later. "We've been wondering why you hadn't called before this. You must have been managing to lead this O'Brian guy on a merry chase without our help, eh?"

"Yes, I've been doing fine, thanks. And I don't know if you've heard, but the *Dispatch* has a guest reporter here from L.A. He's come to do a story on our Santa."

"Sitting right there listening, is he?"

"Yes, exactly. At any rate, we'd like to come and talk to you and Norm this afternoon. Will you be around?"

"We'll be wherever you want us, Claudia. Here or not here."

She thought rapidly and decided she might want to use the *not here* excuse for something else. "Oh...oh, dear," she said. "That's a bit of a problem, then.

"O'Brian?" she added, glancing at him. "Their road hasn't been plowed yet. Not since yesterday's snowfall. So it isn't passable."

"Was there *that* much snow?"

"There was up by their place. Which means that if we go, we'll have to walk in from the main road."

"Nice ploy," Gord said into her ear.

"How far from the road to their house?" O'Brian asked.

"It's a good hike."

"Well, what about your snowmobile rather than the Jeep?"

"No, it's been a little temperamental lately, so I wouldn't trust it out in the middle of nowhere at the moment. Not until Dad finds time to look at it for me."

O'Brian eyed her for a minute, as if he was wondering if she'd made that up. "So that leaves walking in or not going," he said at last.

"Right. And if we walked, the snow's so deep we'd need snowshoes."

"Do you have any?"

She was about to lie, then remembered he'd been in the basement. "Yes," she admitted.

"Good. Then I'm up to it if you are. We could wear our snowmobile suits again. You were right about them, they're really warm."

She forced a smile and said into the phone, "We'll see you in a while, Gord."

"Claudia? You *do* know our road's clean as a whistle, don't you?"

"Yes, of course. We'll have to deal with that."

"Norm and I will give it some thought before you get here," he promised.

"OKAY, BOY," MIKE SAID, opening the Jeep's back door for the dog. When Morgan gazed longingly at the warm house, he quietly added, "I can relate to that, fella."

Claudia, though, leaned across from the driver's seat and said, "Get in, Morgan. You've been darn lazy lately, and walking in to the Nilssons' will be good exercise."

After the dog reluctantly did as he'd been told, Mike climbed into the front and carefully buckled his seat belt. By this point, he knew what kind of trip to expect with Claudia at the wheel.

Sure enough, once they cleared town she accelerated until the passing scenery was little more than a white blur. He checked the speedometer and decided Indy 500 drivers would be impressed. Especially given all the ice and snow.

"What's the matter?" she asked.

Glancing over, he discovered she was looking at him—which sent a shiver down his spine. He'd far rather she kept her eyes glued to the highway.

"You seem nervous," she said.

"Oh . . . I was just thinking you drive a little fast."

"Ahh, your opinion's improving, then. The other day, you told me I drove like a maniac. But don't worry. I've never had an accident."

"Never?"

"Well, nothing serious."

Wondering about her definition of *serious,* he went back to looking out the window, imagining how she'd take to driving around L.A. Ten minutes in gridlock, he decided, and she'd probably be tearing her hair.

He looked over at her again, the thought of her being in L.A. reminding him of something. "That bush pilot who flew me up from Sudbury?"

"Uh-huh?"

"He said most young people leave Victoria Falls."

"He was right. There aren't many jobs, except in the mines. And that's hard, dangerous work."

"But you're still here."

"Very perceptive," she teased, flashing him a smile. "I had an option, other than the mines. I'd been working for the *Dispatch* while I was in high school. And when I graduated, Iggy offered me a full-time job. The rest, as they say, is history."

There was, Mike suspected, a little more than that to the story. Claudia didn't strike him as having the kind of small-town mentality that kept some people tied to the place they were born.

"You didn't want to see more of the world?" he asked. "Explore different options?"

"Well...yes. Actually, I'd intended to spend a year backpacking around Europe. Then I was going to settle in Toronto and study journalism."

"But you didn't do either."

"No," she said quietly. "It was only a couple of months before I graduated that my mother died, and I didn't want to leave my father on his own right away. Then, as time went by... Oh, you know how it goes."

He wanted to ask if she regretted how it had gone but wasn't sure he should. So instead, he asked, "And what about your friend Annie?"

"Oh, she's a different story, of course. She went away to university. But she's one of the rare ones who came back after graduating."

"Because?"

Claudia didn't reply for a minute, then said, "It'll sound silly to you, but it was because of a guy who wasn't even here anymore. A fellow she'd been crazy about all through high school."

"A case of unrequited love?"

"No, not at all. He loved her, too, and they'd planned on getting married in a few years. But then he suddenly left town."

"Why?"

"Oh . . . personal reasons. He was going through a bad patch. At any rate, Annie never stopped loving him, and she was convinced he'd come back someday and they'd pick up where they left off. So when she finished university, she got a job with the district school."

"But this guy never did come back?"

"No."

Mike lapsed into silence, thinking how peoples' lives seldom worked out the way they expected. Then he discovered his gaze had drifted to Claudia again.

He sat watching her, reminding himself she didn't want anything to happen between them. But the more time he spent with her, the harder it was to keep that in mind.

In fact, he was having trouble keeping a lot of things in mind, because all he seemed to be thinking about was her. Foolish as it might be, he knew he'd been falling for Claudia Paquette since the first moment he'd laid eyes on her.

Just when he was about to look away, she glanced over and smiled her gorgeous smile. "Have you snowshoed before?"

"No. It's not difficult, is it?"

"It takes a little getting used to, but I'm sure you'll make out all right. What do you weigh? About one-eighty?"

"About."

"Then that extra pair will be perfect for you."

He nodded, curious about why she had an extra pair perfect for a hundred-and-eighty pounder. Finally he said, "Whose snowshoes am I borrowing?"

"Oh, just a friend's. His name's Chet Summerly, and he's with the provincial police. They transferred him to the detachment at Red Lake a while back, and neither of us remembered his snowshoes were stored in my basement until after he'd gone."

Mike didn't let himself ask how far Red Lake was. If this Chet was with the provincial police, though, he'd been transferred within Ontario—not far enough from Victoria Falls to keep him from eventually coming back for his snowshoes. And possibly for other things.

When that thought wouldn't stop gnawing away at him, Mike began to suspect he'd been falling for Claudia even harder than he'd realized. So what the hell was he going to do about it?

"WE'RE HERE." Claudia pulled off the road and parked next to the snowbank. It was so high there was a solid white wall beside O'Brian's window. "You'll have to slide under the steering wheel," she added, opening her door.

"Really? You mean I can't just roll down my window and tunnel through the snow?"

"Very funny." She climbed out into the cold and opened the back door for Morgan.

By the time she'd retrieved the snowshoes from the cargo area, O'Brian was standing beside the Cherokee—a very different-looking man from the one who'd gotten out of the plane in a bomber jacket and cowboy boots.

Today, in addition to his snowmobile suit, mitts and mukluks, he had a long scarf wrapped around his neck and pulled up over his chin. He was also wearing the earmuffs she'd dug out for him and had his toque tugged down to his eyes. He might be stubborn, but at least he learned from experience.

The only thing she didn't approve of was that camera bag slung across his shoulder.

"Why does *here,*" he asked, "look like the middle of nowhere?"

"We walk to the Nilssons' from here. Actually, that woods is part of their property, and cutting through it is the shortest way to the house."

"Shorter than walking along their road?"

She nodded guiltily. It was a lie, of course, but O'Brian was an extremely hard man to wear down. A walk through those woods, especially when he'd never used snowshoes before, just might do the trick. With any luck, by the time she got him home he wouldn't be able to move for the rest of the week.

"Here," she said, handing him Chet's snowshoes. "We'll have to climb over the snowbank before we put these on. And you'd be smart to leave your camera behind in case you fall."

"I won't."

The odds he actually wouldn't were one in a million, so she tried again. "It's *possible* you might. Morgan has a thing about people wearing snowshoes, so he'll probably give you some trouble." Which, naturally, was the main reason she'd made the dog come along.

"Paquette, I'm going to want to take pictures of the Nilssons, aren't I."

"Well, yes, I guess you will. But at least give the camera to me. You're a novice, and if by any chance you *did* fall, a hundred and eighty pounds landing on your Nikon wouldn't do it any good."

"Has anyone ever told you you're a bit of a nag?" he muttered, reluctantly handing her the camera bag.

She put the strap safely around her neck while he began examining his snowshoes.

"Why," he asked, "are mine so much rounder than yours?"

"Oh, yours are called bear paws. They're made to support heavier weight than the pointier ones. The wider surface means you won't sink too far with each step."

"Ahh."

She didn't mention that bear paws also had a down side. He'd discover that soon enough.

"Wait," Claudia said as they reached the top of the snowbank.

Mike waited. Morgan raced down the far side and charged full steam ahead toward the trees.

"Stop just short of the bottom," Claudia continued, "and put your snowshoes on there. Otherwise, you'll end up waist-high in snow."

The holes Morgan's paws had made were only three or four inches deep, but the dog probably didn't even weigh half as much as Mike did. And he could see that Claudia wasn't exaggerating about the depth of the snow. Several bushes between the bank and the trees were almost entirely buried, with only a few stark branches poking up from beneath the blanket of white.

Cautiously, he edged down the bank, making sure he took longer than Claudia so he could check out how she went about strapping on her snowshoes.

Seeing that there didn't seem to be any trick to it, he tugged off his mitts and started putting on one of his own shoes. When he figured he had the straps adjusted right, he gingerly eased his foot forward, testing it on the level surface.

Relieved that it didn't sink, he went to work on the second shoe—which proved far trickier. He had to keep his feet spread wide apart so that one snowshoe didn't end up half on top of the other, which meant stretching way over to one side to adjust the straps. And that, thanks to the fall he'd taken the other day, made his butt ache like hell.

Then Morgan came racing back from the trees and decided to play tug-of-war with the end of a snowshoe.

"Beat it," Mike told him. "At least give me a fighting chance."

"Morgan," Claudia said sternly. "Morgan, you come over here with me."

The dog gave a final yank on the snowshoe—this one so hard Mike was amazed he didn't completely lose his balance—then plowed through the snow to where Claudia was standing.

Mike turned his attention back to the task at hand. His fingers growing more numb by the second, he eventually managed to get the second set of straps tight enough. Then he pulled his mitts back on and took a few cautious steps. Because of the awkward way he was walking, that pain in his backside stabbed with each one.

"What am I doing wrong?" he asked Claudia.

"Nothing."

"No, I mean how do I walk without practically doing the splits?"

"Well, I'm afraid you really can't. Not without tripping yourself up. That's kind of a problem with bear paws."

"You aren't serious."

The expression on her face told him she was.

"Who designed these damn things?" he demanded. "The same guy who invented torture chambers?"

"Oh, I don't think it could have been. Snowshoes have only been around for a few hundred years, but torture chambers date back to medieval times, don't they?"

"Paquette? If anybody ever tells you you'd make a good stand-up comic, don't believe them."

He took a couple of awkward steps forward, doing his best to ignore the pain. Then he stepped on one showshoe with the other and promptly fell onto his nose.

JUST AFTER MORGAN WENT dashing off in pursuit of a rabbit, Claudia said, "There's the Nilssons' place up ahead. That's the back of it. The front faces onto Lost Lake."

Mike had been keeping his eyes on his snowshoes because it was when he stopped watching what his feet were doing that he fell. But the news they'd almost reached their destination made the risk of looking up worthwhile. As Claudia had promised, the Nilssons' place was in sight.

It was a chalet large enough to border on enormous. If he'd forgotten the brothers were computer millionaires, the size alone would have reminded him. But the significant thing at the moment was that it wasn't much farther. He'd have cheered about that if he hadn't been so exhausted. He wasn't sure how far they'd walked, but every muscle from his waist down was begging for rest.

The chalet was nestled in a clearing, and as they reached it a man came out onto the deck.

"That's Gord," Claudia said, waving to him. "He's a couple of years younger than Norm."

In his midfifties, Gord was of average weight and a little above average height, with glasses and thinning gray hair. Imagining him in a white beard and red suit, Mike decided he might be a passable Santa. Especially in the dead of night.

"Well, I wondered if you'd actually make it," he said as they neared the deck. "I guess I shouldn't have had any doubt, though," he added, focusing on Mike. "If that article in yesterday's paper was even halfway accurate, you can walk on water."

Mike managed a weary grin. "I probably should have read past the caption, then. When I read Santa Thumbs Nose at L.A. Reporter, I figured Iggy'd made me out to be an idiot."

"I see I don't have to worry about introductions," Claudia put in, "so O'Brian and I will just get our snowshoes off and come inside where it's warm, okay?''

Thinking he'd never heard such a terrific suggestion in his life, Mike collapsed onto the deck's stairs and started removing his bear paws.

"You're not going to believe this," Gord said to Claudia, "but the snowplow arrived only ten minutes after you called. You could have driven right up to the house, after all.''

Mike stifled a groan.

"Oh, well," Claudia said, "walking was good exercise.''

"Yeah, but it's quite a hike. After you'd hung up, I realized I should have told you to give us a call from the highway. Then Norm and I could have hopped on the snowmobiles and picked you up.''

"There's nowhere nearby to phone from, is there?''

"No, but isn't that new cell phone of yours working all right?''

Mike glanced at Claudia. She was wearing a strange expression, and he figured he knew why. If she had a cellular, it was news to him.

Sure enough, she said, "I don't have a cell phone.''

"What? Of course you do," Gord insisted. "I ran into you in Bentley's while you were buying it, remember?''

"Oh. Right . . . in Bentley's. Ahh . . . Well, I wasn't actually buying one. I was just looking at them.''

"No, you were signing the charge slip and you said . . . Oh, just looking. I didn't realize that, but I guess I wasn't really paying attention.''

Freeing his second foot from its snowshoe, Mike put the pair of them on the deck without taking his eyes off Claudia. That little exchange hadn't rung true.

And the look on her face said it was because she'd been lying.

Wondering why, he shoved himself up off the steps and hobbled into the house after the others, his legs feeling rubbery and stiff at the same time.

"That pot of coffee's fresh," Gord said, gesturing across the kitchen. "Just help yourselves to some once you get out of those snowmobile suits. Take it on into the living room and have a look at our Christmas tree. Norm's upstairs surfing the Internet, so I'll go get him."

"O'Brian?" Claudia said once they'd taken off their suits. "Coffee?"

"Sure, sounds great."

She put his camera bag on the table and took a couple of mugs from a cupboard.

He watched her for a second, tempted to press her about that cell phone thing. Then, deciding to leave it until later, he glanced around the kitchen while she poured the coffee.

Almost entirely comprised of windows, and stretching solariumlike across the entire back of the chalet, it was furnished with good-looking pine antiques and better-quality appliances than he'd seen in some restaurant kitchens.

"The living room's through here," Claudia said, handing him a mug and leading the way.

The rubbery feeling in his legs had faded, he was glad to discover. Now he only had a few aches and pains to contend with. But he quickly forgot about even those when he saw the Nilssons' tree.

"Holy smoke," he said, stopping to stare at it. "That's bigger than the one in Rockefeller Center."

Claudia smiled. "I don't think it has *quite* as many lights, though. But do you see what I see?"

"What?"

"You're too tall to be at the right angle, but if you crouch a little, you can see a little stack of presents hidden at the back."

He ducked, then followed her gaze and glanced at her again. "I assume you mean those ones wrapped in red foil? With green bows?"

"Uh-huh. Just like Santa's."

Putting down his coffee, he moved a branch aside to get a better look. "I told you we'd need the camera, Paquette. I'll bet that's my proof sitting back there."

She began to say something, but stopped at the sound of footsteps behind them.

Mike looked around. And what he saw surprised him speechless.

CHAPTER NINE

"MIKE," GORD SAID, "meet my brother, Norman."

Mike shot Claudia a glance to tell her she might at least have warned him, then looked at Norm Nilsson again.

The man's hair was curly, almost shoulder length and pure white. His blue eyes were twinkling, his smile was merry and there was little doubt that if he laughed his belly would shake like a bowl full of jelly. Mike almost expected him to lay a finger aside of his nose and give a nod.

Instead, he extended his hand, saying, "Nice to meet you, Mike. How are you liking it up here in the great white north?"

"It's terrific. All the snow is really..."

"Christmasy?" Claudia suggested.

He nodded. It was probably a better word to go with than cold or wet or slippery.

"So," Norm said, "that was quite the article Iggy wrote about you, eh?"

"Well, actually, I haven't gotten around to reading it yet. But I gather he said Santa's really going to give me a run for my money." As he spoke, his eyes were trying their darnedest to stray back in the direction of those Santa presents. He forced them to remain on the Nilssons, though. He didn't want to miss their reactions to anything.

Gord shook his head. "That Iggy. One paragraph he's telling us how you've tracked down gang lords and terrorists all over the world, and the next he's trying to make us believe you'll have trouble figuring out who Santa is."

"Just wishful thinking," Norm said. "I'll bet you already know, don't you, Mike?"

He couldn't help grinning. "Well, there do seem to be a couple of obvious suspects. Paquette and I couldn't help noticing that stack of presents at the back of your tree. The ones wrapped in red," he added, gesturing toward them when both Nilssons looked blank.

Gord stepped forward and peered through the branches, then gave his brother an annoyed glance. "Why did you leave those there, Norm? Those *red* ones."

"Oh," Norm said, peering at them. "Hmm... Well, I know you like to keep them out of sight every year, but I've always thought your notion that somebody's liable to open them by mistake is darn silly. Hey, look, there's Morgan."

Mike glanced toward the windows. The dog was sitting on the deck, which wrapped around the entire house, staring at them.

"Do you want to let him in, Claudia?" Gord asked.

"No, he'll be okay." She turned to Norm, adding, "You were telling us about those presents."

"Oh, right. Well, they're for our nephews. Our sister's two boys. You've met them, Claudia. They always come up from Toronto for part of the Christmas break," he told Mike.

"At any rate," Norm continued, "we give them their gifts when they get here instead of mailing them.

But Gord always wants to hide them away until after Christmas Day. Like I said, he's got this crazy idea somebody might open them by mistake."

"Ahh," Mike said, thinking Norm Nilsson just might be the worst liar he'd heard in his entire life.

"The reason we noticed them," Claudia said, "is that all the presents Santa's delivered have been wrapped in red foil and topped off with green bows. Just like those."

"Really?" Norm said. "Imagine that." He shot Gord a look that was so obviously a plea for help Mike almost laughed.

"Well, I guess Santa shops at The Bay, then," Gord offered. "That's where we got those. That's how they're wrapping their gifts this year."

"The Bay?" Mike said to Claudia.

"It's a major department store chain. There's probably a branch in just about every decent-sized town."

"Uh-huh, their stores are everywhere," Gord agreed. "That's why we buy the boys' gifts there. You know teenagers. If it's not exactly right, they'll never use it. But as long as we buy from a Bay store, they can exchange things down in Toronto."

"Ahh," Mike said again. Then he let the silence grow and watched the Nilssons getting more and more uneasy.

"Mike?" Gord finally said. "You look as if something's puzzling you."

"Well, it's just that I can't help wondering if *your* shopping at the Bay and *Santa's* shopping there is more than a coincidence."

His words hung in the air for a moment, then Norm started to laugh. And sure enough, his stomach *did* shake like a bowl full of jelly.

"Claudia," Gord said, "Mike here doesn't really suspect us, does he? Didn't you tell him you'd already asked us?"

She nodded. "But he thinks you might have been holding out on me. And you can't really blame him. After all, almost everybody figures it's you two playing Santa. Even Dad and Lucille."

"It's not, though?" Mike asked. If the Nilssons weren't ready to come clean, he'd have to go along with them and see where it got him.

"You mean you *really* haven't figured out who it is yet?" Norm asked. "I thought you were just putting us on. Just pretending you suspected us."

"Well . . . no. But if it's not you, then who is it?"

"Well, *think,* Mike. Who's got the most to gain from having this Santa running around creating a newsworthy story?"

"It's going to be a whole *series,* " Gord reminded his brother.

"Whatever. Mike, who's hoping your series will be enough to save his newspaper?"

"*Iggy?* You're trying to tell me that Iggy's Santa?"

"Bingo," the brothers said in unison.

Mike glanced at Claudia, certain the Nilssons were only making an amateurish attempt to throw him off track. Surprisingly, she didn't look *entirely* skeptical, so he said, "Could Iggy possibly have enough money?"

"Of course he's got enough money," Gord put in before she had a chance to reply. "Remember, Claudia, a couple of years back, when Iggy wanted us to try to buy the *Dispatch* from that Ferris Wentworth guy?"

"Yes, I remember."

"Well, when we said we weren't interested, he tried to convince us to at least come up with half of what he figured Wentworth would go for. Said he'd put up the rest and we'd be partners."

"Just who we'd love to be partners with," Norm muttered.

"I've never heard that version of the story before," Claudia said. "All I ever heard was that Iggy wanted *you* to buy it."

Gord shrugged. "Even in Victoria Falls, people don't always hear every detail of every story. But the point is that neither Norm nor I is playing Santa. So let's not waste any more time talking about it, 'cuz I've got something for you."

"Oh?"

"Uh-huh. Your dad was saying you haven't had a chance to get a Christmas tree yet. So when you said you were coming up, I went out and cut down a real nice spruce for you. How about we hop on a snowmobile and go get your Jeep? Then we can tie it on the roof.

"And, Norm?" he added, glancing at his brother. "Maybe Mike would like a tour of the house."

"I'd love one," he said. He hadn't bought the idea that Iggy might be Santa for a minute. He *knew* who Santa was. Which meant there was probably a whole stash of hampers and presents somewhere in this house. A tour would give him the chance to find out exactly where.

"MIND IF I GRAB MY CAMERA, Norm?" Mike asked as the front door closed behind Claudia and Gord. "Even though Santa isn't you or Gord, I'll have to write an article about you as suspects—since so many people figure it *is* you. And Iggy might want some pictures to run with it."

Norm flashed one of his merry smiles. "Iggy should start filling the entire *Dispatch* with pictures. They'd be a darn sight more interesting than most of the articles he prints. Except for Claudia's," he added quickly. "It's Iggy and that nephew of his who can't write worth a damn."

Taking that as a "yes" to his question, Mike limped off and retrieved his camera from the kitchen. After he got a few shots of the tree, he said, "When Gord gets back, I'll want a couple of the two of you in front of that. But in the meantime, I'm ready for the tour. Does it run from the top down or the basement up?"

"Oh, I'm afraid the basement's off-limits, Mike. Nothing personal, but even though Gord and I are officially retired, we're still computer nerds. And we do our serious, confidential work in the basement. Got it all set up as a secure computing room. You know, electrically isolated, lead shields, the whole ball of wax."

Mike nodded, although he couldn't imagine they'd actually gone to those extremes when they were way out in the middle of nowhere. But even if they had, the basement of this place would be huge. So they could probably have a secure computing room the size of the Pentagon's and still have enough space to store a ton of Santa goodies.

Norm showed him around the rest of the main floor, then led the way upstairs. "There's a master suite at either end up here," he said as they reached the second floor. "Gord and I both need our own space. This is my area," he added, ushering Mike through an open doorway.

In addition to the bedroom and bath, the suite had a huge living area containing an entertainment center with all the bells and whistles imaginable—along with enough high-tech equipment to fill an IBM warehouse.

"I'm surprised that you've got anything left to put in the basement," Mike said.

"Oh, these are just my toys." Norm touched a computer key and the screen came alive with space invaders. Hitting another one produced a horse race. He pushed a third and the screen went blank again. "But I sometimes think..."

A phone had started ringing somewhere. Norm listened for a second, then said, "That's Gord's line. And I know he's expecting an important call, so I'd better answer it. I won't be long, but feel free to poke around."

It wasn't often that an investigative reporter got issued an invitation to poke around, Mike thought as Norm hurried from his suite. Which probably meant there wasn't a shred of Santa evidence in here, let alone proof.

He wandered into the lavish bathroom-sauna area, then across the bedroom to a wall of sliding closet doors. They weren't completely closed at one end, and he absently glanced inside. Then his eyes locked on something that was a deep burgundy red.

Telling himself it had to be a dressing gown, he slid the door further along. And discovered that what he'd spotted was a velvet Santa suit. A flowing white beard hung from the hanger beside it. And on the closet floor he found a pair of high black boots with big brass buckles.

Grinning, he lined the boots up beneath the suit, hooked the beard over it and clicked off a few pictures. Then he put the beard and boots back where they'd been and slid the door partly closed, leaving it far enough open to expose the suit even more than before.

Just as he got everything set, Norm reappeared. His gaze flashed immediately to the closet. Then he glanced at Mike.

"I couldn't help noticing there's something red hanging in there," he said. "But I guess it wouldn't be a Santa suit...would it?"

Norm eyed him for a good ten seconds, then smiled. "That's exactly what it is, Mike. I'll be wearing it at our next poker party."

"You play Mr. Dressup at your poker parties?" he said, doing his darnedest to keep a straight face. But even if he'd just fallen off a turnip truck, he wouldn't buy that story.

"Oh, I don't wear costumes at every game. Not by a long shot. But there's Halloween, of course. And Thanksgiving. And Canada Day. That's sort of like your Fourth of July."

"Ahh. So you just do it when there's a good excuse."

"Exactly," Norm agreed. "Oh, and you've got to see the great rabbit suit I wear at Easter." He slid one of the doors open and began rummaging around.

"Shoot," he muttered after a minute. "The damn thing must still be at the cleaners. I'd better remember to pick it up or they'll start charging me a storage fee."

Mike rubbed his jaw, trying to decide where he went from here. Norm Nilsson's Santa suit was for wearing on his nocturnal deliveries, not for any damn poker party. But those pictures of a suit hanging in his closet weren't solid proof that he was Santa. So it looked as if another night of surveillance was in order. This time, though, he'd do it alone.

A man could only handle so much frustration. And another night of sitting in the dark with Claudia, now that she'd told him to keep his hands to himself, would be just too much.

WITH THE CHRISTMAS TREE tied securely to the Cherokee's roof rack, Morgan snoring in the back seat and O'Brian telling her about the tour Norm had given him, Claudia turned onto the highway that would take them home.

Pressing down on the accelerator, she ignored the disapproving look O'Brian gave her. She didn't like driving on icy roads at night, and darkness was already gathering.

"So," he said, getting back to what he'd been saying, "I ended up seeing practically every inch of that house except for the basement. That's the one place they could be storing hampers and things."

"But they're not going to let you check down there."

"No. So the only way to get our proof is by watching the chalet for a night or two. See if one of them leaves on delivery."

"Mmm. Not tonight, though. You've already gone almost two full days without sleep. And you look absolutely drained," she added, glancing over at him. He really did, too, which gave her a sharp pang of guilt.

The idea of slowing him down by completely wearing him out hadn't bothered her much. But she certainly didn't want him dropping dead from exhaustion.

"Well, I don't know," he said. "What about that list you've got? Of all the families that were hit by the layoffs. You've been keeping track of which ones Santa's already delivered to, haven't you?"

"Uh-huh."

"And how many are left? How many more nights do you figure he'll be going out?"

"A lot more than one," she said quickly. "Besides, you've got a story for your second article now, so you're well ahead of the game."

"Yeah. But I assumed that when I wrote about the Nilssons I'd be revealing them as Santa. Not writing about how I figured finding that suit clinched things until Norm told me he likes wearing funny clothes when he plays cards."

Claudia laughed. "See how tired you are, O'Brian? You're losing your sense of humor."

"I am?"

"Yes, because that's a great twist. I mean, first we figure the mystery's solved when we spot those Santa presents. But the Nilssons explain them away."

"Some explanation."

"I didn't say it was brilliant, I just said they came up with an excuse. At any rate, next you think you've got Norm dead to rights with the suit and he hits you with that crazy costume story. The readers will love it. And you'll make Iggy so happy he'll be dancing in the street."

"Maybe that's an angle I should follow up on."

"What? Iggy dancing in the street?"

"Very funny, Paquette."

She waited uneasily for him to tell her what angle he'd really meant. The man never quit, and it was making her very nervous, especially now that he was gradually learning things she didn't want him to know. About her buying that cell phone, for example.

She was certain he hadn't believed she'd been simply looking at them. And even though he seemed to have forgotten about her little exchange with Gord, he was bound to remember it sooner or later.

Of course, she'd thought of a cover story for when he did. But she still didn't like the fact he just kept gnawing away at things like Morgan with a bone.

"I meant," he finally said, "the dressing in costumes for poker parties angle. As you pointed out, Norm came up with that story on the spur of the moment."

She nodded. "If he'd actually ever played poker dressed like a giant rabbit, a team of wild horses couldn't have kept Dad from telling me about it."

"Then maybe I should talk to your dad. And to whoever else plays cards with the Nilssons. Get statements refuting what Norm told me."

"Uh-uh. You wouldn't have a prayer. I'll bet we weren't even off their property before Norm was on the phone telling his buddies that they should go along with the line he fed you."

"Yeah, you're probably right. But, dammit, this whole deal is really starting to bother me. We talk to Greenaway, and it's obvious he's hiding something. We talk to the Nilssons, and they give us ridiculous explanations for things. Now we'll have Norm's buddies trying to help lead me down the garden path.''

"But you'll know better than to believe what they say.''

"I'm starting to figure I shouldn't believe anything *anyone* says. And I hate it when everyone's lying to me but I can't prove it.''

"Oh, I'm sure you'll eventually sort things out.'' Claudia shot him a sympathetic smile, hoping he wouldn't realize who'd been lying to him the most.

They drove the remainder of the way home in silence, then wearily wrestled the Christmas tree off the roof rack.

"You don't want to put this up tonight, do you?'' O'Brian asked, sounding desperately afraid she might.

"No.'' She smiled at the look of relief that appeared on his face. "I don't even want to take it inside. It'll be fine just standing in the snow for the time being.''

While he shoved the bottom of the trunk into a drift beside the house, she headed for the door and discovered a note from her father sticking out of the mailbox.

"Dad stopped by and checked my snowmobile,'' she said, reading the message. "The problem wasn't serious—just something with the timing.''

O'Brian nodded, slowly making his way up the steps.

"A little stiff?'' she asked.

"A little,'' he admitted.

When she opened the door, Morgan dashed inside—displaying far more energy than she had. Probably more than she and O'Brian put together.

"Why don't you go soak in the tub while I throw something together for dinner," she suggested. "Then we should both go straight to bed."

His gaze caught hers as she finished speaking. And tired as they both were, she knew the word *bed* was lingering in his mind, as it was in hers.

She was liking the man more and more all the time. In fact, despite having known him only a few days, she suspected she was quickly moving beyond mere liking. And when you added that to the way she started feeling hot and bothered every time she so much as looked at him...

Lord, even when she wasn't looking at him she kept catching herself thinking about last night. About how the heat of his kisses had made her oblivious to the cold. About how being in his arms had made her feel more wonderful than she'd ever felt before. And if he could make her feel like that by merely holding her, did she really want to go through the rest of her life not knowing what making love with him would be like?

Tired as she was, she still recognized a dangerous thought when she had one, so she forced her eyes from his and began tugging off her boots.

CLAUDIA TRIED SANTA'S number one more time, and when there was still no answer her anxiety level inched up even further. She put the phone down on top of the duvet and checked her bedside clock again.

It had been barely eight when she'd started calling, and here it was after ten. So where had he been all evening? And wherever he was, why didn't he have the cellular with him?

She rubbed her eyes, so weary she could hardly stay awake. O'Brian had stumbled off to bed right after they'd eaten dinner, and he'd probably been dead to the world in three seconds flat. But she wasn't going to sleep until she got an update on how many more nights of deliveries were left.

Santa had said that with any luck he could finish up on Monday or Tuesday, and by now he might know for sure. Either way, she told herself, it wasn't *that* much longer. Just another day or two. And night or two, of course. But she could make it. Then, after that, Santa would go to ground and she'd be able to stop spending every single minute worrying about O'Brian's next move.

O'Brian. She let her eyes close, reminding herself, one more time, that falling for him was an incredibly foolish thing to do. He lived a million miles away, so she'd probably never see him again once he'd left. And just in case geography wasn't reason enough, there was the little matter of what she was doing. If he ever learned the truth about that, he'd want to murder her.

She opened her eyes again, ordering herself to stop thinking about him. Given the circumstances, she'd be better off thinking about any other man in the world. Even Iggy Brooks.

Yes, actually, thinking about Iggy wasn't a bad idea. Or, rather, thinking about that story the Nilssons had concocted. They'd really gone all out to help. Not only had they followed her father's suggestions for muddying the waters, they'd come up with their own red herring—that story about Iggy saying he'd put up half the money to buy the *Dispatch*. In reality, he didn't have two cents to rub together.

Of course, O'Brian had barely nibbled at the idea that Iggy could be Santa. He hadn't even raised it in conversation after they'd left the Nilssons'. But the more possibilities he had to consider, the better. And maybe, if she worked at it, she could bring him around to suspecting Iggy.

For a minute, she tried to figure out how. Then, realizing she was too tired to do any worthwhile plotting, she picked up the phone and pushed redial.

This time, Santa answered.

"Where on earth have you been?" she demanded.

"Just out on the snowmobile."

"That's not very safe, is it? So early at night, I mean? What if you'd run into someone?"

"Claudia, I'm getting cabin fever hanging around here on my own. And I didn't go anywhere near a town or anything. But if you didn't want anything in particular, I—"

"I wanted to know how much longer I have to keep O'Brian running in circles, because I'm getting at least as dizzy as he is."

"Well, hopefully I'll just need tonight and tomorrow."

"Oh, that's good news." Come Tuesday, then, she'd be able to breathe a lot more easily. Santa would still be in the vicinity, of course, but at least there wouldn't be any chance of O'Brian catching up with him on his rounds.

"And I've got some more good news. Well, interesting news, at least. But you need to put on your reporter's hat for this story."

"What story?" She sat up a little straighter in bed.

"Well, like I said, while I was out, I was steering clear of where I figured anyone might be—and I ended up near the Hillstead offices. Which, as you know," he added quickly, "aren't near any town. And I'd never have figured anybody'd be in the offices after hours.''

''But there was?''

''Uh-huh.''

''Nobody saw you, did they?'' she said anxiously, thinking that Wayne Greenaway must have been back there working for the second night in a row—which was very curious indeed.

''No, nobody saw me. Anyway, when I spotted a light, I parked the snowmobile and went on over to have a look.''

She resisted the urge to ask why he'd take such a risk, knowing that was just the way he was. ''And you saw?'' she said instead.

''It had to be that Wayne Greenaway guy you've talked about. The only thing parked outside was a red Blazer with plates reading Wayne G. That his?''

''Yes.''

''Yeah, I knew it couldn't be anyone else. Especially after I sneaked inside. Turned out the guy was working in an office with Greenaway's name on the door.''

''You sneaked inside?'' she repeated, her heart hammering.

''Hey, don't have a fit, Claudia. Everything was cool. I'd just wandered over to have a look through the window when the guy got up and walked out of the office. Then, a minute later, lights started going on along one side of the building. I mean, I could tell he was heading toward the far end and turning the lights on as he went. So I just nipped into his office for a second to see what he'd been working on.''

She closed her eyes. All these years, and he was still doing things he shouldn't, so why did tonight's little escapade surprise her? It wasn't any worse than insisting he was going to continue playing Santa despite O'Brian's arrival.

"Look," he continued, "I know you're thinking I shouldn't have been taking chances, but I was curious. And when I tried the front door it wasn't locked—which was practically an invitation to just go on in, right?"

"But how could you—"

"No, listen, because this is where we get to the interesting reporter-type stuff."

"All right," she said slowly, reminding herself the incident was over and done with and he hadn't been caught.

"You know what was on his desk?"

"No. What?"

"A bunch of assay report forms from the Croply Labs."

She waited to hear what the interesting reporter-type stuff was. It certainly wasn't that Hillstead's mine manager had a bunch of assay reports. Mines were constantly having the quality of veins officially assayed.

"And what I thought was strange," he went on, "was that there was a little stack of blank ones."

"Blank whats?"

"Assay report forms. Croply Lab ones. Already stamped with an official assayer's stamp, but blank. Doesn't that seem unusual to you?"

Tired as she was, every reporter's instinct she'd done her best to develop went on alert. Santa might just have stumbled across the secret she and O'Brian had suspected Wayne Greenaway was keeping.

Those assay reports eventually went to Toronto, where they became part of what Hillstead's directors based their management decisions on. And if Greenaway had a stack of officially stamped blank forms, what would stop him from filling in whatever information he wanted to feed head office?

CHAPTER TEN

MIKE WOKE TO Monday-morning sunshine streaming through the bedroom window. Checking his watch, he discovered it wasn't quite eight. But since he'd gone to bed right after dinner, he'd slept more than twelve hours straight. And he felt terrific—until he swung his legs out of bed and they screamed reminders about yesterday's snowshoeing.

He forced himself to his feet, anyway. He was dying for a cup of coffee, and Claudia would undoubtedly have some waiting in the kitchen.

To his disappointment, she didn't. He could see the Jeep in the driveway, so he knew she hadn't gone anywhere. But her bedroom door was closed and there was no sign of life in the house—except for Morgan, who was sitting at the front door with a desperate look in his eyes.

He let the dog out, then had a quick shower and shave. By the time he'd gotten dressed, he was positively starving. But Claudia still wasn't up, and since she'd hardly had any more sleep than he had lately, he didn't want to wake her with the smell of cooking.

Writing her a quick note to say he wouldn't be gone long, he pulled on his borrowed outdoor clothing. Then, through force of habit, he grabbed his Nikon and started off for Main Street. The other day he'd noticed a place called Betty's Café that couldn't be more than a fifteen-minute walk.

An hour later he was feeling much better. So good, in fact, he decided to stretch his muscles a little more and wander along to Earl's garage. He'd still like to have his own wheels, and there was always a chance one of those loaners had been turned in.

When he reached the garage, there were two people inside. Behind the counter was a kid of eighteen or nineteen, wearing a grease-stained parka with the name Frank stitched on the pocket. He was dealing with an angry customer in his late thirties.

"Well what's it doing out back?" the customer was demanding. "When I left on Friday, it was parked right out front. How the hell are you going to sell it for me if nobody can see it?"

Sell it? If *it* was a car, Mike was interested.

Frank shrugged. "All I know is first thing Saturday mornin', Earl told me to move it out back and take the For Sale sign off it."

"Well what kind of asinine idea was that? I could sell it better in my own driveway. At least a few people would see the damn thing there."

Mike cleared his throat.

"Be with ya in a minute, sir," Frank told him.

"Hey," the other man said, "you're that guy whose picture was in the Saturday paper, aren't you."

"Mike O'Brian," he offered, extending his hand.

"Right. Iggy's guy from L.A. I'm Jack MacDougal, assistant manager at the bank."

"Then you're a good man to know. If I run short while I'm here, I'll come see you. But I couldn't help overhearing your conversation. Is it a car you've got for sale?"

"Yeah, an '87 Civic. The wife just had another baby, so I bought a minivan from my brother."

"But the Civic runs okay?"

"It runs fine. You're not in the market, though, are you?"

"Well, not to buy," he said, thinking that if he submitted an expense account that said he'd bought a car—even an old car—his editor's face would turn purple. "I'm not expecting to be here beyond the weekend, but if you'd be interested in renting it for a few days, I'd like to work something out."

"Renting it, eh?" Jack said. "Well, I don't know. I'd really like to just unload it, and—"

"I wouldn't be tying it up for long. And I'd pay cash," Mike added quietly, turning away so Frank wouldn't hear the details. "Let's say three hundred bucks for the rest of the week," he suggested, digging out his wallet and counting off the bills. "That would buy a few Christmas presents for the kids."

"Yeah, it would, wouldn't it? And there's a sweater in Bentley's the wife's got her heart set on."

Jack reached for the money, then looked back at Frank. "Give Mr. O'Brian the keys I left with Earl, Frankie. The insurance and ownership, too. And tell Earl *maybe* I'll give him another shot at selling it after Christmas."

Frankie nodded, then looked at Mike. "You want me to gas it up for you, sir?"

"Sure, thanks."

"Well," Jack said, extending his hand again. "I've got to get back to the bank, but it was a pleasure doing business with you. And good luck catching Santa, eh?"

"Thanks," Mike said again, then waited inside while Jack headed off down Main and Frank went out back to get the Civic.

By the time the kid had brought it out front and was pumping gas into it, Mike had recalled Claudia mentioning that Earl was another of her father's poker buddies. Then he started thinking about how many times he and Claudia had driven by Earl's in the past couple of days.

If he'd seen a car for sale any of those times, he'd have come in and tried to do exactly what he'd just done. So wasn't it interesting how, on Friday evening, Raymond Paquette had volunteered to line up a car for him and then, first thing Saturday morning, Raymond's friend Earl had told Frank to move that Civic out of sight.

It didn't take an investigative reporter to put those two things together. Which meant Raymond's friendly-guy routine had been nothing more than an act. And that meant Santa hadn't been the only one who'd thumbed his nose at Iggy's L.A. reporter.

He muttered under his breath about that for a minute, wondering what had happened to his normally suspicious nature. How could he have let Raymond Paquette suck him in with nothing more than a little fine Scotch and some high-octane moose milk? He knew better than to take people at face value. But when it had come to Claudia's father...

"Damn," he said aloud. Yesterday, when he'd told her he was starting to think he shouldn't believe anything anyone told him, he'd never dreamed that would include Raymond. From here on, though, he'd be taking everything *anybody* told him with a grain of salt.

Looking down at his borrowed clothes, he wished they belonged to someone other than Raymond. The idea of a shopping spree had suddenly become very tempting, but since Big Jim Souto wouldn't be any happier to see clothes on an expense account than he would a car, a little pride-swallowing was probably in order.

Turning his thoughts back to the matter at hand, he asked himself why Raymond had wanted to keep him from getting hold of a car.

Maybe because Claudia had asked him to?

After a few seconds' consideration, he decided there wasn't any logical reason she would. Regardless of what she'd said, getting stuck playing chauffeur had to be a pain in the butt.

So maybe it was the Nilssons who'd asked Raymond for a little help. Maybe they'd figured they'd be better off if Iggy's investigative reporter couldn't come snooping around their place on his own, anytime he liked.

With a whole lot more questions than answers on his mind, he wandered out into the cold and over to the gas pumps.

"Here's the insurance and ownership," Frankie said, digging them out.

Mike nodded, absently sticking them into his own pocket. "Earl's not around anywhere?"

"Not right now. But if there's somethin' else you need, maybe I can help?"

"No, it's okay. I was just going to introduce myself. Raymond Paquette mentioned that Earl was a friend of his."

"Oh. Yeah. They're good buddies. Ray even works here if we're busy. He's a genius with anything mechanical. But you met him, eh?"

"Uh-huh. I had dinner at his place the other night."

"Yeah? Oh, right. I guess I heard you was stayin' with Claudia."

The trace of a smirk had appeared on the kid's face, and Mike found it damn annoying. Claudia wasn't the type of woman the smirk implied. Hell, if anyone knew that, he did.

"Ray didn't offer to lend you one of his trucks, eh? He's usually real generous about stuff like that."

"Trucks?" Mike repeated, thinking back to Friday night. He was absolutely sure there'd only been one truck in the Paquette driveway. One truck and one snowmobile.

"Yeah, he bought a new one a couple of weeks back. I mean, not a *new* one. Ray's got no more money than anyone else in this town. But it was one Earl was sellin' off the lot, and I think they worked out some deal—that Ray does free work for part of it or somethin'."

"So now he's got *two* trucks?" Mike said, steering the conversation back in that interesting direction.

"Far's I know. I haven't heard he's been lookin' to get rid of his old one. Fact, I see him still drivin' it around. So he must of got the new one for Mrs. Paquette or somethin'."

"Well...I don't know. The subject of his trucks never came up."

Frank shrugged. "Guess it musta been for her, eh? Don't know why she'd want a truck, though, 'stead of a car. Far as that goes, don't know why she'd want *anythin'* in the winter. Not when she's got her snowmobile." He glanced at the pump and added, "I filled you up with windshield washer, so that and the gas is twenty bucks."

Mike dug out his wallet again, trying to decide what he wanted to do first. Have a talk with Raymond or go back and pay the Nilssons an *unexpected* visit.

WHEN MIKE PULLED UP in front of Raymond Paquette's house, there was only one snowmobile parked in the driveway—and no sign of one truck, never mind two, so he assumed nobody was home. But just as he was about to drive off, Lucille opened the side door and tossed out some chunks of bread for the birds.

Very curious about what the deal was with the unaccounted-for truck, he cut the ignition and climbed out of the Civic. On his way to the house, he glanced over at the snowmobile, noting it was the same one he'd seen the other night. The one with Raymond's name written on the chassis.

Something about it sitting there by itself began bothering him, and he started up the steps trying to figure out what it was. His memory of the last part of Friday night was pretty foggy, but he thought he recalled Claudia telling him Lucille's snowmobile was in for repairs.

Raymond had tuned Claudia's right in her driveway, though, so why would he take Lucille's somewhere else?

Silently answering his own question, Mike told himself it had probably needed more extensive work than anyone would want to do outside in the cold. But if that was the case, wouldn't Raymond have taken it to his friend Earl's? And if he had, wouldn't Frankie have mentioned it was in the shop?

Of course he would have. So if the snowmobile wasn't at Earl's and it wasn't here, where was it?

Thinking he was now up to *two* unaccounted-for vehicles, Mike rang the bell.

"Why, hello," Lucille said, opening the door a minute later. "What a nice surprise. But where's Claudia?"

"She was still asleep when I got up, so I came out on my own."

"Oh, well bring yourself in out of the cold. Would you like some coffee? Or are you hungry?" she added, ushering him inside and closing the door.

"No, I'm fine, thanks. I had breakfast at Betty's Café. Then," he continued, following Lucille into the living room, "I hiked to Earl's garage."

"Oh?"

"Uh-huh, and have a look out there." He pointed through the window at the Civic. "I really got lucky. Jack MacDougal was at Earl's talking about selling his car, so I rented it from him for the week."

"Oh. Oh, my, that *was* a stroke of luck, wasn't it? Does Claudia know about it?"

"Not yet. I haven't been back to the house. I wanted to stop by and let Raymond know."

"Well, I'm afraid he's out, but I'll certainly tell him for you."

"Good. And be sure to thank him again, would you? I know how hard he's been trying to line something up."

Lucille nodded. "He must have been on the phone to a hundred different people."

Sure he was, Mike said under his breath. Apparently, whatever Raymond's game was, Lucille was in on it. Which meant he'd badly misread her as well.

Victoria Falls certainly seemed to have its share of sneaky people.

Wondering if any more of them were related to Claudia, he gave Lucille one of his warmest phony smiles and said, "Well, I'd better get going."

He started toward the door, waiting for the right moment to pull that old Columbo trick of almost leaving, then having a question or two just happen to come to mind.

Before he could play that card, though, Lucille said, "Oh, don't rush away, Mike. Stay for a minute and tell me how your Santa search is going."

Stopping and turning back, he warned himself to be careful. Maybe he didn't know exactly what Lucille's role was in all this, but he knew she had one. And he'd bet his bottom dollar that whatever he said to her would be repeated to Raymond and the Nilssons and heaven only knew who else. "Actually," he told her, "tracking Santa down isn't turning out to be as easy as I'd expected."

"Oh?"

He could tell she liked that news. "No, Claudia took me up to visit the Nilssons yesterday, and I've decided they're not Santa after all."

"They're not? Are you sure?"

"As sure as I can be," he lied. "Norm gave me a tour of the whole house, and I didn't see anything suspicious."

"You didn't? Nothing?"

She obviously found that very difficult to believe, so he said, "Well, there were a couple of things, but they didn't turn out to be significant. Although seeing a Santa suit in Norm's closet did have me going for a bit."

"A Santa suit? And that wasn't significant?"

"Well, I sure figured it was at first. But only until Norm explained about dressing up for the poker games."

Lucille looked blank for a few seconds, then recovered. "Oh, yes, dressing up."

"And when he told me about wearing a rabbit costume... Well, I can just imagine how comical he'd look. What did Raymond say the first time he saw that outfit?"

"Oh... He just laughed and laughed."

"Ahh." This was getting more fascinating by the minute. According to Claudia, her father had never seen Norm dressed like a giant bunny.

"I mean," Lucille went on, "like you said, it's not hard to imagine how funny Norm would look as a rabbit. But I'm curious about what you thought of the chalet."

Mike mentally complimented her on neatly changing the subject, then said, "I was really impressed. And finding all that high-tech stuff way out in the middle of nowhere really blew my mind."

"Oh, and they have so much fun with it. They're always using it to play tricks on people. Did Norm show you how he could make any of the phone lines ring just by pressing a key on his computer?"

"Ahh... yeah, he did." *That sly fox,* he added silently. It was touching the right computer key that had started Gord's phone ringing. Then Norm had gone off to answer it—but not before issuing his invitation to poke around.

So Norm had *wanted* him to find the Santa suit. Which meant the plot had been to make him certain the Nilssons were Santa. But why? To keep him off someone else's trail?

That would be the obvious explanation. But if he was guessing right, then who was the someone else?

Thinking this situation had more unanswered questions than a game of Trivial Pursuit, he forced his thoughts back to what he'd originally been going to ask.

"Well, Lucille, I'd really better get going. Just before I do, though, when I was at Earl's I was wondering about something."

"Yes?"

"That kid who works there? Frankie?"

"Yes?"

"Does he do a lot of drugs?"

"I . . . why, I don't know. But Ray helps out at the garage sometimes and he's never mentioned anything like that. Why do you ask?"

He shrugged. "Frankie said a couple of strange things—made me wonder if he was kind of disoriented."

"Strange things?"

"Yeah, he told me Raymond bought a new truck a couple of weeks ago. A second truck, I took him to mean. But since there isn't one sitting in the driveway . . ."

He could practically see Lucille's mind whirling away, then she said, "What a peculiar thing for him to say. I wonder why on earth . . . Unless . . .

"Oh, Mike," she said quietly, disappointment spreading across her face. "Oh, Mike, I think you've just spoiled a big surprise."

"What?"

"Oh, and I do so love surprises. That's why Raymond always tries his best to... But it's all right. I know you didn't mean to say anything you shouldn't have, so don't worry about it. I'll just make a real effort to seem surprised on Christmas Day."

"Wait. You've lost me."

"The truck Frankie was talking about," she said. "It's got to be my Christmas present. And Raymond must have it hidden away until the twenty-fifth."

THE PHONE WAS RINGING when Claudia opened the front door, so without even worrying about her boots she raced into the kitchen and grabbed it—practically falling over Morgan, who was welcoming her home.

"Claudia!" Lucille's voice greeted her. "Where on earth have you been? Iggy said you hadn't been by the *Dispatch* yet, and I couldn't get you at home."

"I've been driving around looking for O'Brian. He left me a note saying he was going out for breakfast and would be right back. So when he didn't show, I started panicking about what he might be up to and—"

"He was here. I mean, he was at Betty's Café and then at Earl's and then here. And, Claudia, he got himself a car."

"What?"

"That little red one of Jack MacDougal's. Jack's been trying to sell it, and—"

"Damn! I oversleep *one* morning and look what happens. How could I have gone to bed without setting the alarm?"

"Now, don't go blaming yourself, dear. I don't think there's any real harm done."

"No? Lucille, if the man has a car he can go anywhere he wants, whenever he wants, and I won't know about it. I mean, where is he right now?"

"Well, I don't know. It must be close to an hour since he left here. But I'd better tell you the rest."

"Oh, Lord, I'm not going to want to hear it, am I?"

"It's not really too bad. But Frankie Hess told him about your father buying the truck."

"What? And you don't think that's bad?"

"Not *too* bad, I said. Because I convinced Mike it must be my Christmas present and that Raymond just has it hidden somewhere."

"Oh, good thinking. But you're *sure* you convinced him?"

"Definitely. He apologized for five minutes about spoiling the surprise."

"Thank heavens. Then we don't have to worry that he'll get the license number and go driving all over the countryside looking for it."

"Well...let's hope not."

"You mean you think he might?"

"I'm just a little worried he could run into your father before I fill him in. And if Raymond comes up with some other explanation, one that doesn't ring as true..."

"Oh, Lord," Claudia said again, absently stroking Morgan's neck.

"Claudia, I'm sure we'll be okay. But hold on a second. Your father's just walked through the door. Raymond," she called without bothering to cover the mouthpiece. "Raymond, come into the kitchen right now."

"Taking my boots off," he called back.

"Hurry up," Claudia muttered.

"Raymond?" she could hear Lucille saying a few moments later. "You haven't seen Mike O'Brian this morning, have you?"

"No, why?"

Claudia offered up a little prayer of thanks while Lucille said, "I'll tell you in a minute, dear. As soon as I finish talking to Claudia. Did you hear that?" she asked into the phone.

"Yes. But we still don't know where he is. You've got no idea where he was going when he left your place?"

"No, he didn't say a word about going *anywhere*."

"All right. Well, call again if anything comes up."

"You too, dear. 'Bye."

"'Bye, Lucille." She clicked off, thinking she had a pretty good idea where O'Brian would have gone. Which meant she should call the Nilssons and warn them he was probably on his way. And after that, she'd better call Iggy so he wouldn't be wondering where she was.

She checked the Nilssons' number and punched it in, thinking it was a darn good thing O'Brian had already dropped off his first column at the *Dispatch*. As long as Iggy had that, he wouldn't care if neither of them made it to the office for a while.

And after she talked to Iggy...well, she didn't know what she'd do then. That would depend on what it turned out O'Brian was doing.

The Nilssons' phone rang. And rang. And rang.

"Rats," she said, finally giving up. When they were down in that basement computer room, they couldn't hear the other lines.

"But you'd think," she told Morgan, "that when they spend half their days playing with electronic things, they could remember to turn on an answering machine.''

Calling Iggy, she told him she and O'Brian were going to be following up some hot Santa leads for most of the afternoon. Then she wandered into the living room and stood looking out the window in hopes she'd see her missing houseguest.

When the phone rang again, she raced back into the kitchen, but it was only Lucille calling back.

"Claudia?" she said, sounding nervous. "Claudia, I was just talking to your father, and I think there's something else I'd better tell you."

"What?"

"Well, while Mike was here, he asked me about Norm dressing up in costumes for poker parties. And I didn't know what to say so I pretended I knew what he was talking about. But Raymond says Norm's never done that, so..."

"Oh, no. O'Brian's onto the Nilssons for sure, then."

"I screwed up," Lucille said.

"It wasn't your fault. You couldn't have known. But is there anything else?"

"Not that I can think of."

"All right, then, don't worry. You misled him about the truck, and that was the important thing. We knew Gord and Norm wouldn't be able to keep him off-balance forever."

Hanging up, she tried the Nilssons' again. When there was still no answer, she sank onto a kitchen chair and told herself that fretting about O'Brian was only wasting energy. She'd be far better off thinking about something else entirely—like that little bombshell Santa had dropped last night.

She still hadn't figured out what the story could be
with those blank assay forms. But since the fate of the
whole area's economy depended on the mines, she
desperately wanted to know what was going on. So
how was she going to keep protecting Santa *and* find
out what Wayne Greenaway was up to?

It would only be possible, she decided, if O'Brian
was too busy helping her investigate Hillstead to worry
much about Santa. But how was she going to convince him to switch priorities when he'd said yesterday that he couldn't spend time on Hillstead until after
he'd solved the Santa mystery?

Maybe, if she told him a confidential source had
called her with the information about those blank
forms—and impressed on him that it was an *incredibly* important lead—he wouldn't be able to resist following up on it.

Unless, of course, he figured out that the Paquettes
had been playing fast and loose with him since the
moment he'd arrived.

If that happened, he wouldn't be speaking to her, let
alone helping her investigate Hillstead.

MIKE TURNED OFF the main highway and headed
down the secondary road that led to the Nilssons'
place, still mentally kicking himself for not remembering to ask Lucille where her snowmobile had gotten to. And for not thinking to ask a few other things,
as well.

Once he'd raised the issue of that second truck,
though, he'd felt like such a jerk for blowing her
Christmas surprise he hadn't been able to get out of
the house fast enough.

At least he'd learned that the Nilssons probably weren't Santa. Which meant he had more important things to worry about than an unaccounted-for snowmobile. After all, if Norm and Gord had simply been leading him on, he was back to not having a clue who Santa was.

He drummed his fingers against the steering wheel while a nagging little voice told him it might be Raymond. His gut, on the other hand, said it wasn't. Aside from anything else, if it was Raymond, Claudia would surely know. And if she did, she'd have spilled the beans long before this.

The better Mike got to know her, the more certain he was that she didn't have a deceitful bone in her body. She couldn't possibly have spent the past few days lying through her teeth to him.

He thought about that for a minute and admitted she might have one or two deceitful bones. He hadn't forgotten that little conversation she'd had with Gord about buying a cell phone. Or *not* buying one, as she'd claimed.

Yes, she *had* seemed to be lying then. But maybe there was some perfectly logical explanation she simply hadn't wanted to mention.

At any rate, as far as Santa was concerned, everything ultimately came down to the issue of how much this caper had to be costing. And nothing Mike had seen or heard indicated that Raymond Paquette had tens of thousands of dollars just sitting around growing moldy. So who the hell was playing Mr. Bountiful?

He drove on, certain he was missing an important piece of the puzzle but unable to figure out what it was—and feeling more and more frustrated that he couldn't.

"If Santa," he told himself, making the turn onto the Nilssons' private road, "isn't Norm or Gord or Raymond, I'm out of suspects." And that was enough to make him shudder, given what Iggy had said about his having to stay here until he identified Santa. At the rate things were going, it *would* take till Easter.

Of course, there was one other possible suspect. At least, the Nilssons had pointed a finger at one. And unlikely as it seemed, maybe Iggy *was* his man.

Telling himself he was really reaching on that one, he parked the Civic before he got within sight of the house, then grabbed his camera from the seat beside him. He might have pretty well written off the Nilssons, but there was still a remote chance they had presents and hampers stored in their basement. And if they did, he was going to get proof of it.

Slinging the Nikon over his shoulder, he climbed out of the car and started walking. As he neared the clearing, he stopped and peered through the trees. To this point, he probably hadn't been visible from the chalet. But since it was heavy on windows, he'd need some luck from here on in.

Slowly, he scoped out the situation. Norm's and Gord's snowmobiles were parked outside the house, along with their pair of Ford Explorers. There was no sign of the men themselves.

Taking as deep a breath as was possible through his scarf, he made a mad dash across the clearing and scuttled in under the wraparound deck. If they hadn't seen him by now, he was safe.

His legs complaining bitterly, he began duck-waddling his way along the foundation of the house, pausing to peer in each window. Fortunately, likely because they were hidden under the deck, none of them were covered by curtains.

The basement was unfinished and virtually empty—except for the furnace room and a long walled section on the far side of the house. There were the standard basement-type things stored in the large open section, but no Santa goodies.

He pressed on, and when he got around to the fourth side he grinned to himself. That stretch of the foundation was solid concrete. And inside it, he'd bet, was a wall of lead shields.

They *did* have a secure computing room down there. But it had to be the last place they'd store parcels and hampers. They'd never expose their precious computer equipment to the risk of accidental knocks.

So the Nilssons definitely weren't Santa. Completely convinced of that now, he backed awkwardly away from the foundation.

Reaching the edge of the deck, he grabbed the length of cedar above his head. Then, swinging out and into a standing position, he turned. And found himself staring down the barrel of a rifle.

CHAPTER ELEVEN

"LOOKING FOR SOMETHING?" Gord asked.

"It's me!" Mike tugged his scarf down from over his nose with one hand and ripped off his toque with the other. "Mike O'Brian," he added, anxiously glancing from Gord to Norm, then back at the rifle in Gord's hands.

"Uh-huh. We thought so when we saw you racing across the clearing." Gord didn't smile and he didn't lower the rifle.

"Lucky for you we did," Norm added. "Otherwise, we might have just blown you away."

Mike tried to grin, but his lips refused to cooperate. "Well, I'm sure glad you didn't," he managed to say. "Iggy'd be mad as hell if I wasn't around to write the entire Santa series."

"You know," Norm said, looking at Gord. "That's true. If you killed Mike, here, it *would* make Iggy mad as hell. So maybe you should go for it."

"But I'd get charged with murder."

Norm shook his head. "I don't think so. Mike's trespassing, which means it'd be manslaughter at most. And we could say he threatened you. That would make it self-defense."

"Hey, come on, you guys," Mike said. "A joke's a joke, but at least stop aiming that thing at me, huh?"

"Well . . ." Gord hesitated, then pointed the rifle at the ground.

Joke or not, Mike began breathing more easily. "Look, I apologize for snooping. But you've got to admit you were kind of asking for it—leading me on the way you did yesterday."

"Leading you on?" Norm repeated.

"Yeah, I asked Claudia a few questions about you two, then tried the same ones on Lucille. And I didn't exactly get the same answers."

"Oh," the brothers said in unison.

"And Lucille told me about your phone-ringing trick."

"Oh," they said again.

"And I know Raymond put you up to everything," he bluffed. He wasn't entirely sure about that part. But since he was ninety-nine percent convinced that Raymond had asked Earl to hide Jack MacDougal's car away, it was a pretty safe guess he'd been behind the Nilssons' performance.

"What makes you figure it was Raymond?" Norm asked.

"I don't figure, I *know*. I told you, I've been talking to both Claudia and Lucille."

"I didn't think Ray was going to say anything to Claudia," Gord muttered to his brother.

Norm merely shrugged.

"So the bottom line," Mike tried, deciding he might as well take a shot in the dark, "is that Raymond wanted you to convince me you were Santa so I wouldn't realize it was actually him."

"What?" Norm said.

"You think Raymond's Santa?" Gord asked. "Good grief, Mike, are you sure you won a Pulitzer?"

"You're not an imposter, are you?" Norm demanded. "I wouldn't put it past Iggy to try breezing a ringer by people."

"What in blazes would make you think Ray has that kind of money?" Gord put in. "Often as not, when he loses at poker he has to settle up with an IOU."

Reminding himself he hadn't actually figured it could be Raymond, anyway, Mike said, "All right, so he's not Santa. But he *did* ask you to try to convince me *you* were, didn't he?"

"Well . . ." Norm said.

"Why?" Mike pressed.

"You think we should tell him?" Norm asked his brother.

"Hey, come on. You two have had a lot of fun at my expense. The least you can do is not make me drive all the way back to town and have to go looking for Raymond to get an answer."

"I guess Raymond *will* tell him," Gord said.

Norm nodded. "Then I guess it wouldn't hurt to fill him in, now that he's on to us anyway."

"So?" Mike said when neither brother volunteered more.

"Well . . ." Norm finally began, "Raymond asked us to help him out because he was pissed off at Iggy— for taking Claudia's big story away from her."

"What?"

"What do you mean, *what?* I'm talking about the Santa story, of course. We've never had anybody running around playing Santa before."

"Probably never will again, either," Gord added.

"Exactly. So when Iggy gave the story to Claudia instead of his own nephew, she was darned excited. And Raymond was real happy for her. But then, the next thing they knew, Iggy had some hotshot California reporter coming and—"

"Norm?" Gord interrupted, shooting his brother a warning look.

"Oh," Norm said. "Sorry, Mike, don't take the hotshot bit personally. That's just what Claudia and Raymond were calling you at first."

"Norm was only trying to make the point that Raymond was really mad at Iggy," Gord explained. "Ray didn't think it was right to bring in a hired gun. And he decided the longer he could keep you from figuring out who the *real* Santa was, the better."

"Because the longer it took," Norm added, "the more worried Iggy would get that your series might not be the big success he was hoping for."

"And, of course," Gord put in, "if you didn't manage to identify Santa at all, you wouldn't have much of an ending, would you. The series would just kind of fizzle out and leave people with a bad taste instead of a good one."

Mike rubbed his jaw, trying to decide how much sense that all made. "There's a major problem with Raymond's logic," he said at last.

"What?" Gord asked.

"Well, Iggy's counting on my series to build up his readership, but if it's a flop, it won't do that. In which case, the *Dispatch* would still be in the red and Ferris Wentworth would pull the plug. And if that happens, Claudia's out of a job. So Raymond's attempt to make the series a flop seems awfully dumb, doesn't it?"

"Not *awfully*," Norm said. "Because it's only a matter of time until the paper goes under, anyway. Raymond knows that, and I'm sure Claudia does, too. Even if your series is terrific, it's only going to give the *Dispatch* a temporary boost. A month or two from now, things will have slipped right back to where they were."

"You might be right," Mike admitted. In fact, it seemed virtually inevitable. And given that, he could understand why Raymond might have said to hell with it and tried to get a little revenge on Claudia's behalf.

"So, now that you know the truth," Gord said, "how about a coffee? You must be freezing."

"I am. And thanks, but I'd better get going. I left Claudia a note telling her I wouldn't be long, and that was hours ago. If I don't show up soon, she'll figure aliens abducted me or something."

"Well, drive safely," Norm told him.

With a goodbye wave, Mike headed back to his car and started for home—more aware of the passing countryside now that he'd gotten the answers to at least a few of his questions.

The stretch of secondary road that led to the main highway was deserted and snow-covered, but there didn't seem to be any icy patches. And doing his own driving, he was beginning to see why someone like Claudia, who was used to the road conditions, didn't worry about speeding.

That thought was still in his head when, from nowhere, a deer stepped onto the road less than fifty yards in front of him.

He slammed on the brakes and wrenched the wheel to the right, sending the car spinning in a dizzy circle.

It crashed against a snowbank, bounced off and went into another spin.

The last thing he saw was the front end plowing into a solid wall of white.

The last thing he felt was the impact flinging him forward and the seat belt wrenching him back.

CLAUDIA ZOOMED ALONG the highway at a speed even she'd admit was excessive. But it was nearly two hours since Gord had called to report on O'Brian's visit.

And since O'Brian had said he was heading straight back to her place, a drive that should take forty minutes tops, she was so certain something had gone wrong that her throat was aching with apprehension. She pressed down even harder on the accelerator, berating herself for not having dealt with this situation nearly as well as she should have.

By the time she'd decided O'Brian had to be lying dead someplace, she'd been in such a panic state her mind had stopped working. All she'd been able to think about was finding him as quickly as she could. But now that she was thinking straight again, she realized she should have phoned Gord back and asked him and Norm to go out looking from their end. And she should have called the police, as well.

She drove on, spotting no sign of an accident along the main highway. As she reached the secondary road that led to the Nilssons', she was hoping against hope this was just a wild-goose chase, that O'Brian had simply decided to make a detour on his way back to town.

Hitting the brakes, she half drove, half slid onto the side road. Then she accelerated again, and only about a kilometer along, she saw it. A little red car half-buried in a snowbank.

She skidded to a stop beside it and leapt out of the Cherokee, her heart beating wildly. The driver's side of the Civic was badly dented and the car's windows were so fogged up she couldn't see inside—couldn't see whether O'Brian was dead or alive. Fear pounding in her ears, she tried to open the door. When she couldn't, tears began streaming down her cheeks. Then she realized someone was wiping the window from inside.

"Paquette!" O'Brian yelled. "Thank heavens! There was a deer. I didn't hit it but—"

He was still talking, but all she could hear was a roar in her ears. If he *had* hit a deer with this little car, he really would have been dead. Even slamming into that snowbank could have caused serious damage.

"Are you all right?" she demanded, interrupting whatever he was telling her.

"No! I'm a damn icicle! This door's stuck shut, the other's wedged tight against the snowbank and I'm dying of hypothermia, so what the hell are you laughing about?"

"I'm not laughing, I'm . . ." But suddenly she was. Half laughing, at least. Her tears had turned into tears of relief, and she was half laughing, half crying.

"Can you get me out of here?"

"Yes, just let me find something." She raced back to the Cherokee and dug out the tire iron, telling herself that if she wasn't able to pry the door open she could drive on to the Nilssons' for help.

But when she got the iron jammed in between the door and the frame and pried with all her might, the door creaked open.

"Oh, O'Brian," she cried, reaching in and throwing her arms around his neck. "I thought I was going to find a dead body."

"Ten minutes more and you might have," he muttered, his teeth chattering. "But since I'm still alive, what the hell am I supposed to do about this car?"

"Don't worry about it right now. You can talk to Jack MacDougal later," she added, taking O'Brian's hands to help him out.

"My Lord," she whispered when he seemed barely able to move. "Do you think anything's broken?"

"No, but I think forty-six different things are frozen solid. So let's get out of here, huh? I've never been so cold in my entire life. And that includes our ice-fishing excursion."

At least he was alive, and that made her heart sing. She hadn't realized how desperately she'd come to care for him, but she was so happy to have found him safe that she just wanted to hold him and never let him go.

Instead, she pulled him from the frigid little car and helped him into the Cherokee. Then she grabbed the car blanket and tucked it around him, saying, "I'll take you to the Nilssons'. That's the nearest warm place."

"No, I don't want to see the Nilssons again. Just take me home, Claudia. Just take me home."

MIKE WAS SO COLD his brain should have been too frozen to function. Amazingly, though, it began chugging away the minute Claudia started the Jeep.

And even more amazing were the thoughts it was generating. Thoughts about how, after only a few days in Victoria Falls, he was madly in love with her.

Of course, they'd been spending practically every minute together, which added up to much longer than a few days in standard dating time. Still, he'd always figured he was immune to the fast-striking, overwhelming kind of love that sometimes hit people. But it had felled him like a bad case of the flu.

No, that was a terrible analogy. Hell, falling in love with her was wonderful. And *she* was wonderful—everything he'd ever wanted in a woman, even if he hadn't consciously realized he'd been wanting it until he'd met her. But she was beautiful and funny and kind and she'd just saved his life. What more could a man want?

Of course, he'd rather she didn't have a devious, conniving, lying father, but she was hardly responsible for Raymond's behavior. And from the way the Nilssons had been talking, he doubted she had the slightest idea what Ray had been up to.

"Claudia?"

She glanced at him and smiled. "Do you realize you've started calling me Claudia? Until a few minutes ago, it was never anything but Paquette."

"Really?"

"Uh-huh."

"Oh. Would you rather I stuck with Paquette?"

"No, Claudia's just fine . . . Mike."

Mike. He liked the way his name sounded on her lips. Or maybe he just liked her lips. "I want to ask you about something," he said, forcing his thoughts back to where they'd been.

"Yes?"

"Did you know your father was incredibly angry at Iggy for giving me the Santa story?"

She shrugged. "It wasn't particularly because he gave it to *you*. What got him mad was the principle of the thing—that one minute it was my story and the next it wasn't."

"Yeah, but that's not exactly what I was getting at. I meant, did you know he's been throwing road-blocks in my way? Trying to keep me from tracking down Santa?"

"What?" She glanced over with such an innocent expression she couldn't possibly be faking it. "You're not serious."

"I am. Gord and Norm told me the whole story. Your dad asked them to try and mislead me into thinking they were Santa—to drag things out and make Iggy sweat."

"Make Iggy sweat?"

"Yeah, the theory was that when he realized I wasn't getting anywhere with finding Santa, he'd start worrying I might not manage to ID him at all. Then there wouldn't be a good wrap-up for the series."

"Really? Dad came up with a plan like that? I didn't realize he was quite so angry."

"Well, he was. And I don't think it was only the Nilssons he had helping him out. I'm almost positive he's been asking people not to let me get my hands on a car."

"Oh, Mike, I don't think he'd—"

"It's okay. I was darned annoyed at him earlier, but I don't hold grudges. Does he?"

"Does he?" she repeated.

Mike nodded. "Did you know he bought a truck for Lucille? As her Christmas present?"

"Ahh...yes, he told me."

"Well, I heard he'd bought it but I didn't know it was a present. That it was going to be a surprise, I mean. At any rate, I dropped by their place this morning and kind of blew the surprise, so if your dad finds out, he's not going to be happy."

"Oh. I see. Well, no, you're safe. He's not a grudge-holder, either."

Claudia gazed ahead at the highway again, feeling positively ill. Despite her determination not to let herself start liking him too much, she knew she'd already fallen in love with Mike O'Brian. It was the only possible explanation for how frantic she'd gotten when she'd thought he might be dead.

So, foolish as she'd been to let it happen, it had. Which meant things were going to be downright awful once he headed back to where he belonged.

In the meantime, though, she wished with all her heart she didn't have to keep lying to him. If she could trust him with the truth, she'd tell him the whole story right this minute. But she *couldn't* trust him. He'd come to Victoria Falls for the sole purpose of revealing Santa's identity to the world. And she'd be dreaming if she thought asking him not to would do any good.

Just the other day, she'd tiptoed around that idea. And what had he said? He'd asked if she was out of her mind. Told her he'd never let some local yokel in a red suit best him. Pointed out he'd be a laughing-stock if he couldn't figure out who Santa was—that if he failed to, he'd never be able to show his face around the *Gazette* again.

No, as much as she wished she could confide in him, she just couldn't risk it. Not when Santa's life might well be in danger.

"YOU KNOW," MIKE SAID when they reached town, "I don't feel chilled right to the bone anymore. So how about stopping by the bank? The sooner I tell Jack MacDougal the bad news, the better I'll feel."

"Do you want me to come in with you?" Claudia offered. "I know him pretty well. He's Annie's next-door neighbor."

"Well, I think I can get through the conversation without moral support, but you don't want to sit out here and freeze."

"I won't. I'll go and pop into the *Dispatch*—tell Iggy you've been back to the Nilssons'. He always likes to be updated on what's happening."

When she pulled up outside the bank, Mike headed in and down to the offices at the back. Jack Mac-Dougal looked pleased to see him—for about the first thirty seconds. By the time Mike had finished his story, though, Jack was shaking his head. "And it's in pretty bad shape, eh?" he said.

"I'm afraid so. I imagine your insurance company's going to give you a settlement rather than have it repaired."

"Damn," he muttered. "When they write off a car they only give you book value. Which means you take a beating."

"I realize that. So what were you asking for it?"

Jack eyed him for a second, then said, "Three thousand."

Mike gritted his teeth. His helpful banker shouldn't be out anything, but he'd bet book value was a whole lot less than that. And there was no way the *Gazette* was going to pick up the entire shortfall.

"Okay, then, here's what we'll do," he said. "If you can get a number from the insurance people fast, I'll give you a check for the difference before I leave town. If they drag their feet, I'll give you a check for a thousand and you can let me know if I owe you more."

"Oh...well...that's really decent of you, Mike. I figured I was going to be out of luck on this. But look, you already paid me three hundred, and I wouldn't have gotten the whole three thousand. So...well, I'll talk to my insurance agent right away and get back to you, eh?"

"Sure. I'm staying at Claudia Paquette's."

Given the way Jack merely nodded, the information had to be common knowledge.

"I'll call you there. And thanks for being so fair about this. If there's anything I can do for you while you're still in town..."

"Well, if you happen to hear who Santa is, be sure to let me know."

Jack grinned. "I'll do that, Mike. I'll definitely do that."

ONCE THEY FINALLY arrived home, Morgan performed a three-minute welcome dance, then pressed his nose against the door asking to be let out.

When Mike opened it, the gust of icy air that rushed in made him shiver.

"You're still awfully cold, aren't you," Claudia said.

"I'm not exactly roasting."

"And I'll bet you didn't have any lunch, did you." He shook his head.

"Then go crawl into bed while I make you something hot. Leave your clothes on and pull the blankets up over your head."

"Old northern trick?"

"You'll see. It's the quickest way to get warm."

"Either I get warm or I suffocate, right? In which case it won't matter if I'm cold."

"Very funny. Just do it."

After hanging up his parka and tugging off his mukluks, he did as he'd been told. And as he climbed into bed, still wearing his jeans and sweatshirt, he was aware of the same feeling he'd had the very first night he'd been in Victoria Falls. The feeling that it was nice to have someone worry about his welfare.

No, that wasn't specific enough. It was nice to have *Claudia* worry about him. So nice, in fact, he'd started thinking he wanted to spend the rest of his life with her caring what was happening to him.

In the back of his mind, though, something was warning him to slow down. After all, his feelings for her had developed incredibly fast, especially considering how certain he'd always been that commitment wasn't for him. An investigative reporter's life-style was darned hard on a relationship.

Of course, Claudia was a reporter herself, so when he had to cancel plans because he was chasing a story, she'd probably be more understanding than most women. But there were a lot of other reasons he'd always figured *no strings, no commitments* was the best way to live his life. Strangely, he couldn't think of a single one of them at the moment.

All he could think was that he didn't want to fly home in a few days and leave Claudia behind. Because it seemed as if he'd suddenly reached the right time for something permanent in his life. And that he'd found the right woman. The only thing wrong was the place he'd found her.

But Claudia was hardly chained to Victoria Falls, was she?

The question lingered in his mind as he lay listening to her let the dog in. And while he heard her giving Morgan a biscuit and telling him not to leave crumbs on the floor. By the time she appeared in the bedroom with a tray, he'd decided he'd be the biggest fool ever born not to find out what the answer was.

"Chicken soup," she announced, setting the tray on the bedside table. "Homemade. I mean, it's gone the freezer and microwave route, but I *did* make it myself."

He pushed the covers off and swung his feet onto the floor, then tried the soup. Pronouncing it delicious, he put the spoon down and smiled at her. How could he even think of life without this woman who made her own fabulous chicken soup?

"Aren't you going to sit with me while I eat?" he said, patting the bed beside him.

"You're not eating," she pointed out.

"It's a bit hot. I'd better let it cool some."

She hesitated, then sat down.

"I was just thinking about something," he told her. "You know my sisters?"

"Not personally," she teased. "But I know what you've told me about them. Their names are Sarah and Rachel. They live in L.A., and each has two children."

"And a husband. They both have husbands."

"Well that's a nice arrangement. Especially when there are children involved."

"And they both fell in love at first sight and got married in no time flat."

"Really. That's quite a coincidence."

"Uh-huh, exactly what I've always thought. But lately I've been wondering if it might be something genetic."

Claudia's pulse had already been beating faster than normal, and those words sent it into double time.

"You mean," she said at last, "your parents fell in love at first sight, too?"

"No, they dated off and on for years. But a lot of genetic traits skip generations."

"I see," she said, although she wasn't sure she saw at all. Or maybe she was just afraid to believe she did.

She waited for Mike to continue, her pulse now doing triple time.

He gazed at her for a long moment, then reached for her hands. "Remember what you were telling me yesterday? About how you'd intended to see more of the world? But that you stayed here when circumstances got in the way?"

She nodded, afraid to trust her voice.

"Well, I was wondering . . ."

"Yes?" she whispered.

"You didn't decide, sometime since then, that you'd never leave Victoria Falls, did you?"

"No. I just stayed on because... I guess because, by the time things got straightened around, I'd settled into an adult life here."

"Ahh."

He gazed at her for another moment, his eyes telling her even more than his words had.

He was thinking of a possible future for them. And she'd be more than happy to think about one, too.

"You know," he said softly, "maybe you could start off seeing more of the world by coming down to visit L.A. Sometime soon, I mean."

"I think I'd like that," she whispered.

"Good, because I think I'd like it, too." He gave her a smile that made her heart skip ten beats. Then he took her face between his hands and kissed her, precipitating a sweet surge of desire.

It was such a hungry kiss that she knew if she didn't walk out of his room within the next thirty seconds, they'd end up making love. And then she found herself thinking it was a safe time of the month, and realized there was no question of *if*.

"Claudia?" he finally murmured against her lips. "Do you believe in love at first sight?"

She took a long, slow breath. "I never used to. But I think I might be revising my views."

Drawing away an inch or so, he smiled again, this time so warmly she felt heat clear down to her toes. Then he rested his hand on her shoulder and began gently brushing his fingers along the side of her throat.

His touch sent shock waves of need through her. And even though they made it extremely difficult to think, she knew she had to. She was about to make love with a man she'd been deceiving since the moment they'd met, and she couldn't do that.

"Mike?" she forced herself to say.

"It's okay," he murmured kissing her ear, "I've got a clean bill of health. So unless this is a dangerous time..."

"No, but that wasn't—"

"Good," he whispered, "because I want you so badly I think I'd die if you told me we couldn't."

"Me, too, only..." Her words trailed off as he slid his hands possessively down her body and pulled her closer.

She was positively aching for him, but she *had* to tell him the truth. She couldn't, though. Not without being certain he wouldn't reveal it.

And then, while she was still mentally arguing with herself, he eased her down onto the bed.

The length of his body pressing against hers started a throbbing urgency within her—so strong it made every thought in her head fade like smoke in the wind.

Only the awareness of physical sensations remained—of scent and taste and touch. He smelled of a frosty winter woods, but there was only warmth in his kisses. And in his caress.

His mouth was hot and hard against hers. His hands, after he slipped them under her sweater, lingered seductively on her rib cage and made her shiver with anticipation.

"You're cold," he said, pulling the blankets over them, then taking her in his arms again. This time, he pushed her sweater up and kissed her stomach. When he began working his way to her breasts, she murmured his name and shifted so he could pull the sweater over her head.

He shrugged out of his sweatshirt, then unhooked her bra and slid it off. Cupping her breasts, he began to cover them with kisses. "Mmm," she whispered, smoothing her hands across the muscles of his shoulders and down his sides, delighting in the solid heat of his body against hers.

When he began teasing her nipples with his tongue, her need grew stronger still. She moaned, skimming her hands lower and making him moan in return. Quickly, he unzipped his jeans and yanked off the rest of his clothes, then drew her hand down to his hard arousal.

Caressing him started a liquid fire of excitement between her legs. And as he rested his hand there, she was swept by a wave of longing so strong it made her gasp.

He unsnapped her jeans and helped her out of them, then began touching her again, stoking the fire of her need until she was hot and wet and absolutely desperate for him.

"Oh, Mike," she whispered, her breathing so fast and shallow she was barely able to speak at all.

She arched against his hand, over and over, wanting him inside her yet not wanting him to stop what he was doing.

He didn't stop. But he moved a little and found one of her nipples with his mouth again. It sent fresh shock waves through her; she felt as if she was standing on the edge of a precipice. And just when she was certain she was about to die of excruciating desire, another white-hot surge of heat seized her. Then she shattered and the world shattered around her.

She could neither breathe nor speak; she was totally lost to the shudders of release that gradually brought her down from the height of passion.

And then Mike kissed her throat and more shudders seized her.

"You okay?" he murmured as her body grew still a second time.

"Okay?" She felt like laughing and crying at once. "Mike," she managed to say, "I've never been more okay in my life."

"Ahh."

Her eyes were closed, but she could hear him smile. Smiling herself, she slid her hands down his body and drew him to her. He buried his hands in her hair and entered her—hot and hard and primordial male.

His thrusts aroused her yet again. And when he came, collapsing against her, she shattered once more.

Her final conscious thought was a wish that the moment could last forever.

CHAPTER TWELVE

THE LATE-AFTERNOON sunlight dancing through the bedroom window promised heat, but Mike knew it was a false promise. Even though he and Claudia were warm as toast in bed, the house was chilly.

Cuddling her more closely to him, he sleepily considered how much more enjoyable it was to lie here with her than it would be to get up and write his articles.

He loved the softness of her naked body against his, the way her lips were red from kissing him, the way her hair was messed from their lovemaking and the way her long lashes looked so dark against her skin.

Then she smiled, her eyes still closed, and he loved that, too.

"What?" he whispered.

"Afterglow," she whispered back.

"Afterglow. Is that what this is called?"

"Mmm," she said, lazily opening her eyes. "I'm not sure if that's really the right word when the sun's shining, but I can't think of another one."

"And you call yourself a newspaperwoman? You should never be at a loss for words."

"Oh, sometimes, when one finds oneself in extraordinary circumstances, I think it's allowed."

That made him laugh. These were extraordinary circumstances, all right. His entire world had turned upside down, leaving him happier than he could ever remember being. He was just wondering if he should tell Claudia that when the phone began to ring.

"Rats," she said, rolling out of bed.

He watched her for a moment—until she grabbed his robe from the chair and tugged it on, spoiling his view.

As she dashed from the room, he snuggled down into the warmth of the bed once more, thinking he might have time for a catnap. But she was back a minute later, the cordless to her ear and Morgan on her heels.

She mouthed that it was Iggy on the phone, then said, "Ville-Marie? That's quite a drive, Iggy."

After a moment's pause, she said, "Yes, I realize a house fire right before Christmas makes for a great tearjerker, but couldn't I just call somebody and get the story over the phone?

"Oh. You want pictures. Well, all right, I'll hit the road first thing in the morning. But I wish our budget wasn't so tight and we could afford a real photographer."

There were a few more moments of silence, then she waved crossed fingers at Mike, saying, "As a matter of fact he's writing it this very minute. But sure you can talk to him.

"Iggy's just about to leave for the day," she explained, handing over the phone. "And before he does, he wants to know how you're coming with the second article."

"No problems," he told the editor after their initial hellos. "I'm just finishing Wednesday's, and I'll write Thursday's now, as well. They both focus on the Nilssons—kind of a miniseries within the series."

"But they're not Santa," Iggy said.

"No, and that's what I'll be concluding in the Thursday piece. The two of them led me on a merry chase, though, so I'm emphasizing the humor again. You figured it worked all right in the first article?"

"Yeah, it's funny as hell. And the picture of you with that fish came out great. I'm running it front page center."

"Claudia gets photo credit," he said, smiling at her. She'd shut Morgan out of the room and crawled back into bed—nicely shedding his robe on the way. And now she was nibbling at his shoulder, which made him fervently hope Iggy wasn't in the mood to ramble on.

"But what about who Santa *is?*" Iggy asked as Claudia began tangling Mike's chest hair around her finger. "Have you figured that out yet?"

"Still working on it."

"But you've got a pretty good idea?"

"Getting close."

"So am I," Claudia whispered, trailing kisses downward.

"Close doesn't count," Iggy said. "I didn't think a reporter of your caliber would have any trouble ferreting out our Santa, but unless you've got a serious suspect you're not telling me about..."

Mike swallowed hard, unsuccessfully trying to ignore what Claudia was doing.

"O'Brian?" Iggy said. "Are you okay? Did you just groan?"

"No. Must be a problem on the line. But listen, I'll drop by in the morning with the articles, okay?"

"Yeah, that'd be fine. And we should do a little brainstorming. It sounds as if you could use some help, and bouncing a few ideas around might do the trick. Maybe I'll get Pete to sit in on it, too."

While Iggy was talking, Mike covered the speaker and urgently whispered, "Claudia, give me a break."

Instead, she gave him a wet kiss on the stomach that all but made him groan again.

"Well, speak of the devil," Iggy went on. "Pete just walked in and he wants something. See you in the morning, huh? In the meantime, keep on with what you're doing."

"Yeah, okay, Iggy. See you in the morning." He clicked the phone off. Then, trying not to grin, he said, "Iggy told me to keep on with what I'm doing."

Claudia snuggled closer. "Well, Iggy's the boss."

AN HOUR OR SO LATER, Mike stretched lazily in the bed, then gave Claudia's bare shoulder a kiss and said, "You know what I want to do?"

"No." She smiled to herself. She might not know what he *wanted* to do, but unless he was completely insatiable she knew what he couldn't possibly have in mind.

"Let's put up your Christmas tree. It's been years since I decorated one."

"Really? You poor, deprived man. I've never *not* decorated one."

He gave her shoulder another kiss. "I knew that."

"You didn't know any such thing."

"Sure I did. That's the type of woman you are."

"Oh? You think you have me pegged, do you?"

"Perfectly. I know all your secrets. I'll bet you couldn't keep one from me if you tried."

She was just smiling to herself again—guiltily, this time—when he went on. "Unless, of course, it was a secret about a cell phone or something."

"What?" she said, her blood running cold.

"That cellular Gord was talking about. You *did* buy one, didn't you."

She ordered herself to relax and said, "I guess you're right. I really can't keep secrets from you."

He grinned at her, looking pleased as punch with himself. "So?" he pressed. "Why were you trying to convince Gord you *didn't* buy it?"

"Because it's my Christmas gift to Annie, and Gord often doesn't think before he speaks. You never know who he might mention things to.

"At any rate," she continued when Mike seemed to accept the explanation, "do you want to decorate the tree *before* you write those articles you promised Iggy, or after?"

"Before. They're already written in my head, so they won't take long."

"All right, then we'd better get dressed because the tree's still sitting outside."

"In the cold," Mike added unhappily.

He looked so miserable about the prospect of having to go out that she took pity on him.

"I'll tell you what," she offered. "I'm used to the cold, so I'll bring in the tree. You go down to the basement and get the decorations."

"And risk being conked over the head again?" he said with an utterly horrified expression.

"That's my best offer. Take it or leave it."

"I'll take it. I'd kill to not have to go out into that cold again today."

"Killing won't be necessary. You'll just owe me one." She crawled out of bed and gathered her clothes up from the floor. "The decorations are to the right of the furnace," she told him, starting for her own room.

Mike lingered in the warmth of the bed for a couple of minutes, then forced himself to get up. Deciding he really shouldn't make Claudia brave the outdoors alone, he dug into the drawer for an extra sweatshirt.

But while he was doing that, he heard her heading down the hall, talking to Morgan. A moment later, the front door opened and closed.

Telling himself she'd only be outside a couple of minutes, not long enough to get totally frozen, he pulled on his jeans and headed for the basement.

This time, he was careful to turn on the light before he started down the stairs. Today, though, the only other living things he spotted were Ghost and a spider. It was crawling across the concrete wall, just above the cat's pawing range. But Ghost was watching it intently, clearly waiting for one false move.

The boxes of tree ornaments were exactly where Claudia had told him, carefully labeled with a felt pen. Beside them were some cartons marked Books, some marked Miscellaneous, and one labeled Pictures.

The flaps on the pictures box were standing open, so he stepped over to rectify the situation, figuring dust must be getting in. When he absently glanced into the box, he saw there were some photo albums in it, neatly stacked. And on top of those were three framed photographs that looked as if they'd been tossed in hurriedly. Curious, he took them out for a closer look.

On top was one of Claudia and Annie, taken, he'd guess, when they were seventeen or eighteen. The next had obviously been shot in the same place on the same day. There was a boy in this one, though—roughly their age—standing with an arm around each girl.

The final picture was of the boy alone. But he was a grown man in this one. Probably in his late twenties. Tanned and broad-shouldered, he was leaning on the railing of a good-sized cabin cruiser, an easy smile on his face.

Mike eyed the photo for a minute, wondering who the guy was. The fellow Claudia used to go with? That Chet who'd been transferred to wherever?

Probably not, he decided, because she'd said Chet was with the provincial police, and the guy in the picture had hair far longer than any police force would tolerate. Unless, of course, the provincial police had an undercover unit. So who was he?

Stifling his curiosity, Mike put the pictures back, closed the carton and reached for the boxes of decorations.

"MORGAN, DON'T YOU even think about it," Claudia warned, coming back into the living room with the rest of the presents.

The dog ignored her and continued to sniff eagerly at the tree.

"Morgan! This is the house, not the great outdoors."

He listened that time. And once he'd skulked away a couple of feet, Claudia knelt to arrange the gifts under the bottom branches.

That done, she stepped back and watched Mike add the final touch—the treetop angel her mother had loved.

"Yes, you've got it exactly right," she told him when he glanced over for her approval. "And the tree looks beautiful."

"Of course it does." He stepped down from the chair. "Just because I haven't decorated one for years doesn't mean I forgot how."

"Oh? And I had nothing to do with it? I wasn't the one who finally got the lights to work?"

"I never claimed to be an electrician." He stood beside her looking at the tree for a minute, then his gaze wandered to the gifts beneath it. "Which one of those is Annie's phone?"

Her pulse gave an anxious little skip. "That one," she said, pointing to Annie's gift and thanking her lucky stars it was a believable shape.

"Looks like a shoe box."

"It is. The old disguise-something-to-look-like-slippers trick is one of my favorites."

When Mike smiled, she smiled back. Then she looked at the tree again. It really *was* beautiful. And the pizza they'd ordered for dinner had been delicious. And being here with Mike... Well, words couldn't describe how wonderful *that* was.

The only fly in the ointment was the guilt that wouldn't stop nagging at her. She was going to feel immensely better once she'd come clean. And she'd do that the moment she was sure it was safe. She only hoped Mike wouldn't be *too* angry when she finally told him the truth.

"You know," he said, draping his arm around her and pulling her close, "what I *did* forget was how sleepy decorating a tree makes me. I could really use a nap. How about you?"

"A nap," she repeated, managing not to smile. "No, I don't think so. You've still got those articles to write. And there's something I want to tell you about."

"Mmm?" he said, nuzzling her neck. "Couldn't you have told me while we were decorating the tree?"

"No, because I wanted your full attention. So are you going to sit down and give it to me?" she asked, taking his hand and leading him over to the couch.

"All you want is my attention?"

"At the moment, yes."

"Anyone ever tell you you're a spoilsport?"

"Probably, but listen to this. I think we were right about Hillstead—that there's definitely something going on there. And whatever it is, Wayne Greenaway's involved."

"You heard something?"

"I sure did."

She proceeded to explain that Wayne had been in his office again last night, and about the blank Croply Lab assay forms. Then she provided a two-minute explanation of how a major mining company operates.

"All right," Mike said when she finished. "The first question is, how reliable is your source?"

"Very."

"He's not just some guy with a grudge against Greenaway?"

"No."

"Okay then, let's figure out what we've got. This assay routine sounds straightforward. I mean, unless I'm missing something, all Croply does is get ore samples from Hillstead and analyze them, right? To determine how much valuable metal they contain?"

She nodded. "But from our perspective, the important thing is that after Greenaway's seen an assay report he forwards it to Toronto. And head office relies on them in its strategic planning."

"So," Mike said slowly, "if Greenaway has blank assay forms from Croply Labs, and for some reason he wanted to influence top management's decisions..."

"Exactly. Or it could be that somebody at head office wants to see specific results—and has Wayne sending reports saying whatever that somebody wants them to."

"Ahh. Good thinking. Greenaway isn't necessarily the instigator. He might just be a flunkie. Either way, it sounds as if he's as crooked as a dog's hind leg."

"Quaint saying for a California guy," she teased.

"Hey, they can't keep all the quaint sayings in the Deep South. But I take it this is making you want to investigate Hillstead even more."

"It sure is. I was hoping we could spend some time on it tomorrow. After I get back from Ville-Marie."

"Well..."

"Mike? I know you said you had to get the Santa mystery wrapped up first, but if Greenaway *is* up to no good, it's really important that somebody finds out exactly what's going on."

"I know. And believe me, I'd far rather sink my teeth into that than keep on doing what I've been doing. But I'm not getting *anywhere* with Santa. In fact, unless you think the Nilssons weren't just trying to mislead me about Iggy, I'm completely out of suspects."

Still wishing she could drop the pretense, she tried to look as if she was giving the possibility of Iggy's being Santa serious consideration.

"We shouldn't forget it was Pete who gave you that welcome on Main Street," she offered at last. "Which means Iggy certainly has access to a Santa suit. And maybe he *does* have money squirreled away. Who knows?"

Mike didn't look convinced. "You can't think of *anyone* else it might be?"

She shook her head. She'd reached the bottom of her bag of tricks.

"Then let's get back to your Hillstead problem. I can at least try to give you some ideas about where to start digging, so tell me everything else you know. Has anything unusual happened in the company lately?"

"Well, the layoffs were certainly unexpected."

"And they sent the share prices tumbling?"

"Yes. You're thinking stock manipulation?"

"It's pretty common in the industry. So you should check recent insider trading records. See if anyone in the company's been buying or selling."

"I know someone I can call about that—a business reporter with the *Toronto Star* who has access to all kinds of data bases. I'll fill her in and see what she can come up with. But what about those blank assay forms?"

"Well, Greenaway must keep copies of whatever he sends head office, right?"

"I'd imagine."

"Then you need to compare what he's been sending with the original assay records at Coply Labs. I mean, we might be off base here. Maybe he's forwarding the real thing. But if he's using those blank forms to get creative, a simple comparison will show it."

Claudia smiled. All she needed was a simple comparison. Then she thought about how she'd have to get it and her smile faded. "Having a look at Greenaway's records... That's not exactly ethical, is it."

"Not *exactly*," Mike said slowly. "But it's the sort of thing investigative reporters run up against all the time."

"So you just ignore the finer points of the law?"

"Sometimes. I decided long ago that the only thing I can do is consider each situation on its own merit."

"As in, does the end justify the means?"

He nodded. "I'll bet every reporter I work with has done things he—or she—could get arrested for. But sometimes bending the rules is the only way to expose the truth."

"And in this case...?"

"I don't know enough details to judge. But it won't hurt to phone your contact at the *Star* and see what that gets you."

"Then I'll call her right away. Tonight. Because I can't stop wondering if head office decided on those layoffs because of falsified reports and whether Hillstead might shut down operations permanently if nobody exposes the truth."

"Okay, then make your phone call. And if anything suspicious turns up... Well, don't do anything risky without me."

"That means you'll give me a hand?"

"If your contact finds something interesting, I'll do what I can."

"Thank you," she said, giving him a quick kiss.

He smiled. "I just wish identifying Santa was as easy as getting a peek at some files."

His words banished her thoughts about Hillstead. "Mike? You're still convinced you've *got* to ID him? I mean, Iggy said he liked the first article, didn't he?"

"Uh-huh, but—"

"And I'm sure the rest of them will be great. So readers are certain to get a kick out of the series and—"

"Claudia? I think we've had this conversation before, and the bottom line hasn't changed. Ending my series without revealing who Santa is would be like ending a murder mystery without revealing the murderer's identity."

Exhaling slowly, she told herself she might as well get used to feeling guilty. Because she was certainly no closer to being able to tell Mike the truth.

He stretched, then grinned at her. "I'm going to give Iggy a picture of Santa to splash across the front page if it kills me."

She tried to smile but couldn't. Not when she knew who a picture of Santa splashed across the front page might really kill.

THE RINGING PHONE startled Mike awake. Claudia's bedroom was pitch-black, the clock radio read 4:07 a.m., and beside him she was sitting up and reaching out in the darkness to switch on the bedside lamp.

He closed his eyes against the sudden light and listened to her anxious "Hello?"

A minute later, she whispered, "Mike?"

When he opened his eyes, she had her hand over the speaker.

"It's Jack MacDougal. He says he's got to talk to you."

He reached for the phone, but she held it away.

"Wait a minute so he'll think I had to go and wake you."

Grinning sleepily, he sat admiring the way her silky nightshirt clung to her curves until she decided enough time had passed.

"Jack?" he said once she finally gave him the phone. "What's happening?"

"Santa."

"What?"

"Santa's happening," Jack said. "And he's right next door. At Annie Robidoux's."

"At Annie's?"

"What about Annie?" Claudia demanded loudly enough to make Morgan sit up and look at her.

"Yeah," Jack said. "The baby was crying, and it was my turn to get up with her. And when I came into the kitchen and looked out the window, there it was in Annie's drive. Santa's snowmobile."

"You're sure it's his? And it's still there?"

"Yeah, I'm looking out at it right this minute. It's got bells hanging on the front and a big sled with a hamper sitting on it."

"But you didn't see Santa himself?"

"Santa?" Claudia practically yelled.

"No," Jack said. "He's got to be in her house, though."

"I'm on my way. And thanks, Jack."

"Santa's at Annie's," he told Claudia, handing her the phone and watching her closely. Annie was her best friend. So if Annie knew who Santa was, why didn't Claudia? Yet the way she was staring at him, her expression a combination of shock and horror, made him certain the news had surprised the hell out of her.

"Let's go," he added, rolling out of bed and grabbing his robe. "I'll be ready in thirty seconds. You *do* want to come, don't you?" he asked when she didn't move. "Hell, you *have* to come. I don't know where Annie lives."

"Yes. Yes, of course. Go get dressed."

For a few seconds after Mike headed to the other bedroom Claudia simply sat in stunned silence. Then, the phone still in her hand, she raced into the bathroom and locked the door. Turning the sink tap on full, she punched in Annie's number.

"Listen," she whispered when Annie picked up, "get him out of there. Mike's on his way."

"Claudia! How could you have kept this from me! You had to know—"

"Annie, he made me promise not to say a word. But he must have explained that to you, and—"

"You still should have told me! You—"

"Annie, listen! There's no time to talk right now. Just tell him Mike's on his way and get him out of there."

Hanging up before Annie could say another word, Claudia raced back into her bedroom and grabbed some clothes, her thoughts whirling.

What on earth had he been thinking of, going to Annie's? Well, she *knew* what he'd been thinking of, but why had he done it?

"Because," she muttered under her breath, "he's never had a risk-averse bone in his body."

As for poor Annie, she'd sounded as if she were in a state of shock. And mad as hell, which made Claudia feel like two cents. Annie never stayed angry, though, so once she calmed down things would be fine between them.

"Claudia?" Mike called. "Ready?"

"Almost," she called back, telling herself to hurry. If she didn't look as if she was just as anxious to get there as him, he'd be suspicious for sure. And she'd already taken so long that Morgan had curled up and gone back to sleep.

By the time she rushed out of her room, Mike was impatiently waiting in his snowmobile suit.

"I thought we should take the snowmobile, right? In case he makes a run for it and we have to follow him cross-country?"

The prospect of a chase scene through the night made her stomach knot. But surely he'd be gone from Annie's well before they arrived.

Quickly pulling on her own suit and boots, she grabbed the helmets and they headed out into the darkness.

CHAPTER THIRTEEN

To CLAUDIA'S VAST RELIEF, when Annie's house came into view there was no sign of a snowmobile. Only her car was in the drive, and the house was as dark and quiet as the night enveloping them.

Next door, Jack MacDougal's living room and front lights were on. And as Claudia pulled her snowmobile to a stop, he came out onto the porch.

She whipped off her helmet just in time to hear him call, "They're gone!"

"What?" Mike asked.

"They?" she said, her sense of relief vanishing.

Jack headed down his front steps, waiting until Mike had taken off his helmet. "I said, they're gone. They went flying out of here just a few minutes after I phoned you."

"They?" Claudia tried again.

Jack nodded. "I watched for a couple of minutes after I talked to Mike, then figured I'd better go wake Mary. She'd have hated to miss any excitement. But by the time I got back to the kitchen, Santa was sitting on the snowmobile."

"Dressed in his red suit and all?" Mike asked.

"He sure was. At any rate, I was thinking I should maybe run out and try to stop him from leaving for you. But before I could, Annie came racing out of the house with a suitcase."

"A suitcase," Claudia repeated numbly. This was getting more unbelievable by the second.

"Uh-huh," Jack said. "She just tossed it into the sled, climbed on behind Santa and away they went."

"Dammit to hell," Mike muttered. "How could we come this close and miss him? But you didn't recognize him, Jack?"

"No, I only saw him sitting on the snowmobile in the dark. And only from the back."

"Well, tell me anything you noticed. Was he short or tall?"

"Mike, he was sitting on the snowmobile and I was looking down from the kitchen."

"All right, then, skinny or fat? Young or old?"

"Jeez, look, I'm really sorry, but it was impossible to tell much. I mean, I guess he looked kind of heavy, but that could have just been his Santa disguise. Or a snowmobile suit under his outfit."

"So are you saying that he could have been almost anybody?" Claudia put in.

"Hell, Claudia, he could have been the man in the moon for all I could make out."

"Then the question is," Mike said, "who would Annie run off with in the middle of the night?"

Claudia and Jack looked at each other.

"Well?" Mike demanded. "There can't be a list of a hundred possible names."

"Sorry," Jack said. "But I'm her next-door neighbor and I can't think of even one."

"I can beat that," Claudia told him. "I'm her best friend, and I can't, either."

SINCE CLAUDIA HAD HEADED off for Ville-Marie before Mike showered and shaved on Tuesday morning, he was left without a ride to the *Dispatch*. And even though he bundled up for the walk, by the time he reached the bottom of the front steps his nose was so cold that he gave her snowmobile a contemplative glance. He'd be a little rusty. It had been years since he'd driven one. But he could probably handle it well enough.

He considered the idea for another second, then remembered she'd said that driving snowmobiles on Main Street was really frowned upon. With that in mind, he reluctantly started up the street.

Trudging through the cold, he tried once again to make sense of the latest episode in the Santa caper. But he simply couldn't. Both Claudia and Jack claimed that Annie almost never dated, that packing a bag and riding off into the night with someone was decidedly out of character. So who the hell could Santa be?

Not Iggy, an imaginary voice whispered.

It made Mike frown. Ruling out Iggy would leave absolutely no suspects. Even a highly improbable one was better than none at all, but after last night...

Well, a sixtyish, potbellied, married man had to be one of the last people Annie would have run off with. Unless there was some bizarre explanation. Like Annie being Iggy's secret daughter or some such thing. And she'd taken off with him in the middle of the night because...

Mike was still trying to think of an even semiplausible reason when he arrived at the paper.

Pete Doleman greeted him from the central area, where he was sitting in front of one of the computers; Iggy was by the door, putting on his parka. "Morning," he said. "You've got those articles for me?"

Mike nodded.

"Good. I'm just on my way out for a few minutes, but while you're waiting you can dig around in Claudia's computer and check her notes on the Santa story."

"Oh, I don't know, Iggy. I'd feel funny poking around in somebody else's files without asking first."

"Well, it's hard to ask when she's not here, isn't it? And something just might leap out at you."

"She won't mind," Pete put in. "We're always using each other's notes."

"If I'm not back by the time you finish that," Iggy added as he headed out, "you and Pete start the brainstorming without me."

Mike nodded, thinking his timing couldn't have been better. Now he had a chance to run the Iggy-as-Santa theory by Pete before entirely scrapping it. And it made sense to ask a few questions about Annie, as well.

Not that he'd gotten the sense Claudia and Jack were lying last night. But an incredibly high proportion of the Victoria Falls population *did* seem to be into deception.

After hanging up his parka, Mike sat down at Claudia's desk and switched on her computer. While it was going through its warm-up checks, he swiveled the chair in Pete's direction and said, "Mind if I ask something?"

"Ask away," Pete told him, looking over.

"Is Annie Robidoux involved with anyone?"

"Annie? You're interested in Annie?" The delighted look that appeared on Pete's face reminded Mike the guy had a thing for Claudia.

"Well...no, not interested. Just curious."

The admission clearly wasn't what Pete had hoped to hear, but he simply shrugged and said, "No, she's not going with anyone." Then he turned back to his computer, leaving Mike to come up with a not-too-obvious way of asking about Iggy.

Before he managed to, Pete stopped what he was doing and looked over at him again. "How are you coming with Santa? Iggy says you've ruled out the Nilssons, so who does that leave?"

Mike tried not to grin, but it was tough when he'd just been handed a perfect opening. "Well, I've got an interesting lead. Got it from the Nilssons, in fact."

"Yeah? Who do they figure it is?"

"Well, according to them, it's your uncle."

"Really? Which uncle?"

"Iggy."

Pete didn't reply for a minute, but his expression said he figured Mike was one snowshoe short of a pair.

"Those Nilssons have got a really warped sense of humor," he finally said. "Iggy doesn't have any money to be playing Santa."

"They told me he did."

"Then they're nuts."

"You're sure?"

"Absolutely. Did Iggy happen to mention that his wife, my aunt Alma, had surgery last month?"

"Uh-huh, he said something about it."

"And did he also mention a specialist in Toronto did the operation? That they had to fly down there for it?"

Mike shook his head. "He didn't go into the details."

"Then I guess he didn't tell you he had to borrow fifteen hundred bucks from my father to pay for the plane tickets and hotel. Now does that sound like a man who'd be giving away sleigh loads of presents?"

"Ahh. Since you put it like that, I guess I'd better start looking through Claudia's files."

When that made Pete laugh, Mike turned his chair to face the computer. For a minute, he simply sat staring at the screen saver and thinking back to the earlier part of last night, when he'd asked Claudia if she figured Iggy could possibly be Santa.

She certainly hadn't said he couldn't be. In fact, she'd sounded as if she thought it was worth checking into. But maybe she hadn't heard the story about his borrowing that money. Assuming, of course, Pete hadn't simply made it up. Feeling as if the question of the week was, "Who can you trust?" Mike touched the mouse.

At least, he thought as the Windows program manager screen appeared, Claudia didn't have some weird software he wasn't familiar with. He called up the word processing directory. And just as he'd expected, there was a file named "Santa"—which had to be the one he wanted. But when it popped onto the screen, it wasn't.

Instead of notes for the Santa articles she'd written, the file consisted of a list of names with items beside them.

Susan Abbot, age 8. Dollhouse, animal jigsaw puzzles, sand art kit, hat and scarf—pink.

The next entry was *Brian Benton, age 10. Three-speed bike, fishing rod, any of Dr. Horrific's lab kits except the Brain Juice one.*

Mike stared at that for a second, asking himself what the hell was going on. This was a kids' Christmas wish list.

Scrolling down to the name Nowiki, he read through the items.

Angela Nowiki, age 2, no letter. Maybe stuffed toy, bath toys, big wooden blocks, doll furniture.

Becky Nowiki, age 7. Baby-Walks-and-Talks, finger paints and paper, walkie-talkies.

Tommy Nowiki, age 10. Hockey gloves, Maple Leaf hockey jersey—number 16, radio-controlled racing car (the faster the better).

Vance Nowiki, age 6. Beginner's in-line skates, toboggan, Big-Boy carpenter bench.

"Well, I'll be," he muttered under his breath. He'd seen every one of those items at May Nowiki's house, but when he'd asked Claudia how she figured Santa could have known what the kids wanted, she'd said she didn't have a clue. So how many other things had she been pretending to know nothing about?

He could feel his anger quickly heating to the boiling point. Obviously, she'd been lying to him all along. And that *really* burned him. If she'd been in on her father's plot to throw him off Santa's trail, she was every bit as devious and conniving as Raymond. Hell, for all he knew, it had even been *her* plot. Maybe *she'd* been the one who'd been angry at Iggy for taking the story away from her. So angry that *she'd* decided to make him sweat. If it turned out she *had* been behind the game of making Mike O'Brian look like an idiot, he knew he was going to feel like killing her.

"You say something?" Pete asked.

"Oh, sorry, must have been muttering to myself. I assumed this file called Santa would be the one I was after, but it seems to be a list of what kids want for Christmas."

"Oh, yeah, Claudia's been looking after the letters-to-Santa thing. You know, the kids all write care of the paper, and she supposedly forwards their letters to the North Pole. I think she even got the teachers to make it a project at school."

"But why would she have drawn up a master list of what they want?"

"I... Well, I don't know. I didn't realize she had. Maybe... No," Pete concluded, shaking his head. "You've got me. I don't have a clue why she would."

Mike hesitated. He had no idea whether he could trust Pete any more than he could trust anyone else around here—including, apparently, the woman he'd merrily fallen in love with.

Telling himself he'd worry about that little problem later, he said, "Pete? Would you mind having a look at this list?"

Pete came over from his own desk and glanced at the screen. "What am I looking for?"

"Is this pretty well *all* the local kids? Or only ones from families that were hit by the layoffs?"

"Just the layoffs," he said after Mike had scrolled through about half the names.

"You're positive?"

"Absolutely. Those are all miners' kids. Nobody else's."

Mike spent a minute trying to come up with something significant he might be missing. But since he could think of only one possible reason that list existed, what did he have to lose by filling Pete in on a few of the bits and pieces? Hell, with any luck, Pete would do some filling in of his own.

"You want to hear something interesting?"

"Sure," Pete said.

"Santa delivered to the Nowikis' place the other night, and I got May Nowiki to open the presents he left."

"Yeah?"

"Uh-huh, and they were straight off this list. Every last one of them."

"No bull?"

"No bull."

"You mean you think Claudia . . . ?"

"It looks that way, doesn't it."

"It sure does. She's been helping Santa."

"So who is he?"

Pete grinned, looking as excited as a thirteen-year-old with a new boom box. "Claudia sneaking around helping Santa. I'd never have figured her to do anything like that. But maybe there's some other good stuff in her files. Why don't you start checking them while I look through her desk?"

For half a second, Mike thought about objecting to that invasion of privacy, but it was a very brief half a second. Claudia didn't deserve his looking out for her welfare. Not when she'd been playing games with him from the first minute he'd laid eyes on her.

Pete had already yanked out her top drawer, dumped the contents onto the desk and begun pawing through it. "Not much here except handwritten notes for articles. And a little stack of receipts from Bentley's. Let's see, a pair of slippers, a shirt, something that just says cosmetics—probably all Christmas gifts. Oh, here's a more interesting one. A cell phone. I wonder who she got that for."

"Annie," Mike told him.

"Annie? Annie Robidoux?"

Mike nodded.

"No, it wouldn't be for her. She already has one."

"What? Are you sure?"

"Uh-huh. She's got to make that drive out to the district school every day. And her car's getting pretty old, so she bought a cellular last winter—said it was a lot cheaper than buying a new car."

"Let me look at that receipt, will you?"

Pete handed it over.

"Well, here's something *else* interesting. There's a phone number written on this. Do you figure it's for the cellular? That they wrote it down when they activated the phone?"

"Makes sense to me," Pete said as Mike reached for the phone on the desk.

He carefully punched in the number, wondering if the phone Claudia had bought was actually in that box beneath her tree or if someone was about to answer it. But even if it *was* sitting in her living room, why had she said she'd gotten it for Annie?

Listening to it ring, he pictured Morgan trying to figure out why one of the boxes had started making a noise. Then a man answered, and he stopped imagining the dog.

"Hello?" Mike said. "Who's this?"

"You've got the wrong number," the man told him.

"Oh? Isn't this 555-1629?"

There was a brief pause, then the man said, "No, sorry," and broke the connection.

"A guy," Mike told Pete. "In his thirties, I'd guess."

"So what's the deal? If a man calls, hang up?"

"Could be," Mike said, "but whatever the deal is, I think we've got Santa's number."

"Really? Claudia bought the phone for *him?*"

"I think she must have. She made a list of what he should get for all those kids. And it's suddenly obvious that she's been trying to keep me from tracking him down. Doesn't it make sense that she bought the cellular so they'd be able to keep in touch?"

"But wouldn't he have a regular phone?"

Mike shook his head. "I don't know. Maybe it's not in a private place or... Well, I need more time to think everything through, but there's probably a good reason why they wanted a cellular."

He pressed the redial button, then handed Pete the receiver. "You try him this time. See if you recognize his voice."

This time nobody answered. The number simply kept ringing until they gave up.

"IT LOOKS LIKE the cell phone's our only clue to who Santa is," Pete said.

Mike nodded. He'd checked the rest of Claudia's computer files while Pete had gone through the other drawers in her desk, but they'd turned up nothing else of interest.

"If we went to Bentley's," Pete suggested, "I could probably get them to tell me whose name the phone's in."

"It'll be in Claudia's. She wouldn't go to all this effort to keep Santa's identity a secret, then put the phone in his name."

"Yeah, I guess you're right. So what do we do next?"

"I'll confront her," Mike said. Damned if he was going to pussyfoot around, waiting for a chance to trip her up, when all the while she'd be thinking she was still putting one over on him.

"I'll go straight back to her place from here," he added. "And the minute she walks through the door, I'll nail her to the wall."

"And you figure that'll do it? I mean, like you said, she's gone to a lot of trouble. She might hang tough."

Mike shrugged. "I earn my living getting information that people are trying to keep secret. And if I can't convince *her* to talk, there's always Raymond or Lucille."

"They've been in on things, too?"

"Uh-huh. But listen, don't say a word to Iggy yet, huh? Not about any of this."

When Pete gave him a curious look, he shrugged. He was so damn mad at Claudia for playing him for a fool that he was half inclined to just throw her to the wolves. Or to Iggy, as the case might be. But he'd learned, years ago, never to do anything rash without knowing the whole story.

"If we told your uncle what's been going on," he said to Pete, "he'd be *really* pissed off at Claudia, wouldn't he."

"Yeah, he's getting pretty uneasy about how long it's taking you to ID Santa. So if he knew she... Well, yeah, I think really pissed off would pretty much describe it."

"Then let's wait before we tell him anything. Steamed as I am at her, I'd hate to see anybody get fired right before Christmas."

"Well, I don't know if Iggy'd go *that* far. He might, though."

"Exactly. And even if he didn't, it would cause a lot of conflict and he'd never trust her again. So let's wait until we know what the entire deal is."

"Yeah. I guess that's only fair."

"Okay, good. Now, I'm going to clear out of here before Iggy gets back."

"He's not going to like that. He wants to brainstorm, remember?"

Mike shrugged and got up from the desk. "If we sat around brainstorming and couldn't come up with any suspects, he wouldn't like that, either.

"So," he added, heading over to the coatrack, "just tell him you tried to keep me here but I insisted on leaving. Say I spotted a terrific clue in Claudia's notes or something and said I wanted to follow up on it right away."

"Well . . . okay."

"Great."

"And, Mike? Once you finally learn who Santa is, I guess you'll just bang out the rest of your articles and take off, eh? Head back to L.A.?"

Right. Pete's thing for Claudia. Well, he sure didn't have to worry about competition from Mike O'Brian. Not at this point. Any sane man would run like the wind from a woman who made Mata Hari look like an amateur. A woman who lied with the skill of a psychopath. Hell, for all he knew, she *was* a psychopath.

"Iggy wants me to stay till Saturday," he said, pulling on his parka, "but I expect to be leaving then."

"And in the meantime, you'll let me know what happens when Claudia gets home?"

"Sure. I'll give you a call later." Heading out into the cold, he started back in the direction of Claudia's place, wondering if he'd ever been so thoroughly sucked in before. The only time he could think of was way back when he'd been three years old—when his mother told him that having his tonsils out would be a real treat because they'd give him ice cream afterward.

He'd always figured that was when his suspicious nature had begun to develop. But when it came to Claudia, with her angelic expression and those big, innocent eyes...

Tugging his scarf up over his nose, he tried to figure out why he'd been so damn trusting and how he could have tumbled head over heels for her when that had never happened with any other woman.

He turned off Main onto Claudia's street, remembering that only yesterday he'd been asking himself how he could possibly have fallen in love so fast. It had obviously been a very sensible question, and maybe the fact that he'd asked it meant he hadn't truly fallen in love at all. Maybe he'd only fallen in lust.

He mulled over the possibility. The longer he thought about it, the more likely it seemed. After all, surely he couldn't really be in love with a scheming liar. Regardless of how good she looked and how wonderful she smelled and the fact that her body fit perfectly with his.

Walking on, he felt incredibly relieved to have everything straight in his head. He wasn't actually in love with Claudia, so he had no real problem. Once this week was over, it would be out of sight, out of mind. But since he was so relieved, why did his throat hurt and his chest feel hollow? And even though it was out of the question at this point, why did he still desperately want her to come and visit him in L.A.?

SOMETHING WAS UP with both Iggy and Pete. Claudia could feel it in her bones the whole time she was writing her piece on the house fire in Ville-Marie.

Iggy was hiding out in his office, so mad he'd barely spoken to her when she'd walked in. She couldn't figure out *why* he was angry, though. Not when the one thing he *had* told her was that Mike was off chasing some hot clue—which should have made Iggy happy.

She couldn't figure out what the hot clue might be, either, but she was refusing to worry about it. Without a car, Mike wouldn't be going far enough to turn up anything really significant. And the story about him wrecking Jack's Civic had to be all over town by now, so there wouldn't exactly be a lineup of people willing to lend him wheels.

While she was trying to think of a good final line for the article, she glanced over at Pete—and wondered again what *his* problem was. He was acting as anxious as a kid watching the sky on Christmas Eve. And the minute she'd arrived, he'd wanted to know whether she'd stopped by her house before coming to the paper. It had struck her as a peculiar question, but when she'd asked why he cared, he'd put on an innocent expression and simply said, "No reason."

Turning back to her computer, she typed in a last line she hoped would fly. Then she clicked back to her opening, read through what she'd written and pressed the print command. Iggy only edited from hard copy.

Pete looked over from his desk the instant the printer stopped. "So, you're on your way home now?"

"I guess," she said.

Since Mike was off wherever, following his lead, she had no great urge to get right home. On the other hand, she didn't really want to stick around here when there were so many strange vibes in the air. Plus, she desperately wanted to talk to Santa and Annie—find out exactly what was what. But she could hardly call them from here.

Picking up her article, she took it and the film she'd shot this morning into Iggy's office. That earned her a grunt.

"I got pictures of both the burned-out house and the dispossessed family," she told him. "There's even a shot of a charred teddy bear lying in the snow, so I'm sure there'll be something you'll like."

"What I'd really like," he muttered, "is for you and O'Brian to figure out who Santa is."

"We're working on it, Iggy."

"Yeah, that's his line, too."

When she started to back out of the office, Iggy said, "Close that door behind you, eh?"

She pulled it shut, mouthed "I'm outta here" to Pete, then headed straight for the coatrack. As she was putting on her jacket, the phone rang and Pete grabbed it.

"Just a sec," he said a moment later. "I'll see if she's here. For you," he told her, covering the speaker. "But I don't recognize the voice. Want me to take a message?"

When she nodded, he listened for a minute, then said, "Wait. She just walked in the door."

Covering the speaker again, he added, "It's someone named Beth Robertson from the *Toronto Star*. She says it's urgent she talk to you as soon as possible."

Claudia raced back across the office and took the phone from Pete. "Beth? You found something for me?"

"I sure did. That was a good guess about the insider trading. It turns out Hillstead's vice president of finance has been under investigation by the Securities

Commission. But that's not the biggie. Just listen to this—there's a fire burning out of control at Hill-stead's head offices.''

"You mean right this minute?"

"Yes. And the news crews on the scene are reporting that most of the company's records have gone up in smoke."

"Arson?" Claudia said excitedly.

"I expect. But arson or not, if you're right about somebody fudging those assay reports, and the head office records are toast, the only proof is sitting up there in Victoria Falls."

"Then I *have* to get to the reports."

"Claudia, you have to get to them *fast*. Otherwise, odds are that something will happen to them. It might be too late already."

"What?" Pete demanded as she hung up. "I heard the word arson. Have we got a fire?"

"No, not here. There's an out-of-control fire at Hillstead's head offices. But, look, I don't have time to go into details. I've got to get to the mine offices right now."

"There's no one there. The place is shut down tight for the holidays."

"I know, but... Oh, when Iggy shows his face, just tell him to hold tomorrow's front page until he hears from me. This might be nothing, but it might be an incredible story."

CHAPTER FOURTEEN

"WELL, MORGAN?" MIKE SAID, turning away from the living room window and looking at the dog. "Where on earth is she? She's been gone long enough to drive to this Ville-Marie place and back three times."

Morgan offered a few thumps of his tail in reply.

"Damn," Mike muttered, glancing out the window again. She had him so upset he was expecting answers from a dog. But who wouldn't be upset?

He gazed over toward the tree, at the shoe box that had supposedly held Annie's cellular. Actually, it contained a pair of fluffy blue slippers.

And the story about that phone had been only one in a whole string of lies. Claudia had layered falsehoods on top of half truths on top of total fabrications he should have seen right through. And he probably would have if his emotions hadn't blinded him. And if she hadn't had so many people helping her.

Hell, never mind a Santa caper, this was a full-blown Santa conspiracy. He'd bet even Wayne Greenaway was in on things. And that those blank assay forms were nothing but a figment of Claudia's imagination. The big investigation she'd asked for help with had been just another ploy to keep Mike O'Brian from catching up with Santa—for whatever reason.

Of course, he was pretty sure he had things figured out. Santa wanted to remain anonymous. And Claudia had been helping him do that because she was in love with him. Whoever he was, she loved him so much she'd used every trick she could think of to protect him. Including sleeping with the enemy.

That, Mike thought, wearily shaking his head, hurt worse than anything else. He'd figured she was falling in love with him, but she'd merely been acting. She'd only made love with him to help another man.

After staring out at the street for a little longer, he checked his watch once more. He was growing more certain by the minute that she'd been in an accident. And even though he knew he was an idiot to worry about her after all she'd done, he couldn't make himself stop. Finally, he fished Iggy's card out of his wallet, picked up the phone and dialed the paper.

"Dispatch," Pete answered.

"It's Mike O'Brian, Pete. Claudia's not there, is she?"

"She was, but she left fifteen or twenty minutes ago."

"Fifteen or twenty minutes?" he repeated uneasily. The paper was about a four-minute drive away. "Then why isn't she home by now?"

"She wasn't heading for home. She had a call from some reporter in Toronto. She's gone after a lead."

"To Hillstead?"

"Yeah, how'd you know?"

"It's not important. But she went alone?"

"Uh-huh."

"Pete, what did that reporter say? Do you know?"

"Not all of it. But apparently there's a fire burning at Hillstead's headquarters down in Toronto. And for some reason Claudia decided she had to get to the mine offices right away. I told her they were closed, but she took off, anyway.''

"There must be at least a watchman there, mustn't there?"

"No, this isn't the big city. We don't have any problems with vandals. And there's nothing of value up there. I mean, we're just talking admin offices, not an operating mine site."

Mike realized his heart was pounding and tried telling himself Claudia would be fine. But he wasn't a hundred percent sure of that. It sounded as if those assay forms weren't a figment of her imagination, after all. If she figured she had to get to Hillstead right away, she had to be hoping to beat someone else there.

He hesitated for half a second, then said, "Pete, can I borrow your car?"

"You mean now?"

"Yes."

"Sorry, no can do. Iggy's got a story for me to cover. I was just about to leave when you called."

"Look, this could be really important, so how about telling Iggy—"

"Mike, *I'm* the one who had to tell Iggy you'd gone off chasing a clue instead of sticking around to brainstorm—which did *not* please him. And at the moment he's holed up in his office like a bear in a cave, so trying to tell him anything would be worth my life."

"Then let me talk to him."

"He's on the other line."

"Then interrupt him, okay? Maybe I can use his Chevy."

"Uh-uh. It wouldn't start this morning. But why don't you check out Earl's garage?"

"Yeah, good idea." Swearing to himself, Mike hung up. He didn't have the time to argue with Pete or Iggy or to check out anything. Not if his gut feeling was right.

Jamming his hands into the pockets of his jeans, he reminded himself that Claudia was the most deceitful woman he'd ever had the misfortune to meet. And that she'd done nothing but lie to him and lead him down dead ends. And that she was in love with another man. So even if something *did* happen to her...

"Damn," he muttered. Whether he liked it or not, he knew that if anything happened to her, it would haunt him for the rest of his life.

THE DRIVE TO HILLSTEAD had given Claudia a chance to think things through carefully, checking for possible flaws in her logic. But by the time she turned into the long driveway leading to the mining offices, she'd decided that everything Beth had told her fit in with the hypothesis she and Mike had touched on last night—that those blank assay forms were part of a scheme to manipulate Hillstead share prices.

The Securities Commission's investigation certainly supported that theory. And assuming the fire in Toronto really was the work of an arsonist, it must have been set to take care of the records there.

So, if Wayne *had* been forging Coply Lab reports, the records here were the only remaining proof of it. Of course, he might already have destroyed anything incriminating. But if the reports were still in his files, she had to get at them now because they wouldn't be there for long.

After driving around the entire exterior of the building, satisfying herself that nobody else was there, she parked by the rear door. Wayne's office was near the *front* door, of course, but there was no way she was going to try to get in the side of the building that was visible from the road.

Climbing out of the Cherokee, she slung her purse over her shoulder. Then, her heart in her throat, she approached the door and stood staring at it.

It was metal—probably solid steel—and windowless. She took a credit card out of her wallet and tried wiggling it between the door frame and the lock. Effective as that was in the movies, it got her nowhere. And when the nail file she tried next didn't work, either, she decided she might have to smash a window.

She found one about halfway along the building that was low to the ground. Luckily, it proved to be the window of the staff kitchen, not a storage area that might be locked from the outside.

Carefully pulling the sleeve of her jacket down over her mitt, she made a fist, assuring herself she couldn't possibly get cut through all that fabric. Then she hesitated. Nobody around here ever bothered locking up at home. And even in the dead of winter, people sometimes opened a window for a breath of fresh air. So just maybe...

Sure enough, the window opened. Telling herself that was a good omen, Claudia wriggled inside, then slid the window down again and quickly started for Wayne Greenaway's office.

Not much daylight reached the hallways, and the empty building seemed incredibly spooky. But the last thing she wanted was company, so she did her best to ignore the way her heart was hammering and simply hurried to her destination.

There was a photocopier in the reception area outside Wayne's office, and seeing it gave her pause. Once she found those reports, should she just take them and run? Or would it be smarter to make copies so Wayne wouldn't realize anyone was on to him?

She remembered Chet once telling her that it gave the police an advantage if a suspect wasn't aware they were building a case against him. With that in mind, she turned on the copier. Then, praying Wayne's door wasn't locked, she tried it. The handle turned, the door opened, and she breathed a sigh of relief—only to discover, seconds later, that both his filing cabinet and desk *were* locked.

Think, she told herself. Almost everybody keeps a set of spare keys around. So where would his be?

She looked in every likely place in the office without finding them. Next, she tried the *unlikely* places. When that produced nothing, she began to panic. Forcing herself to look around slowly, hoping to spot something she'd missed, she noticed the receptionist's desk beyond the open doorway.

Heading back out of the office she hit pay dirt. In the back of the receptionist's top drawer were three keys on a ring with a tag that read Mr. G.'s Office.

Grabbing them, she raced into the office again and unlocked the filing cabinet. There were all kinds of assay reports in it, but the most recent ones were a year old. She needed the latest ones, the ones management would have been basing its decisions on for the past few months. Had they already been destroyed?

She tried the desk next, and when she opened the top drawer her pulse jumped. Wayne had a gun in there, a little silver automatic. She eyed it curiously for a moment. A lot of people in the area owned rifles for hunting, her father included. But with Canada's strict gun laws, there were very few handguns around. Maybe wandering onto the wrong side of the law had turned Wayne into the nervous type.

Closing the top drawer, she opened the bottom one—and found what she was looking for. Feeling weak with relief, she took the little stack of assay reports from the drawer. Now all she had to do was copy them and she could get out of here.

But just as she was pushing back the chair, someone said, "What the hell do you think you're doing?"

IT HAD TAKEN MIKE a little longer than he'd hoped to get to Hillstead on Claudia's snowmobile. He'd thought he remembered exactly where to turn, but he'd cut off the main road too soon and it had cost him time.

Swinging into the driveway, he began breathing more easily. Up ahead, he could see Wayne Greenaway's red Blazer, but there was no sign of the Jeep. Which had to mean—whatever had transpired— Claudia had been and gone.

Just as he was about to pull a U-turn and leave, something told him not to be too hasty. He drove along the side of the building, and there it was in the back lot. Claudia's Cherokee.

Parking beside it, he tugged off his helmet. Then he ran to the back door and gave it a yank, swearing when he discovered it was locked. He started jogging along the back of the building, looking for a way in.

Claudia must have broken a window or something, but since he didn't see any sign of that, he kept moving—up the side of the building and across the front, his head lowered so nobody would see him from inside.

She'd told him her source had just slipped in the front door the other night, that Greenaway hadn't locked it while he was in there working. With any luck, he hadn't locked it today, either.

Reaching the front steps, Mike walked quietly up them and tentatively pulled on the door—then thanked the powers that be when it opened.

Once inside, he started silently to his right, which led him to a reception area, quiet except for the hum of a photocopier. Above that, he could hear the murmur of voices coming through an open office door. Claudia's voice. And Greenaway's. But he couldn't make out the words.

Cautiously, he edged closer until he could see in. And what he saw stopped him in his tracks. He'd never met a woman half as full of surprises as Claudia, but this one took the cake. She was standing behind the desk, pointing a pistol at Greenaway.

Since the side of the desk was parallel to the door, neither of them was going to notice Mike unless they broke eye contact with each other. From the looks of things, that wouldn't be happening for a while, so he merely stood there and waited for the scene to play out. After all, Claudia was in no danger. She had the gun.

"Okay, look," Greenaway was saying, "we're *both* in big trouble if anybody learns about this."

"I don't think so," Claudia told him.

"No? Well in case it hasn't occurred to you, I can have you charged with breaking and entering. Plus espionage or something for snooping through private company files. You'd end up in jail."

"Possibly. But not for nearly as long as you're going to. Why did you do it, Wayne? Just for the money?"

He shrugged. "Not exactly. I got an offer I couldn't refuse. Either I went along with the scheme or I was going to be out and somebody more cooperative would be in."

"Then the prosecutors probably won't be as tough on you. In fact, why don't we call the police right now? If you explain you were forced into this, and hand over the files voluntarily, you'll be in a far better position."

"Well ... You know, maybe you're right. Maybe that *would* be the smartest thing."

Suddenly, Mike's adrenaline began pumping like crazy. Something had crept into Greenaway's tone that was setting off alarm bells. But just as he began moving, Greenaway threw himself across the desk at Claudia.

In the seconds it took to reach them, Greenaway had wrenched the gun from her hand.

"All right," he snarled, oblivious to Mike's presence. "Let's reconsider things."

Mike didn't waste any time. Grabbing Greenaway's arm and forcing it to the side, he slammed the guy's hand against the desk. Greenaway screamed; the gun went flying. And while Claudia scrambled to her feet and raced to pick it up, Mike jammed his knee into the small of the other man's back, flattening him to the floor.

"Now," he said. "Claudia came here after a story. And if you're prepared to give her some juicy details, I'm prepared not to break any bones."

ONTARIO PROVINCIAL Police Constable Harry Charlton glanced across Greenaway's office at his partner—who Mike had decided should be named Silent Sam.

When Sam nodded, Charlton closed his notebook. "All right," he said, "We seem to have all we need from you two. But it's sure a lucky thing you decided to come and talk to Greenaway, Claudia."

She nodded. "As I said earlier, I didn't know for sure he'd be here, but after that call from Toronto, I thought it was worth a shot."

"Well, it's sure a lucky thing," Charlton said again. "Otherwise, these assay reports would have disappeared. And hell, Greenaway might have been on his way to South America by now."

It was also a lucky thing, Mike couldn't help thinking, that Harry Charlton happened to be an old schoolmate of Claudia's. Otherwise, he and his partner might not have been so quick to accept Mike and Claudia's version of how the events had unfolded. Especially not when they'd concocted their story in about two minutes' worth of whispers while they were holding Greenaway at gunpoint and waiting for the OPP to arrive.

But the constables seemed quite content to believe that both reporters had arrived after Greenaway was already here, that Claudia had simply walked in the unlocked front door and discovered him with the files.

"Harry?" she said.

Charlton looked at her.

"Wayne Greenaway's going to get a serious jail term, isn't he?"

"Definitely. Why?"

"Oh, I was just thinking about Maureen and the kids. It'll be so hard on them, and they had nothing at all to do with what he was up to."

"She's got her family," Charlton said. "And her old man's pretty well off. They'll be okay."

"I didn't mean financially. I meant . . . It'll just be awfully tough."

When Charlton merely shrugged, Mike said, "Stuff happens, Claudia. Maybe not up here very often, but stuff happens all the time. And innocent people get hurt. There's nothing you can do about it."

"I guess," she murmured. But his philosophizing obviously hadn't made her feel any better.

"You know, Claudia," Charlton said, "getting back to what happened here, there's one more thing I'm curious about."

Mike held his breath, sensing the old Columbo trick was coming.

"What's that?" she asked.

"Why did you and O'Brian park around back?"

Mike swore under his breath. He'd forgotten all about that minor detail. They should have moved the Jeep and snowmobile around to the front before they even called the police.

"Well," Claudia said, "as we explained, I'd asked Mike to meet me here. But when I arrived first and there was only Wayne's Blazer out front . . . Oh, you know how people love to gossip, Harry. So maybe it was silly, but I thought, what if somebody drives by and sees Wayne's Blazer and my Jeep parked out there when they know the offices are closed?"

Harry grinned. "Right. I figured you'd have a good explanation. But why," he asked, glancing at Mike, "did you leave the snowmobile back there?"

"Because that's where the Jeep was," he said as smoothly as he could. "When I first arrived, I didn't think Claudia was here yet, so I drove around back to have a look at the property. Then, once I realized she *was* here, I parked beside her. We were going to be coming out together, so it only made sense."

"Ahh," Harry said, nodding slowly. "That must be everything, then."

"Would you mind if I make one quick call before we leave?" Claudia said. "I have to tell Iggy I've got a major story—I know he'll want to clear the front page for it."

Picking up the phone, she looked at Mike. "I'll be bumping the famous Mike O'Brian to page two," she teased. Then she gave him such a sweet smile his chest hurt.

She didn't know yet that he was on to her. That he'd discovered how she'd schemed and lied. He hadn't had a chance to confront her, because they hadn't been alone for even a second. But they'd almost reached the moment of truth. As soon as they got out of here, he'd tell her he knew what she'd been up to and ask the sixty-four-thousand-dollar question.

Who was she in love with, and why had she done everything in her power to help him keep his identity a secret?

Watching her talk animatedly to Iggy, Mike wished he could make himself hate her. But despite everything, he merely had to look at her to feel warm inside. He knew he could tell himself he didn't really love her until he was blue in the face, but it still wouldn't be the truth.

She didn't love him, though. So, come Saturday, he'd leave Victoria Falls behind and start trying to forget her.

As Harry Charlton and Silent Sam pulled away, Claudia and Mike started for the back parking lot. The minute they got around the side of the building, she stopped and smiled an invitation. "Hold me?"

For a second, she thought something was dreadfully wrong. Then he wrapped his arms around her and pulled her close. She snuggled against the cold fabric of his snowmobile suit and hugged him hard, so full of love she could hardly keep it all inside.

"For old time's sake," he said against her hair.

"What?"

She looked up at him, and then she *knew* something was wrong.

He let his arms drop to his sides and took a backward step.

"Mike? What is it?"

"It's that I'm a lot closer to the truth than I was last night, Claudia. This morning, I talked to Santa on the phone. Just called him up at 555-1629 and said hello. So I know you really bought that cellular for *him*. And I know you've had the whole town trying to make a fool of me from the moment I arrived."

"Oh, Lord," she murmured. Her stomach was suddenly in knots, her heart was racing and she felt icy cold. She also felt like crying, because it was obvious he was every bit as angry as she'd known he'd be.

"Mike, *nobody's* been trying to make a fool of you. Especially not me."

"Oh? Then what do you call it?"

She shook her head, not wanting to meet his eyes. They were usually full of warmth, but at the moment they were hard blue steel. And she was terrified that meant her lies had destroyed his feelings for her.

"I was only trying to keep you away from Santa," she whispered. "But... Why did you come after me when you knew?"

"I owed you one, remember?"

"No," she said, blinking back tears.

"Yesterday. When you volunteered to bring the tree in out of the cold, you said I owed you one. And I hate owing people."

"Oh, Mike, that isn't even a little bit funny."

"Well, I'm not in a very humorous mood. But at least we're even now."

"Even? I brought in a Christmas tree and you saved my life."

He didn't reply for a minute, then said, "I might have. So maybe you'd like to finally let me in on who Santa is."

Her heart began to race even faster. She wanted to tell him the entire story, but that meant trusting him to help keep the secret, when only yesterday he'd said he was determined to give Iggy a picture of Santa to splash across the front page.

She loved Mike, though. Desperately. And surely she could never have fallen in love with a man she couldn't trust.

"Are you going to tell me or not?" he pressed.

"First," she said slowly, "I want to tell you something else. I don't normally lie. Or deceive people. But it was just so important that you not find out who Santa was."

"Why?"

"Because if you tell the world who he is, his life will be in danger. I mean, it's already in danger, but if certain people know where he is, if they can pick up his trail..."

"What is he? A criminal?"

"No." She took a deep breath and made her decision. "His name is Dennis. And he's my brother."

CHAPTER FIFTEEN

FOR A LONG MINUTE, Mike simply stared at Claudia.

His first thought was that it was her *brother* she loved so much. And that was wonderful news.

His second thought was that she didn't have a brother. So dammit to hell! She was lying to him again.

"I know you had the impression I was an only child," she said before he could open his mouth to accuse her.

"I had the *impression?* That's what you told me!"

"I didn't *exactly* tell you. I just didn't correct you when you made that assumption, because I realized that if you even knew Dennis existed, you might put two and two together."

"And you didn't figure anyone else would mention him?"

"Nobody did, did they."

"Well...no."

"That's because he's been gone from Victoria Falls for a long time—since way back when our mother died. He took it awfully hard, was in really rough shape for weeks after it happened. Then, one day, he just up and left."

"And never came back?"

Claudia shook her head. "He traveled around for a couple of years, doing odd jobs, then ended up in

Florida. Dad and I have visited him there, but he's never come home before. At any rate, because he'd been gone so long, we figured that with luck nobody would bring up his name. So we stashed away our pictures of him and—"

"We?"

"Dad and Lucille and I."

"Those photographs in your basement? Of you and Annie and some guy? That was your brother?"

"You saw them?"

He nodded. "The carton was open and "

"It was?"

"Yes, but never mind that. Who else was in on this? Aside from Annie and the Nilssons and Earl and—"

"Nobody. None of them. Only Dad and Lucille and me. I mean, Dad asked Earl to do what he could to keep you from getting a car. And he got the Nilssons to run you around in circles. But none of them know Dennis is here. They all thought Dad's agenda was exactly what he told them—just to give Iggy a hard time for taking the Santa story away from me.

"As for Annie, remember I told you she was madly in love with somebody back in high school?"

"Dennis?" Mike guessed. "He's the one who left and never came back? But why?"

"Oh, a lot of reasons. Partly because there wasn't really anything for him to do here. Nothing he wanted to do, at least. But in Florida he got a job taking tourists out deep-sea fishing, which he loved. He said it was like a permanent vacation.

"So he was down there and Annie was away at university. Then, as time passed, he got it into his head that he wasn't good enough for her. He convinced himself that if she ever spent any time with him again, she'd realize that. So, illogical as it was, he finally cut off what little contact they'd maintained.''

"But he still loved her?''

"I'm sure he did. I think there was more pride involved than anything else. The few times I tried talking to him about it, he asked what a French teacher would want with a guy who bummed around in a boat all day, barely making enough to support himself, let alone a family. And I guess the longer he was away...

"Oh, I didn't always understand how his mind worked. But getting back to the present, he called a few weeks ago, right out of the blue, saying he was in trouble and needed help. And he made us promise not to tell Annie he was here. I think he was afraid to face her after all those years. Afraid he was still in love with her but it was far too late for them.''

"Then how does last night figure in?''

Claudia shook her head. "I have no idea. I haven't talked to either of them since.''

"All right, tell me the rest of the story about why he's hiding out. No, wait. Before you explain any more, you *are* telling me the truth now, aren't you? You've told me so damn many lies that—''

"I'm sorry about that, Mike. More sorry than I can say. I didn't want to lie to you. Not after I started getting to know you. But you kept talking about how you *had* to ID Santa and how you just *couldn't* let him best you and... And yes, I *am* telling the truth now.''

"Why?''

"Because I can't lie to you any longer. And because I've come to know you well enough that I trust you to do what's right—not to put Dennis's safety in jeopardy.''

He waited, willing her to say, *And because I love you*. She didn't, though, so he said, "I wouldn't put your brother's safety in jeopardy."

"I know. But I wasn't sure enough of it before. I was afraid you'd care more about getting your story than anything else."

"That doesn't say much for me, does it. I do have *some* integrity, you know."

"Of course I know—now. But all I knew at first was that you have a reputation for going after a story like a fox after a rabbit and for not giving up until you expose whatever it is you set out to investigate."

"All right," he said slowly. "I guess it makes sense that you wouldn't trust me at first."

"It does? Then you don't hate me?"

"No, I don't hate you. In fact . . ."

"In fact?" she whispered.

He hesitated, but one of them had to say it first. "In fact, I love you, Claudia Paquette."

She smiled one of those smiles that lit up her entire face. Then she wrapped her arms around his neck and kissed him until he thought she was never going to stop—which was the most appealing prospect he'd faced in his entire life.

Eventually, she drew away a little and smiled at him once more. "I'm glad you love me, Mike O'Brian. Very glad. Because I love you, too."

"What a terrific coincidence," he murmured, pulling her close again.

"But you know what's going to happen if we keep this up?"

"Absolutely. I'm just not sure we should let it happen out here where it's forty below."

She laughed at that—a laugh that reminded him of silver bells.

"No," she finally said, "not *that*. What would happen is our lips would freeze together."

"I can think of worse fates."

"But I wouldn't be able to finish the story."

"Ahh. Well, I suppose I *would* like to hear the rest of it."

"Fine. Then before we both end up with frostbite, I want you to follow me somewhere."

For half a second he drew a blank—then remembered they had both the snowmobile and the Jeep. "Follow you where? Back to town so you can write your lead for Iggy?"

"No, Iggy can wait."

"Then?"

"I want to take you to meet my brother. It's *his* story, so you might as well hear the rest of it from him. Besides, after last night, I'm just dying to know where things stand with him and Annie."

THEIR DESTINATION proved to be a large rustic cabin on a frozen lake. It was isolated, but obviously occupied.

The road in had been roughly plowed, there was smoke coming from the chimney, and Mike caught a glimpse of a man's face at a window before it quickly disappeared.

Parked outside were a truck, a snowmobile—complete with sled—and a snowplow.

Mike climbed off Claudia's snowmobile as she got out of the Jeep. "This is where Dennis is staying?"

She nodded. "It's the family cottage. We normally never use it in winter, but the odds of anyone coming by are almost nil, so it was the safest place we could think of."

"And the truck?" he said. "Should I assume it's the one your father bought from Earl? The one that was supposedly Lucille's Christmas present?"

Claudia smiled. "Very good. Do you want to try for another one?" she added, gesturing toward the snow-mobile.

"Lucille's?"

"Give the man a cigar. And the snowplow's borrowed from Earl's."

As Claudia finished speaking, the cabin door opened partway and an extremely nervous-looking Annie poked her head out.

"Claudia? Mike? What are you doing here?"

"We came to talk to Dennis," Claudia explained, taking Mike's hand and starting for the door.

"Dennis? Dennis who?"

"It's okay, Annie, Mike knows. And everything's fine. He's not going to say a word."

"Claudia?" she said, looking more worried than convinced. "Are you sure you know what you're doing?"

"Yes. So can we come in before you let *all* the heat escape?"

At that, the door opened more widely and the man from the photograph wrapped his arm around Annie, shifting her away from the door.

When Mike and Claudia hurried in out of the cold, Dennis gave his sister a quick hug, then extended his hand to Mike.

"If Claudia says I can trust you, that's good enough for me."

Dennis had a firm handshake and a broad smile that made Mike like him immediately.

"I told Mike you'd fill him in on why you're here," Claudia explained.

"You haven't already told him?"

"No, we've been too busy catching crooks. You were right about Wayne Greenaway being up to no good."

"Oh?" Dennis said. "Then let's all sit down," he suggested, indicating the couches on either side of the fireplace. "I want to hear the details."

The heat from the fire made Mike realize just how cold he was. But by the time Claudia had filled the others in, it had warmed him to his toes.

"Do you think," Annie demanded the moment Claudia finished, "that Wayne would have actually killed you?"

"I don't know. But for those few seconds before I realized Mike was there, I was more frightened than I've ever been. It's your turn now, though," she said to Dennis. "Tell Mike why you had to hide out."

"And I'd kind of like to know why you've been playing Santa, too," Mike told him.

"Well, that's the simplest part of the story, so why don't I start there."

"I'm just going to put on some water for coffee," Annie said. "I've heard all this," she added, heading for the kitchen.

Dennis followed her with his eyes until she disappeared, then turned back. "Well, like Claudia said, I had to hide out, which meant I was all alone and getting more bored by the minute. So what with the mine layoffs, the Santa idea just seemed like a real kick."

"Dennis has *always* been one for real kicks," Annie put in, reappearing from the kitchen.

"I promise you, hon," he said, draping his arm over her shoulders when she sat down again, "I'm not nearly as bad as I used to be."

"Oh? Then why didn't you stop delivering presents after Mike arrived? It couldn't have been because you still love playing with fire, could it?"

"Well, maybe just a little. But it was mostly because of what I told Claudia. When we heard for sure that Mike was coming, I'd only delivered to half the families on my list. How could I have stopped then?"

"You're just as impossible as ever, Dennis, you know that?" Annie told him, smiling.

"What Annie means," Claudia explained, "is the whole time we were growing up Dennis was in and out of trouble."

"Hey, I wasn't Billy the Kid or anything," he protested.

"You were *definitely* Dennis the Menace, though," Annie teased.

"Ah, come on. I was just a bit of a hell-raiser. But let's not get into the story of my ill-spent youth when I haven't even finished telling Mike about the Santa thing.

"As I said," he continued, "it gave me something to do. Claudia got me the list of what the kids wanted, and I made a few shopping trips."

"But if you were supposed to be staying out of sight...?" Mike said.

"I went to stores in Timmins and North Bay, where I didn't know many people even ten years ago. And I wore a balaclava. One clerk thought I'd come in to rob them, but aside from that everything went fine."

"Somebody took you for a robber?" Claudia demanded. "You didn't tell me that. What if they'd called the police and—"

"They didn't," Dennis said, grinning. "Now, don't interrupt or I'll never get to the part about why I'm hiding out."

"And don't forget the part about how Annie ended up here last night," Claudia told him.

There were a few seconds of silence, then both Annie and Dennis started to laugh. "We wondered how long you'd be able to keep from asking about that," Annie said.

"Well, it wasn't as long as I'd hoped. But since it slipped out..." Claudia glanced at Mike. "Can you wait another minute or two for the hiding-out part?"

"Sure. I'm not the one who has to get back to write Iggy's lead."

"So?" she said, turning to Annie again.

Annie shrugged. "About three-thirty last night I heard a noise outside. And when I looked out, there was Santa coming up my front steps."

"After I made my final delivery," Dennis said, "I had a hamper left over. So I decided I'd leave it at Annie's."

"That was the only reason you went there?" Claudia asked, sounding decidedly skeptical.

"Tell her the whole truth," Annie ordered. "Tell her about the picture."

"What picture?" Claudia demanded.

Dennis suddenly looked sheepish. "I don't know quite what happened, but being back here..."

"He got obsessed with the idea of seeing me again," Annie explained. "But he was still being so damn idiotic that he decided he'd make do with a picture.

That's what he was doing in your house, Claudia. He knew you'd have pictures of me, so he was looking for one and—"

"He mugged me," Mike interrupted. "I'd forgotten about that, but you're the one who conked me over the head, Dennis!"

"Well...yeah. I'm really sorry, Mike. If there'd been any other way of handling it..."

"He forgives you," Claudia said.

"Yeah. I guess," Mike said reluctantly. "No hard feelings."

"Great," Dennis said. "Anyway, getting back to last night, I decided to leave the extra hamper for Annie."

"He couldn't make himself stay away from me any longer," she put in.

"Maybe," he admitted. "At any rate, I wasn't exactly sure which house was hers. Claudia had told me where she was living," he explained to Mike, "but it was too dark to see the house number from the driveway. And when I went up onto the porch to check it, Annie opened the door."

"The ironic thing," she interjected, "is that I did it for you, Mike. I decided I'd just take him by surprise and pull down his beard so we'd know who he was. But then, when I did—"

"She was the one who got the *real* surprise," Dennis concluded.

"So what now?" Claudia asked.

The way Annie and Dennis looked at each other, the answer seemed pretty obvious.

ANNIE WENT TO GET the coffee as Dennis began talking about why he'd had to flee Florida.

By the time she brought it into the main room he'd explained that a few weeks back, a couple of guys he'd pegged as lowlifes had chartered his boat for a morning of fishing.

"Anyway," he continued as Annie sat down beside him once more, "they made me uneasy because they kept their jackets on all morning, even though it got pretty warm. It made me figure they must be packing heat. But things went okay. They caught a couple of big fish, so they were happy. And when we got back to port, I said I'd help them carry their gear to the parking lot."

"That was your mistake," Annie said.

Dennis nodded. "It sure was. Because when we got to their car, there were two other characters waiting for them. They said something about wanting to talk, but the next thing I knew my guys had guns out. And they didn't waste any time talking—just emptied their clips into the other two.

"Then one of them said to his buddy, 'Hey, we don't want no witness,' and the next thing I knew, they were both looking at me and reloading. I took off like a bat out of hell."

"They shot at him, though," Claudia said quietly. "If he hadn't been lucky, they'd have killed him."

"Well, they didn't," Dennis said. "But I knew they'd have no trouble tracking me down, so I headed straight to my apartment and packed my bags. I figured I had to buy myself time. I mean, I realize the right thing to do is tell the police what I know and eventually go back to testify, but it seemed ludicrous to hang around with those guys looking for me."

"You'd be in danger if you went back," Annie said anxiously.

"Not necessarily. Not as long as the cops have already arrested them."

"And as long as they don't have a dozen friends who'd be happy to kill you if you showed your face," Claudia said.

"I know," Dennis agreed. "I know I've got to think things through carefully. But where was I with the story?"

"You'd gone back to your apartment and packed," Mike told him.

"Oh, right. Okay, then I headed for the airport, and that's where this gets really unbelievable. Once I'd arranged for a flight, I bought a paper. Just to hide behind, really. But the numbers from the state lottery were in there, so I checked my ticket. And damned if I hadn't won."

"Almost thirty million dollars," Annie said.

"Thirty million?" Mike repeated.

Dennis nodded. "I figured that was worth the risk of sticking around for a few more hours. After all, the last place those guys would be looking for me was the lottery office, so I went and claimed my prize. By the time film of the most recent happy winner was rolling on the evening news, I was thirty-five thousand feet over North Carolina."

"Do you understand now, Mike?" Claudia said, taking his hand. "You see why I was so afraid to tell you the truth? If you'd identified Dennis in your series, if his name, let alone his picture, had ended up in all of Ferris Wentworth's papers, especially the Florida one, those killers would have known where he was."

"But if that had happened," Dennis said, "I'd have left here right away."

"They'd have had a fresh trail to follow, though," Claudia told him. "You *do* see, Mike?" she added.

"Yeah, I see." But he couldn't help wondering how much *they* actually saw. Whether they really figured Dennis was perfectly safe here as long as his picture didn't end up in the news.

"Did you use your real name when you bought your plane ticket, Dennis?" he said.

"I had to. I knew I'd need identification to get into Canada. But I covered my tracks. I flew from Florida to Montreal. Then I bought a ticket as Fred Brown and flew to North Bay. Once I got there, I called Dad and he picked me up. So even if those two came after me, there's no way they'd know I ever left Montreal."

Mike hesitated, not certain how much he should say. Both Claudia and Annie already looked terribly anxious.

"Mike?" Claudia said, eyeing him. "You think they could track him here, don't you."

"Well, finding out this is his hometown wouldn't be that tough." Actually, of course, it would be a piece of cake. "And a hometown is an obvious place to look."

"It's been weeks," Dennis said. "If they were coming they'd have come by now."

"Maybe, but you can't count on people like that always doing the expected. So, if I were you, I'd think about taking off. If you like, I can call a fellow who's a genius at helping people disappear. Then, once you're someplace safe, you can deal with the Florida police from there—through the smartest lawyer you can find."

"Dennis?" Annie said. "What do you think?"

"It's a good idea," Claudia told him.

He nodded slowly, then reached over to where the cellular was sitting and passed it to Mike. "I'd guess I'd better talk to your friend."

Mike dug his notebook from his pocket, and as he was checking for the number, Dennis said to Annie, "Wherever I go, would you come with me? Now that I've got all that money?"

"It was never money I cared about," she said so quietly Mike could barely hear her.

"But you won't let it *keep* you from coming with me, will you?"

She gave him a teasing smile and said, "What about all the kids who expect Mademoiselle Robidoux back to teach them after the Christmas break?"

"What about if I donate some money to the school?" Dennis replied, grinning at her. "Enough that your principal can fly a dozen French teachers over from Paris?"

TWILIGHT WAS FALLING by the time Claudia pulled up in front of her house, and Mike was already there waiting—nonchalantly leaning against the snowmobile. He'd only trailed the Jeep for a few miles after they left the cabin, then he'd taken off cross-country.

"You," she said as he climbed into the Cherokee beside her, "are an absolute speed demon on that thing."

He gave her such a hot kiss it made her pulse race, then said, "I've been here long enough to let Morgan out and back in, have a coffee and vacuum your whole house."

"You didn't really vacuum the house."

"No, but I had time to."

"Very funny," she told him, starting down the street.

As she turned left onto Main, he said, "Aren't we heading straight to the paper? It's almost dark. Iggy must be wondering where the hell you are."

"Well, he'll have to wonder for a little longer. He doesn't *really* have to put the paper to bed till midnight, and I want to give my father and Lucille an update before I do anything else. They're just going to be so, so happy to hear they can stop worrying about Dennis."

And *she* was so, so happy, she thought, glancing at Mike, that things were fine between *them*.

He caught her looking and smiled, which made her even happier.

"You don't think Dennis will have called them?" he asked.

"No, I'm certain Annie won't let him tie up the phone for a second. Not until that friend of yours has gotten in touch. But when do you think he'll get your message?"

"Oh, this guy's always right on top of things, so I'll bet he phones your brother within an hour or two. Dennis and Annie will probably be gone by morning."

"And even *we* won't know where they are?"

"That's the whole point. *Nobody* will. Only temporarily, though."

"Good. I'd hate to think of them having to hide out forever."

She turned onto her father's street, then said, "But now that you've met both of them . . ."

"What?"

"Oh, I don't know. It's just that I almost can't believe they're back together. And you saw the way they are. They've both changed over the years, yet they still seem so..."

"Right?" Mike said as she pulled into the driveway.

She cut the engine, turned off the headlights, then glanced at him again. The look in his eyes started her heart hammering.

"Yes...right for each other," she agreed. "As if there could never be anyone else in the world for either of them."

"Maybe there isn't. Do you think that's the way it is with some people? That they go along for ages and ages not falling in love because they haven't met the right person?"

"I think it happens," she said quietly.

Mike reached for her hands. "I do, too. And I think that when you *do* meet the right person, you have to make sure they don't slip out of your life again."

She breathlessly waited for him to go on, but instead of saying more, he took her face in his hands and kissed her. A long, sweet kiss full of promises.

When it finally ended, he said, "You're still going to come and visit me in L.A.?"

"If you still want me to."

"Well, actually, I've been thinking I'd prefer more than just a visit."

"Oh?" she said, dreadfully afraid he didn't mean what she was praying he did.

He kissed her once more, then whispered, "Marry me, Claudia?"

She tried to say yes, but her throat was so tight not even one word would come out.

"Oh, I know it's awfully fast," he murmured against her hair, "but if I go back home and you're way up here..."

"And falling in love at first sight," she managed to say, "runs in your family. So it would make more sense to worry if it *hadn't* happened fast. Right?"

Drawing back a little, he grinned at her. "Is that a yes?"

"Yes, it is."

"Then there's only one serious problem."

His words sent a chill through her. She didn't want to hear there was any problem, let alone a serious one.

"Which is?" she made herself ask.

"We have to decide what to do first. Give your father and Lucille the update on Dennis or tell them about us." Mike's smile clearly said "Got you."

Claudia exhaled slowly, trying not to let him see he actually *had* scared her, then said, "There are a few far more real problems, Mike."

"Oh?"

Liking the way his smile faded, she went on. "Yes. You've never told me what sort of place you live in. Would it allow Morgan and Ghost?"

"There's no question of allowing. I've got a house in Santa Monica. It's not too big, but I know you'll like it. And Santa Monica's great—more like a small town than a suburb of L.A."

She nodded. "I recall reading a travel piece about it, but I got the impression that only movie stars lived there."

"No, just a few. Most of us are ordinary working folks. But would a furry dog like Morgan be happy in a warm climate?"

"Are you kidding? He hates winter. He'd kill to live in California."

"Killing won't be necessary," Mike teased. "He can just owe me one. So, does that take care of the *real* problems?"

"Not quite," she said, determined not to let him off the hook too easily. "There's a very big one left. How do I know you don't only want to marry me because my brother has thirty million dollars?"

"Oh. Well . . . how about I sign a prenuptial agreement never to take any money from him?"

"Hmm. I guess that might be a possibility."

"Of course," he added as they got out of the Jeep, "that wouldn't stop me from asking him for really neat birthday presents. Maybe a Ferrari the first year and a yacht the second. How does that sound?"

"Very funny."

"Is that what you like best about me?" he asked, following her up the stairs. "My sense of humor? Or is it that I'm so good at decorating Christmas trees? Or so talented at *other* things?"

That made her laugh, and she felt certain he'd always be able to make her smile. "We'll discuss what I like best later," she said, opening the front door and stepping inside.

"Dad? Lucille?" she called. "It's me."

"Maybe they're not home."

"The lights are on. And Dad's truck and snowmobile are in the drive, so they must be here. Dad? Lucille?" she tried again.

"We're in the basement, Claudia," Lucille called back. "In the rec room."

Claudia put her purse on the hall table, tugged off her boots and started through the house.

"You know," Mike said, trailing behind, "I really don't like basements."

"This one's perfectly safe. When we were kids, Dennis and I used to play in it all the time. But if it makes you feel better, you can hold my hand," she added, taking his as they started down the stairs.

"I never imagined I'd ever even consider marrying a man who was afraid of basements," she teased.

"I'm not *afraid* of them."

"No? Well, I think you are. So what's going to happen when a circuit breaker has to be reset? Or the washing machine needs fixing? Or..."

She stopped dead in the rec room doorway, her knees suddenly weak and terror gripping her heart. Her father was lying motionless on the floor, his face half covered in blood, his hair matted with it.

And there were two men with guns. One was pointing his at her. The other was pointing his at Lucille.

CHAPTER SIXTEEN

MIKE'S BLOOD HAD FROZEN in his veins, but his brain was in overdrive, taking in the scene in a split second. The guys with the guns had greased-back hair, deep tans and looked like a couple of punks. They could only be Dennis's lowlifes.

And given the length of clothesline lying beside Raymond, they'd been about to tie him up. Which at least meant he wasn't dead.

"So that's the sister, huh?" the short one was saying to Lucille. "And who's the guy?"

"Just a friend," she told him, her voice filled with fear.

"Dad?" Claudia whispered as if she was coming out of a trance.

When she tried to move forward, Mike grabbed her arms and pulled her closely against his chest.

"That's my father!" she cried to the men. "What have you done to my father?"

"Shut up," the one pointing his gun at her snapped. "He's okay."

"They hit him, Claudia," Lucille said, wiping her eyes. "With a gun."

"You!" The short one waved his pistol toward Mike. "Let go of her and get over by the wall."

"Do whatever they say," he whispered to Claudia. Releasing her, he moved across the room, his heart pounding.

"Awright, change of plans," the short one told his pal. "We can't take three of 'em with us. So you stay with these others."

"Aw, Rocco—"

"You stay," Rocco ordered more firmly. "Claudia here's gonna show me how to get to this cottage."

"Oh, my God," she murmured. "Lucille, you told them where Dennis is."

"I had to! They were going to kill Raymond."

"So this place is an hour from here, right?" Rocco asked Claudia. "That's what *she* said," he added, gesturing at Lucille when he didn't get an answer. "So here's the deal. I got a phone in my car, see, Claudia. And I'm gonna phone back here after I talk to your brother."

"You don't want to *talk* to Dennis! You want to kill him!"

"We'll try talkin' first. See how that goes. But I don't want you directin' me along no scenic route. So if I ain't phoned in—let's say an hour and a half— Pops and Lucille and your friend here are all gonna be dead ducks. You got it?"

"Claudia?" Mike said.

When she looked at him, he willed her to read his thoughts. Because if there was any way on earth he could take out Rocco's pal and come after her, he would.

"Do exactly what the man tells you," he said. "Go straight to the cottage."

"Yeah, you listen to your boyfriend," Rocco told her.

Mike stared at him hard, wanting to kill him so badly he could taste it. "If you do anything to harm her, you're a dead man."

"Yeah, right," Rocco sneered. "I'm shakin'. Let's go," he said, grabbing Claudia by the arm and shoving her out of the room.

Listening to their footsteps on the stairs, Mike was almost shaking with frustration. Claudia was right. The lowlifes hadn't come all this way to *talk* to Dennis. And if they were this worried about a witness to those other murders, they wouldn't be leaving any alive this time around.

So there just couldn't be a "this time."

When he heard the front door open and close, Mike looked at the remaining punk. "What about him?" He nodded toward Raymond. "Can we call a doctor?"

"Oh, yeah, right. Like I want *four* of yous to babysit."

"Then at least let us elevate his head to stop the bleeding." He glanced at Lucille as he said that, silently telling her to give him some help.

She must have gotten the message, because before the creep could say a word she wailed, "He's going to die if we don't stop the bleeding! My Raymond's going to die!"

When she began sobbing hysterically, the man muttered, "Shee-it, woman. All right. Take one of them cushions off the couch.

"Not you!" he snapped when Mike started forward. "Her."

Still sobbing, Lucille looked quickly at Mike.

Praying it had been a meaningful glance, he kept one eye on her as she scurried over to the couch, the other eye on the lowlife and his gun.

"I'll help you with him," Mike said, starting in Lucille's direction again as she grabbed a cushion.

"I told you not to move!" The man wheeled toward him and pointed the gun at the center of his chest.

But he'd gotten close enough—if only Lucille would do something to distract him.

"Hey," he said, slowly raising his hands, palms toward the guy. "I never argue with a man holding a gun."

"Good. Then get the hell back over to the wall."

But before he had to move, Lucille tripped and went down.

As the man swung around, Mike flew forward and hit him with a tackle. They landed half on the floor, half on top of Lucille.

She screamed. Then, an instant later, it was the lowlife screaming.

Mike tore the gun from his hand, pressed it to his throat and looked to see what had happened. Damned if Lucille hadn't grabbed the guy's ear and tried to rip it off.

"Good going," Mike told her. "Now, hand me that clothesline."

Wriggling out from beneath them, she got it and gave it to him.

"Do you know how to use a gun?" he asked.

"Yes."

"And are you up to blowing this guy's brains out if he gives me any trouble?"

"I might blow them out even if he doesn't," she said shakily.

Suspecting she really might, Mike took a moment to try to reassure her. "Raymond's going to be fine," he said quietly. "Head wounds always bleed a lot. So just hold this aimed at our friend's head while I get him tied up."

As quickly as he could, he bound the guy's wrists and ankles. Then he took the gun back from Lucille. "All right, I'm going to the cottage. You phone the doctor, then the police, then Dennis. Where are the keys for Raymond's snowmobile?"

"On the kitchen counter."

"Okay, I'm on my way." He raced from the room and up the stairs. But just as he reached the top, Lucille called after him.

"What?" he demanded impatiently. Every second counted.

"Ray's snowmobile," she said, appearing at the bottom of the stairs. "I just remembered he's been working on it. Half the parts of the engine are sitting on his workbench. You'll have to take the truck."

Swearing to himself, he found the keys and headed for the door. When he opened it, he realized Claudia's Jeep was parked behind the truck.

For half a second he panicked. Then he remembered she'd put her purse down when they came in.

He grabbed it from the hall table, dug through it for her keys and took off into the near darkness. But how in hell was he going to beat Rocco to the cottage if he couldn't go cross-country?

CLAUDIA FURTIVELY GLANCED across the car at Rocco—still frightened half to death. But that was hardly surprising when she knew he was going to kill her once they reached the cottage.

Even though she'd calmed down enough to think straight again, she couldn't come up with any possible way to get out of this. Not alive, at least.

"Turn left up ahead," she made herself say.

"You sure?"

"Yes. We're almost there." As much as she wished that weren't true, it was. If she'd given Rocco the wrong instructions, his buddy would have killed her father and Lucille and Mike.

Not that she had much hope he wouldn't, anyway. But at least, if she cooperated, there was a chance. Just the thought of them dying filled her eyes with tears. She loved them all, and she wanted to marry Mike more than she'd ever wanted anything. But it wasn't going to happen.

"So's your brother got a gun?" Rocco asked.

"No," she lied. There were rifles in the cottage. Which meant that just possibly, Dennis might shoot Rocco before . . . But if he did, Rocco wouldn't phone his partner and the others would die for sure. There was simply no possibility of a happy ending here, and—

"How much farther?" Rocco demanded.

"The driveway's just ahead," she said numbly. "On the right."

As he slowed the car her pulse rate accelerated. She was living the last minutes of her life, and there was nothing she could do to change that.

He started to make the turn; she began praying Dennis and Annie would see the headlights.

Then Rocco switched them off.

Blinking back tears, she tried to tell herself they'd *hear* the car, just as they'd heard her snowmobile earlier. But a snowmobile was an awful lot louder than this car, so the only thing left was to try giving them a few seconds' warning.

She might get a chance to sound the horn. And if she couldn't manage that, she'd at least scream. But the moment she did, she'd be dead.

"Looks like they're expectin' company," he said, stopping the car about a hundred feet from the cabin. "You know anythin' about that?"

She shook her head, then stared out through the windshield, her vision blurred by her unshed tears. She could see that the light was on over the front door. It was shining down onto Lucille's snowmobile and ...

Wiping her eyes, she tried to clear her vision.

"Okay, here's what we're gonna do," Rocco said. "You're gonna open your door and get out—real slow. And my gun's gonna be on you while you're doin' it, so don't even think about tryin' to take off."

She shook her head again, as if the idea had never occurred to her.

"I'm gonna slide over and get out your side and we're gonna walk to the door together, nice and quiet. Then you're gonna knock and tell your brother it's you. That all clear?"

"Yes," she whispered.

"Okay. Let's go."

Her hand trembling, she opened the car door and slowly got out, surreptitiously glancing around in the darkness. She couldn't see anyone or anything unusual. Except that the truck was nowhere in sight. And the snowmobile was parked practically in front of the door. Right under the light so she couldn't possibly miss noticing it wasn't Lucille's at all. It was hers. But how could it be?

Rocco climbed out of the car and grabbed her arm. "You walk in front of me," he ordered. "And remember my gun's at your back."

With each step she took her heart pounded more loudly. It was hammering in her ears by the time they reached her snowmobile. Then the cottage door opened and Annie was standing there.

"Claudia," she said. "What a surprise. And you," she added, glancing at Rocco, "must be the friend who was coming up for Christmas. But I'm sorry, I've forgotten what Claudia told me your name was."

"Uhh...Rocco."

"Well, Dennis has just gone off in the truck to get some beer, but he won't be long. Come on in."

Claudia's legs threatened to give out before she got inside, but she made it—Rocco right behind her.

"Oh," Annie said, "it's so good to see you again." She wrapped her arms around Claudia, pulling her forward in a hug, then said, "Shove that door closed, will you, Rocco?"

Annie's gaze stayed on him for another second, then flashed to Claudia's. Just as she was mouthing the word "down," the door banged shut and there was a dull *thwocking* noise followed by a heavy thud.

In front of Claudia, Dennis stepped out of the kitchen, lowering a rifle. From behind her, Mike said, "It's over."

She whirled around. He was standing beside the door with a pistol in his hand. Rocco lay crumpled on the floor at his feet. Her gaze lingered on the motionless body for a moment, then she looked back up at

Mike, realizing he'd hit Rocco with the gun but not certain where he'd come from.

"Mike was behind the door when I opened it," Annie explained.

And that was when Claudia's legs *did* give out.

Mike scooped her up into his arms before she could fall and carried her over to the couch.

"How did you get away from Rocco's friend?" she managed to say.

"It was a cinch. Then I drove back to your place and got your snowmobile so I could come cross-country. I was just afraid I wouldn't get here soon enough. I was so worried about you," he added, hugging her close to him.

"Me, too," she whispered. "Worried about you, I mean. But what about Dad?"

"I think he's okay. Lucille phoned before I got here, to alert Dennis. At that point the doctor was on her way and your Dad was conscious, saying he was all right."

"Oh, thank heavens. And Rocco's friend?"

"He's either still tied up in the rec room or already under arrest."

"That could only have happened if the police were a lot faster getting there than they've been getting here," Dennis muttered.

As if on cue, a man hammered on the door and yelled, "Police! Open up!"

CLAUDIA, DENNIS AND Annie waited anxiously while Mike talked to his contact in Florida. It had taken the man less than an hour to check out Rocco and his partner—Bernie—and phone back, but it had seemed a lot longer to Claudia. And she knew it had to the others, as well.

They'd filled in the time by calling Lucille to make sure the doctor hadn't found anything seriously wrong with Raymond, and by talking about everything under the sun. But even though they'd pretended differently, they'd been worrying. If Rocco and Bernie were serious gangsters, they'd have friends who'd likely come after Dennis on their behalf.

"You're in luck, Dennis," Mike said. He put down the cell phone and leaned back on the couch, wrapping his arm around Claudia.

The three sighs of relief were audible, then Dennis said, "So what's the story?"

"Basically, Rocco and Bernie are nothing but a couple of two-bit hoods."

"Which means Dennis and I don't have to go into hiding?" Annie asked.

Mike nodded. "From the sound of things, he's safe now. I mean, when he goes back to Florida to testify, he should be careful—just in case those two creeps have any small-time friends with delusions of grandeur. But aside from that, my guy says there's nothing to lose sleep over."

"Lord," Dennis muttered, "what a load off my mind. And yours, too, I guess, Mike," he added with a grin. "Claudia told me Iggy threatened to keep you here till Easter if you couldn't ID Santa. Now you can go ahead and tell everyone the whole story."

"That'll sure make Iggy happy," Mike said.

"Happy?" Claudia repeated. "I just hope he doesn't end up so excited it brings on a heart attack. After all, he's getting the ending he wanted to your series, plus we're giving him the story about Hillstead *and* an exclusive about Rocco and Bernie.''

"My sister," Dennis said dryly, "has never been known to do things halfheartedly.''

Mike laughed. "I've noticed that. But getting back to Iggy," he added, glancing at Claudia once more. "Aren't you going to call in those stories? It's almost ten o'clock. The poor guy might have that heart attack just worrying about his deadline.''

IT WAS NEARLY ELEVEN before Claudia got off the phone and smiled wearily at the others.

"Well?" Dennis said. "Is Iggy as happy as you expected?''

"He's in seventh heaven. He figures circulation's going to go through the ceiling and a hundred new advertisers will be hammering on the door.''

She snuggled closer to Mike on the couch, then added, "The only problem is, he really believes it'll be a permanent improvement, and it won't. Whatever new subscribers and advertisers he gets will gradually drift away again, and that makes me feel a little guilty about going off to L.A.—kind of like I'm deserting a sinking ship.''

"You know," Mike said, kissing her hair, "there's something else Iggy could try. Something that's worked for other small papers.''

"Oh? What's that?''

"Well, you've mentioned how many people have moved away from here over the years. And a lot of them would have at least some interest in reading about what's going on these days.''

"Enough interest to pay for a subscription?" Annie said skeptically.

"Probably not a daily one," Mike told her. "But other papers have tried mailing out free copies of their Saturday issues for a while. I think six months to a year has been pretty standard. After that, a surprising number of people start paying to keep them coming."

"Really?" Claudia said, sitting up a little straighter.

Mike nodded. "I know selling one extra paper a week doesn't sound like much, but all those expatriates add up. And they sometimes order gifts from local merchants—for relatives still living back home. So it helps build up the advertising side, too."

"Then why," Claudia asked, "didn't Ferris Wentworth suggest *his* small-town papers try it?"

"Because it would have cost him money, I suppose. I hear he's the type who decides something one day and wants it done the day before. So, for him, once he decided to shut down his losers, giving them *any* time to turn themselves around was stretching things. But he was obviously only prepared to carry them for a few more weeks."

"If somebody loaned Iggy the money to try the idea, though..." Claudia looked at Dennis. Then Annie looked at Dennis.

"Is this what happens to rich people?" he asked, laughing.

"Well," Claudia said, "you've already played Santa to so many people, one more wouldn't make much difference."

"I guess you've got a point. And if it would let you go off to L.A. without feeling like you're deserting a sinking ship..."

"You know, Dennis," she said, "you're not a half-bad guy for a multimillionaire."

CLAUDIA HADN'T TURNED ON the living room lights when she and Mike finally got home. But moonlight was straying in through the window, and the lights on their tree were twinkling like tiny stars. Beside the couch, both Morgan and Ghost were curled up asleep.

"Happy?" Mike asked, kissing her neck.

"Perfectly. Dennis is safe. My father's going to be all right. And best of all..."

When Mike looked at her, she smiled.

"Me?" he said, smiling back. "I'm best of all?"

"Absolutely." She cuddled even closer to him. "But I was wondering...?"

"Mmm?"

"With Christmas Day being next Wednesday, would the *Gazette* really care if you didn't go back on Saturday?"

"You want me to stay?"

"I'd love you to stay. Lucille makes a wonderful turkey dinner. And since it's the first Christmas in so long that Dennis has been home, and it's *our* first Christmas... But I guess you've already made plans with your own family, haven't you."

"Well...yeah. They're a pretty understanding bunch, though. So as long as I had a good reason for not being there..."

"And am I a good reason?"

"Oh, Claudia, you're the best reason anybody could ever think of."

He gave her a long, loving kiss. Then he leaned back, his arm around her, and they sat contentedly watching the lights twinkle.

"We did one hell of a job on that tree, didn't we?" he said at last.

"Uh-huh, we did. And next year? When we're in Santa Monica? We don't have to have an artificial tree, do we? We can have a real one there, too?"

"We can have whatever you want."

"Oh, Mike," she murmured. "I've already got everything in the world I want, right here in this room."

"What?" he said, looking around. "A real Christmas tree? Morgan and Ghost?"

"Very funny," she whispered. Then she kissed him until he admitted he knew what she meant.

EPILOGUE

Fourteen months later

CLAUDIA DROVE HOME in a daze, barely seeing the palm trees and Mediterranean-style houses that made up the quiet neighborhood she loved.

Absently, she took the mail from the box, then went inside and waited while Morgan performed his dance of the deserted dog. Ghost, who was curled up on the hall table, opened his eyes long enough to give Morgan a disgusted glance.

"Big changes coming, boy," Claudia told the dog, giving him a hearty pat. She let him out into the backyard and stood gazing through the screen, reflecting how almost every day of the past year had brought changes.

First, she and Mike had been married and she'd moved from the frozen north to balmy Santa Monica. Next, she'd enrolled at UCLA as a part-time journalism student. And recently she'd actually sold a free-lance article to a major magazine—only a start, she realized, but a good one.

She glanced through the little stack of mail and read the "wish you were here" postcard from Hawaii. Dennis seemed to be sending their father and Lucille on endless vacations, and they were loving every minute of them.

Not that Dennis and Annie hadn't been seeing a lot of the world themselves. They'd made some decisions regarding their money—which charities they were going to support and that sort of thing. But they were still traveling a lot, trying to decide where they'd like to settle.

Claudia let Morgan back in and set the rest of the mail aside. Then she glanced at her watch, calculating how long it would be until Mike got home.

Deciding she couldn't wait, she hurried back out to her little Miata and headed for the *L.A. Gazette*.

"HEY, O'BRIAN," Howie said from the next desk, "you've got company."

When Mike looked across the newsroom and spotted Claudia, he got the same warm feeling that swept through him every time he saw her—but today it was tinged with apprehension.

Pushing back his chair, he strode over to her, his heart beating hard. She'd gone for an ultrasound this morning, and that had to be why she was here.

"So?" he said, taking her hand as he reached her. "Everything looked all right? I'm still going to be a daddy?"

"Definitely."

He took her in his arms and hugged her. The doctor had said things were fine, but having that confirmed by pictures made it so much easier to believe.

"Mike?" she said, drawing back a little and gazing at him. "You know how you're always saying we should have two children—like your sisters? That two kids make the ideal family?"

"Uh-huh," he said uncertainly.

"Well, you won't mind if we have them both at once, will you?"

"You mean it's twins?"

She nodded.

"Twins," he repeated, feeling himself grinning like an idiot. Pulling her close again, he said, "You know, Paquette, your brother was right. You sure *don't* do things halfheartedly."

"Oh? Well, O'Brian, I hardly did this all on my own, so I guess you don't do things halfheartedly, either."

That made him laugh. "Do you realize how much I love you?"

"Wholeheartedly?"

"Exactly," he told her. And then he kissed her, wholeheartedly, until the entire newsroom erupted into applause and whistles.

FREE VALENTINE'S BROOCH! $9.95 U.S. retail value

This Valentine's Day Harlequin brings you all the essentials—romance, chocolate and jewelry—in:

VALENTINE *Delights*

Matchmaking chocolate-shop owner Papa Valentine dispenses sinful desserts, mouth-watering chocolates…and advice to the lovelorn, in this collection of three delightfully romantic stories by Meryl Sawyer, Kate Hoffmann and Gina Wilkins.

As our special Valentine's Day gift to you, each copy of *Valentine Delights* will have a beautiful, filigreed, heart-shaped brooch attached to the cover.

Make this your most delicious Valentine's Day ever with *Valentine Delights!*

Available in February wherever Harlequin books are sold.

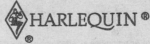

HARLEQUIN ®

VAL97

You are cordially invited to a

HOMETOWN REUNION

September 1996—August 1997

Bad boys, cowboys, babies. Feuding families,
arson, mistaken identity, a mom on the run...
Where can you find romance and adventure?
Tyler, Wisconsin, that's where!

So join us in this not-so-sleepy little town and
experience the love, the laughter and the
tears of those who call it home.

WELCOME TO A
HOMETOWN REUNION

Sheila and Douglas are going to spend their
honeymoon in a wigwam, by choice. But rumor
has it that Rosemary Dusold may be *forced*—by
runny-nosed babies—to live in one if the new
pediatrician follows through on his intention to
renovate her home as an office. Don't miss
Helen Conrad's *Baby Blues,* fifth in
a series you won't want to end....

Available in January 1997
at your favorite retail store.

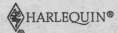

HARLEQUIN®

Look us up on-line at: http://www.romance.net

HTR5

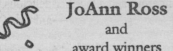

HARLEQUIN ®

Scandals

A passionate story of romance, where bold, daring characters set out to defy their world of propriety and strict social codes.

"Scandals—a story that will make your heart race and your pulse pound. Spectacular!"
—Suzanne Forster

"Devon is daring, dangerous and altogether delicious."
—Amanda Quick

Don't miss this wonderful full-length novel from Regency favorite Georgina Devon.

Available in December, wherever Harlequin books are sold.

Look us up on-line at: http://www.romance.net

The collection of the year!
NEW YORK TIMES BESTSELLING AUTHORS

Linda Lael Miller
Wild About Harry

Janet Dailey
Sweet Promise

Elizabeth Lowell
Reckless Love

Penny Jordan
Love's Choices

and featuring
Nora Roberts
The Calhoun Women

This special trade-size edition features four of the wildly popular titles in the Calhoun miniseries together in one volume—a true collector's item!

Pick up these great authors and a chance to win a weekend for two in New York City at the Marriott Marquis Hotel on Broadway! We'll pay for your flight, your hotel—even a Broadway show!

Available in December at your favorite retail outlet.

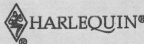

1997
Reader's Engagement Book
A calendar of important dates
and anniversaries for readers to use!

Informative and entertaining—with notable
dates and trivia highlighted throughout the year.

Handy, convenient, pocketbook size to help you
keep track of your own personal important dates.

Added bonus—contains $5.00 worth of coupons
for upcoming Harlequin and Silhouette books.
This calendar more than pays for itself!

Available beginning in November at
your favorite retail outlet.

HARLEQUIN® Silhouette®

Look us up on-line at: http://www.romance.net   CAL97